{A CIRCLE OF SOULS}

{A CIRCLE OF SOULS}

a novel

PREETHAM GRANDHI

iUniverse, Inc.

New York Lincoln Shanghai

A Circle of Souls

iUniverse books may be ordered through booksellers or by contacting:

iUniverse
2021 Pine Lake Road, Suite 100
Lincoln, NE 68512
www.iuniverse.com
1-800-Authors (1-800-288-4677)

Because of the dynamic nature of the Internet, any Web addresses or links contained in this book may have changed since publication and may no longer be valid.

This is a work of fiction. All of the characters, names, incidents, organizations, and dialogue in this novel are either the products of the author's imagination or are used fictitiously.

ISBN: 978-0-595-41672-1 (pbk)
ISBN: 978-0-595-86016-6 (ebk)

Printed in the United States of America

Dedicated to
the devoted staff and precious children of House 5

Special thanks to
my parents for allowing me to explore my dreams;
my sister for sharing my growing experiences;
my in-laws for their continuous support;
my wife for being a part of all my ventures; and
my son for his pure and unconditional love.

{PROLOGUE}

The *slaaf* stumbled along the shore of Willow Lake. The ground was soft from the previous night's rain, and wet leaves made a slippery carpet under his feet. His arms ached from struggling to contain the animal he carried in a coarse gunnysack across his shoulder. The sedative had worn off, and the animal thrashed more and more violently as the slaaf approached the faded red boathouse. Finally, in front of the peeling door, he dropped the squirming sack. The creature inside yelped as the bag hit the ground. The slaaf found the key on his large metal ring, unlocked the padlock, and slipped inside.

He lifted the sack onto a long, wooden workbench near the back of the boathouse, where its contents lay still for a moment. He wiped his sweaty forehead with his arm, while with his other hand, he fingered the small bag of white powder inside the front pocket of his jeans. He sat carefully in a creaky wooden chair against the wall. He wanted to wait, knowing it would be over so quickly … but his hand moved against his will, pulled out the bag, reached in, and took a pinch. He placed the white powder in the palm of his other hand. He snorted it, and his head came alive.

Yes, yes, he thought. He cast his euphoric mind into the ether, searching for his master. Would he come?

But the euphoria didn't last long, and the slaaf, having felt no trace of his master's presence, found himself slammed back into his body. His hands were gripping the arms of the wooden chair. The muscles in his legs had tensed so rigidly that he wondered if he would be able to stand.

"I hate you! I hate you!" he screamed at the top of his lungs. The sound of his panting was interrupted by a low whine from the sack on the workbench. The slaaf snorted more of the cocaine and tried again to reach his master, whom he was certain was toying with him. Again, he failed. It took more and more of the cocaine to reach the ecstatic state he needed to summon his master. And now, the little bag was empty.

His heart raced, and sweat trickled down his spine. He stomped on the wooden floor in frustration.

On the bench, the creature in the sack whimpered again, more loudly this time. "Shut up," the slaaf shouted. His anxiety was immense, unbearable. He seized a long, serrated knife from a rack near the table—and, with all his might, drove it through the sack. Moaning unintelligibly, he plunged the knife through the sack over and over again. The burlap darkened as thick blood seeped out through the holes the slaaf had created.

Finally, he stopped. The silence in the boathouse was almost too much to bear. "Oh, no," the slaaf sobbed.

He had trapped the young coyote the previous night, expecting to catch a smaller animal—a rabbit or a raccoon—to give to his master. Now his plan was ruined. The animal was dead, and his master had abandoned him. His chance at redemption, however temporary, had passed.

Then, just when he thought all hope was lost, a voice called out to him from the doorway of the boathouse. The door had been pushed ajar, and the light coming through the narrow opening blinded the slaaf with the radiance of a god. His master was here. His master told him to crouch down under the bench and wait patiently. The slaaf's heart raced. Had his master come to punish or redeem him?

{CHAPTER ONE}

An Autumn Evening

"I can't wait to get home and have a piece of my mom's apple pie," Janet said as she and Melissa climbed onto the school bus after the bell signaled the end of another day. "Do you want to come over?"

"I can't," Melissa said, frowning. "My mom said I have to come right home and clean my room. I was supposed to do it yesterday. Maybe you could bring me a piece of pie tomorrow."

"I will," Janet said.

She got off at her usual stop. "Bye, Jaaanet!" Melissa sang out from the window as Janet walked down Alden Avenue.

Janet returned the farewell to her best friend as the bus sped away.

Janet was relieved that the day was over. She had been nervous about her math test, and she felt sick when she thought of all the questions she had skipped. "Fifth-grade math shouldn't be so hard," she mumbled to herself, echoing what her father had said when he was trying to help with her homework.

A breeze rustled through the trees, shaking a few red leaves loose. Janet shivered and walked more quickly. The sun was already sinking, and without it, the air grew cold against her bare, slender legs. She skipped a little down the partially paved sidewalk along Alden Avenue and kicked a pebble into a pile of leaves as she came to the T-junction between Alden and Farmington.

She paused, looking right down Farmington, then straight ahead, across Mr. Deed's property. If she took Farmington Avenue, she would be home in less than four minutes. If she climbed Mr. Deed's fence and walked around Willow Lake until she reached her own backyard, it would take her eight. She was chilly, and she really wanted a piece of that pie, but the walk along Willow Lake promised more discovery. Once, as she passed the red boathouse, she had seen a fox and three kits trot into the woods. Another time, she had watched in morbid fascination as a hawk swooped low over Mr. Deed's yard and ascended again with a baby rabbit in its talons.

The sun was setting behind her, and her body cast a long shadow that pointed toward Mr. Deed's property and Willow Lake. Janet ran across Farmington Avenue, and, after making sure no one was around, bent over and shoved her schoolbag through the slats in the peeling white picket fence.

As far as Janet knew, Mr. Deed had lived on the large plot of land since long before she was born. From here, she could hardly see his small house between the neat rows of apple trees that grew on the back side of his property. From the front, the house had the significance of a golf ball on the sprawling lawn. She knew Mr. Deed as a kind, quiet old man who invited his friends and neighbors to pick apples in his orchard every fall. Janet and her parents had just been there the day before and had taken home two five-pound bags.

Janet climbed carefully over the fence, pulling her wool skirt up to avoid snagging it on a rusty nail. She pulled the straps of her book bag up onto her shoulders and darted across the yard, staying at the edge of the property. As she skirted the apple trees, she checked for light in the cottage windows, but there was none.

It took Janet two minutes to reach the point where an old tree stump marked the end of Mr. Deed's land and the beginning of Willow Lake. Janet was breathing hard from her brisk, self-conscious gallop. She was pretty sure nobody had seen her trespass.

She ran down the winding path that bordered the lake. It was quiet there, except for a few birds that called to each other as they flew across the rippling water. Janet slowed to a walk. She was out of breath and had a sharp pain under her ribs. She stopped and bent over, her hands on her knees, and took a few deep breaths. When she looked up again, she saw the old, red boathouse in front of her along the curved path. She had always wondered who it belonged to and what they kept in there. In all the times she had run across Mr. Deed's property, she had never seen anybody enter or leave it, and the door was always locked with a big padlock.

But as she looked at the boathouse, Janet's heart jumped with excitement. Today, the padlock was missing from the door. She looked around but saw no one, so she jogged closer. As she reached out to push the door open, she thought she heard a low moaning sound from inside, like a person or an animal in pain. She froze, startled. Then the eerie groan stopped, leaving only silence. *It was nothing*, she told herself. *Maybe the wind.* Looking over her shoulder again, she pushed the boathouse door open just wide enough to slip inside.

"Hello?" she called. She stood just inside the door as her eyes adjusted to the gloom. The boathouse had a peculiar metallic odor. It seemed as if it had not been cleaned in a very long time. A pile of old, tattered fishing nets sat heaped in the corner to her right. A large cloth tarpaulin lay on the floor. On the far wall, she could just make out a tangle of tools on a long workbench. An old paddle lay on the floor. The boat bay was empty, but the big doors were closed, meaning there likely and simply was no boat. Janet guessed that the wooden deck overlooking the lake would be a daring place to for the neighborhood kids to hang out.

As Janet moved toward the far door that led to the deck, she heard a soft shuffle behind her, from the corner near the workbench. Perhaps there *was* an animal in there, or even a person—maybe someone sick or injured who needed help. Janet was both frightened and exhilarated by the thought of finding a lost child or a homeless person here and rescuing him. She might even be in the paper. She thought of the pie waiting for her at home, but she was sure her mother would want her to be brave and help if she could.

"Do you need help?" she called out toward the workbench.

Suddenly, a huge figure loomed up out of the darkness and lunged toward her. He seemed seven feet tall, as though his head would scrape the low ceiling. He reached out for her, and she backed away in surprise and horror. It was like a bad dream. One huge hand grasped the back of her head while the other covered her mouth. The hands twisted her around until the back of her head rested against the giant's chest.

She couldn't breathe. The hand that covered her mouth also blocked her nostrils. She wanted to scream, but couldn't. She began to struggle, digging into her captor's hands with her fingernails, trying to bite the hand that covered her mouth, to wrestle free of the arm that was now wrapped tightly around her waist. The salty taste of the giant's sweat was in her mouth. She thrashed her legs to kick him. But he didn't budge; she couldn't hurt him. She began to tire. The terror that had helped her to fight like an animal now soothed her like an anesthetic. Her mind floated, reached toward home. She could hear the giant's heavy, rhythmic breathing. She could smell apple pie.

The giant dragged her limp body backward. When he finally took his hand away from her mouth, she could only produce a jagged, squeaky cry that no one would have heard, even from just outside the door. The giant reached around her face again and pressed a damp cloth over her nose and mouth. She held her breath against the unbearably pungent fumes emanating from the cloth, but finally, she had no choice but to breathe. Everything went black.

{CHAPTER TWO}

An Autumn Night

Mrs. Troy stood next to the telephone, fighting tears. Her eyes were puffy from intermittent crying. When Janet hadn't come home from school that afternoon, she had tried hard to rationalize her daughter's absence. Surely Janet had gone to a friend's house or stayed late at school. Soon the phone would ring, and Mrs. Troy would pick it up and hear Janet's sweet, breathless apology. But now, at eleven thirty at night, her mind could travel nowhere but the worst possible places—the places where beautiful young girls were hit by cars and left to die in ditches, or nabbed and subjected to unspeakable tortures.

The telephone rang, echoing hollowly in the living room. Although she had been waiting for this moment, she hesitated now to pick up the phone.

"Hello?" she said finally.

"Catherine." It wasn't Janet's voice, as she had hoped, but her husband's. "We're organizing search parties," Mr. Troy said. "Will you be all right if I go?".

"Yes," Mrs. Troy said softly. Her voice cracked as tears flowed from her eyes. "I called Cliff. He's on his way now from Danbury to sit with me."

Mrs. Troy hung up the telephone and stared at the clock. Only two of the longest minutes of her life had passed since the last time she'd looked at it. Her head pounded. She paced a figure eight through the living room, then walked into the kitchen, where she glared accusingly at the apple pie that sat cold and untouched in the middle of the table. Had she somehow managed to bake an unlucky omen?

It was Janet's favorite dessert. They had all gone apple picking at Mr. Deed's orchard the day before—just in time, before the cold front came in. Mrs. Troy had spent several hours baking the pie. At a quarter to four, she had set it right there, on that table, where it waited for Janet, warm and fresh. By four thirty, she was surprised that Janet hadn't come home yet. Had Mrs. Troy forgotten about some extracurricular activity scheduled that day at the school? She called the school office, but the secretary assured her that everyone but the janitor had gone home for the day.

At five, she had called Melissa's mother to see if Janet had gone over to her best friend's house and forgotten to call home. Melissa said that Janet had gotten off the bus at her usual stop, as she did every day.

Sick with worry, Mrs. Troy had called her husband, Herbert, who worked the evening shift as a manager at Mr. Green's twenty-four-hour grocery shop. He had left work immediately to trace his daughter's path between the bus stop and their house, while Mrs. Troy waited by the phone in case Janet should call. Having found no signs of Janet anywhere, Mr. Troy had dashed to the police station. The officer had sent him home to get a recent picture of Janet. Then, as Mr. Troy waited at the station, four officers had canvassed the houses along Janet's route, questioning several people who lived on Alden and Farmington avenues to find out if they'd seen her. No one had. Finally, the officers had decided to issue an AMBER alert. Janet's name, face, and vital statistics would be broadcast via all radio and television stations across the state through the emergency alert system.

Mrs. Troy sat at the kitchen table, praying silently as she held a framed photograph of Janet. She was a strong woman who usually held up well during emergencies, but now she felt crippled, as though a part of her own body had been ripped away. She gazed down at the girl in the frame: Janet's bright smile, her silky blonde hair, her wide blue eyes with sweeping lashes. Mrs. Troy shut her eyes tightly, knowing that everywhere she looked in the house, she would see reminders of Janet's absence: the tennis shoes by the back door, the report card with A's in every subject but math hanging from the refrigerator … and that untouched apple pie.

The doorbell rang, and Mrs. Troy jumped to her feet. Hope blossomed inside her chest as she ran to open the door.

But it was Mr. Troy, alone. He had left so quickly for the police station that he had forgotten his keys. "Anything?" she asked, trying to still the quaver in her voice. She already knew the answer from the empty expression on her husband's face. She glanced at the clock and realized that it was one o'clock in the morning.

"Nothing so far," Mr. Troy sighed, exhausted. He embraced his wife, whose tense body shuddered in his arms. She held onto him tightly, and he returned her desperation, each of them seeking an impossible comfort. It was the most unbearable moment of their lives.

*   *   *   *

The slaaf lifted the girl in his muscular arms and gently placed her on the wooden workbench at the rear of the boathouse. He molded her supple arms to her sides. She lay still, a perfect little doll.

Once he was satisfied with her positioning, the slaaf pushed the door of the boathouse closed and lit the candle in the holder that hung above the workbench. He stood next to the girl, staring at her beautiful face as flickering shadows moved across it. He watched her chest rise as she took in a short breath. He stroked the side of her face and smoothed a strand of hair back from her forehead. Her cheeks were flushed, and her thin scarlet lips were parted slightly. The slaaf smiled. "He will be happy," he murmured.

He reached up near the girl's head for the cloth and vial. His smile widened. His master had sent the girl as a sign of the redemption to come, he realized. He had been given a second chance! He soaked the cloth with the liquid in the vial until it radiated fumes. He couldn't take the chance of her waking up. He placed the rag over the girl's face and watched her chest as it gradually stilled. He then tucked her pale gray skirt between her thighs, exposing her long legs completely. He rolled the long sleeves of her white blouse up over her shoulders.

He reached into the satchel that lay near the girl's feet. He felt an enveloping sense of calm as his hand closed on the cold handle of a steel instrument. The sharp blade of the scalpel glimmered in the orange candlelight. He admired its smooth contours. The symbol of his massive power felt feather light in his hand.

The slaaf put his left hand over the girl's face and pushed back, tilting her chin up and extending her neck. With his right hand, he pressed the broad end of the blade into the left side of her neck. It sliced through the skin immediately, effortlessly. With one masterful stroke, the slaaf extended the incision all the way across.

Blood gushed as the incision reached the right clavicle. The slaaf watched as his victim turned pale. He felt immense relief as blood poured from the incision and flowed from the workbench onto the floor. He stepped back, trying to avoid the growing pool. He watched the helpless body become listless and cold.

This was just the beginning.

{CHAPTER THREE}

Thursday, Before Dawn

"Dr. Gram, please call extension 239. Dr. Peter Gram, please call extension 239," the speaker in the hallway boomed.

Oh, no. Not again, Peter thought as he lay under a blanket in the doctor's lounge.

It was one in the morning at the Newbury General and Pediatric Hospital, and the hallways outside the physicians' on-call room bustled with activity. Peter had only just lain down fifteen minutes before, curling up under the blanket against the chill of the air-conditioning. He had slid almost immediately into a dream of being crammed into a small, dark space. There was an ache in his joints now, and he stretched his limbs to alleviate it. If he didn't get some uninterrupted sleep, he was sure to be a zombie tomorrow. And his head cold only seemed to be worsening. As he slowly sat up, his pager went off, and he fumbled for it in the dark to stop the infernal beeping.

It had been a busy night for the pediatric emergency-room personnel. The pediatric emergency room at Newbury was one of the busiest ERs in the area. It provided multidisciplinary care for children from birth to eighteen years of age, and it wasn't unusual for some of the young adults who had received care there as children to continue treatment there for the long-term and potentially terminal illnesses the Newbury doctors had diagnosed. The hospital housed every conceivable department available in the medical field and served as a training center for the Newbury Medical

School and University. Medical students, residents, fellows, and other trainees walked the halls every day.

Peter stood and blew his nose loudly. He grabbed the telephone that hung on the wall near the bed, reaching out with his other hand to flick the light switch on the wall. The fluorescent bulb came alive, and he shaded his eyes and dialed 239 on the phone. It took two tries before he could get through to the ER—239 was a popular number, especially at night.

"Pediatric ER. How can I help you?"

"This is Dr. Gram calling. Did somebody page me?"

"Hold on a minute," the voice rasped on the other end. Peter could hear a muffled shout. "Did anybody page Dr. Gram?" Peter waited for a few moments before hearing a distant affirmation in the background. The earpiece rustled as the phone changed hands.

"Hello, Dr. Gram," a woman's voice said. He thought he recognized Alice, a resident. "I paged you. We have a seven-year-old girl who was brought in by emergency medical services, and we need a psychiatry consult for her."

"Why was she brought in?" Peter asked.

"She tried to jump off a balcony."

"Has she been medically cleared?"

"Yes, she's all yours," the resident said with a hint of relief in her voice. If Peter remembered correctly, she was a second-year pediatric resident and had enough to worry about.

"I'll be there in fifteen," he said.

The pediatric emergency room wasn't one of Peter's favorite places to work. The area was so cramped that Peter often struggled to find space to interview a cooperative patient, let alone an uncooperative, unruly, and frightened child. On a busy night, a dozen children could waltz into the ER for psychiatric evaluations. Some were children who had decompensated—become depressed, suicidal, or violent—after running out of medication. Others were in the midst of social crises, such as abuse, neglect, or parental conflict.

It took Peter five minutes to dress and another five to walk from the on-call room, through the connecting hallways, and over to the rear entrance of the pediatric emergency room. He swiped the ID card that hung from his neck, and the heavy automatic doors jerked open. The rear entrance to the ER offered a shortcut around the heavy traffic at the main entrance. Still, as he made his way toward the nurses' station—which was the hub of the ER—Peter found himself blocked by the flow of people in and out of the examination rooms that lined the hallway. The ER often seemed like a well-contained ecosystem that never paused to rest.

Peter had trouble getting the ER clerk's attention. She seemed engrossed in stamping names on completed consultations reports, but Peter knew she must see him there. At over six feet tall, with a shock of dark hair and striking blue eyes, he was difficult to miss. He cleared his throat, but the clerk only looked up and stared at him as though he were an alien who had just landed.

"Dr. Gram," Peter said, offering his ID card as though to prove he belonged there. "I was paged for a child psych consultation."

The clerk rolled her chair toward the doorway behind her and yelled out, "Anybody ask for a child psych consultation?" Getting no immediate response, she rolled back to the counter and continued her work as though their interaction had never occurred.

Peter scanned the list of patient names written on a large dry-erase board on the wall. He looked for the "ψ" symbol that indicated a psychiatry patient. The first one was a twelve-year-old girl whom Peter had evaluated earlier, and the second was Naya Hastings, a seven-year-old girl. He asked the ER clerk to page Alice, the resident in charge of Naya's case. She did so in an automated fashion, without looking up. Peter could hardly hear the page himself above the prominent chatter of the ER. He continued to stand there until the clerk finally looked up and stared into his eyes.

"There," she said and pointed to a phone at the far end of the nursing station. As though on cue, the phone rang. Peter hurried toward it.

"This is Dr. Gram, child-psych fellow, speaking," he said.

"I'll speak with you shortly," the resident said tersely. "You can join Sharon if you like. She's with the child's parents."

Peter didn't like the idea that Sharon, the ER social worker, was interviewing a child and her parents before he had met with them. The few times he had seen Sharon work, she hadn't seemed in tune with the psychological needs of a child. Her demeanor came off as cold, critical, and often insensitive to the child's needs. Her strengths weren't in her bedside manner, but rather in her navigation of the complex bureaucratic rules of hospitals. She was very good at finding beds at various inpatient psychiatric units, as well as dealing with the frustrating procedures of managed care.

Peter grabbed Naya's medical chart from the rack and headed out to room 105, the child-psych exam room, to say hello and find out what had brought the family to the ER. The door to room 105 was shut, and he paused outside to blow his nose again. Then he knocked gently, and the door slid open a few inches with a squeak. The room was dark. As Peter pushed the door open, the fluorescent light from the hallway illuminated the child-size table and chairs, the purple couch, the television, and the toys strewn about the room. At first glance, the room appeared to be empty, but then Peter saw an ER staff member sitting silently in the corner and a small figure covered with a white sheet lying on the couch. He walked over to get a look at his patient, but the child had pulled the sheet over her face, presumably to shield it from the cold air blowing from the vent above.

Peter knew better than to wake her at this hour. In any case, he needed to interview her parents first. He waved at the ER staff member and quietly slipped out of the room, then headed toward the ER conference room—the next best place to hold an interview without being disturbed. He skimmed through Naya's chart on his way.

Peter introduced himself as he entered the conference room. "Hi, I'm Dr. Gram, one of the child-psychiatry fellows. I'll be working with you this evening."

"Fred Hastings," said Naya's father as he leaned forward to shake Peter's outstretched hand. "And this is my wife, Jane."

Mrs. Hastings clasped Peter's fingertips briefly and gave him a small, forced smile. Peter turned to Sharon, who sat opposite the couple at the table with her chair pushed back, her legs crossed, and a notepad resting on her thigh.

"Sharon, how are you?" Peter asked politely.

"Fine, thank you, Dr. Gram," Sharon said without the least bit of warmth.

Peter pulled up a chair next to her and looked across the table at the weary couple. He set Naya's chart on the table, along with his pen.

"Sharon, what have you gathered so far?" Peter inquired, not wanting to subject a pair of already frazzled parents to redundant questions. He noticed with annoyance that Sharon had little stars painted on her fingernails. Who had time for such frivolousness?

"Oh, we just started," Sharon said. "Mr. Hastings was telling me about the difficult time they had bringing their daughter to the emergency room."

Peter looked at the Hastings. They were a Caucasian couple in their forties. Mr. Hastings was a handsome, square-faced man who wore glasses. A few gray streaks in his hair shimmered under the fluorescent light. On his lap, he held a tan cashmere blazer. Mrs. Hastings appeared slightly younger; no gray glinted in the short, blonde hair that partially covered her diamond earrings. She looked pale and tired. She was dressed impeccably in a cream sweater accented by a pale blue neck scarf and dove gray woolen trousers.

From Naya's chart, Peter had gathered that Mr. Hastings was a lawyer and his wife an interior designer. He found that in cases of a child's psychological distress, it was much easier to work with well-educated parents.

"Mr. and Mrs. Hastings, please tell me what brought you here tonight," Peter said.

"Well—our daughter wasn't herself today," said Mr. Hastings.

"What do you mean?"

"I found Naya standing on the second-floor balcony," Mrs. Hastings said shakily, "and I think she thought she could fly away. She was looking at the sky, trying to climb over the balcony wall, and mumbling to herself."

"What was she saying?"

"It sounded like she was saying, 'I do want to come!'"

"Was she speaking to you? Did she know you were in the room at the time?" Peter asked, gauging the possibility of auditory hallucinations.

"No, I don't think she knew I was there," Mrs. Hastings said.

"Was she asleep?"

Mrs. Hastings nodded. "I think so," she said.

"When did you discover her on the balcony?"

"After our dinner," Mr. Hastings said.

Mr. Hastings paused as Peter sneezed into a Kleenex.

"Bless you," he said.

"Thank you," Peter said. He smiled wanly. "I'm beginning to understand the hazards of working with children."

Mrs. Hastings smiled tightly, and Mr. Hastings continued, "My wife went to make sure that Naya was still asleep, and that's when she discovered that Naya wasn't in her room—"

"And that she was trying to climb over the wall," Mrs. Hastings finished.

"Has anything like this ever happened before?"

"No," Mrs. Hastings replied.

"Did anything unusual happen earlier in the day?" Peter asked Mrs. Hastings. He sensed that, although both parents had careers, she was Naya's primary caregiver.

"Nothing that I can think of. She went to school at the same time as always, on the same bus. She came home in a happy mood; she didn't mention that anything had happened at school. She finished her homework and then she spent her free time before bedtime playing with her dolls. It was really a normal day."

"Did she eat anything unusual or feel sick after eating?" Peter asked. The ingestion of a toxic substance could be the reason for the sudden onset of bizarre behavior.

"No," Mrs. Hastings said, and Peter detected a note of defensiveness in her voice. "We had dinner at home. I cook all the meals myself, and I can assure you that they are sanitary, fully cooked, and fully vegetarian."

"Please understand, Mr. and Mrs. Hastings, that I don't think you've done anything to harm your daughter." Peter looked directly into Mrs. Hastings's eyes as he spoke. "But I have to ask these questions to rule out every possibility."

Mrs. Hastings looked down at her lap. Mr. Hastings nodded and took his wife's hand.

"Are you ready to continue?" Peter asked Mrs. Hastings.

"Of course," she said, looking up at him again.

"Do you know if Naya might have ingested any medications unknowingly?"

"We keep all our medications in a locked cabinet," Mrs. Hastings said. "Before we came to the hospital, I checked to see if she might have gotten into the cabinet somehow, but it was still locked, and nothing was missing."

Peter tried to focus on what Mrs. Hastings was saying instead of his now burning, watery eyes and the maddening itch in his nostrils.

"I also have to ask if Naya might have come into contact with any drugs or alcohol."

"Definitely not!" Mrs. Hastings exclaimed.

Peter could see that in spite of his best efforts, Mrs. Hastings was becoming more anxious, so he decided to change the line of questioning.

"How old is Naya?" he asked softly.

"Seven and a half," Mr. Hastings answered.

"Did Naya have any developmental delays or problems when she was younger?"

"Not that I can recall," Mrs. Hastings replied more calmly. "She walked at the right time, talked at the right time, toilet trained early."

"What about her speech and language development?"

"She spoke early, and she loves to read," Mrs. Hastings said proudly.

"Has she had any medical problems?" he asked.

"For the most part, she has always been a healthy, active girl," Mr. Hastings replied. He and his wife looked at each other for a long moment.

"Except for?" Peter asked.

"It started when Naya had just turned six," Mrs. Hastings said, looking from her husband to Peter. "She began having the most horrible nightmares."

"Almost every night," Mr. Hastings added, and Peter could see from the tightening of his lips that the episodes had taken a toll on him. "She would cry out, but then flail her arms and scream when we tried to hold her."

"We thought it was just childish fears, you know, so we waited, but they only got worse. Then, just when we were ready to take her to see a doctor, they stopped.

"But this time, it was different from those other nights. She looked posse—" Mrs. Hastings cut herself off.

"The nightmares started again last week," Mr. Hastings said, "and they've been just terrible. We wake up to her screaming and shouting, and often by the time we get to her room, she's up and out of her bed."

"Are they occurring every night?" Peter asked.

The Hastings looked at each other. "Yes," Mrs. Hastings said.

"Has a neurologist ever evaluated her for an epileptic seizure disorder?" Peter asked.

"No," Mr. Hastings said.

"What kind of girl is Naya generally? Is she happy ... sad ... angry?"

"Oh, she's such a happy girl," Mrs. Hastings said, and her smile wiped the exhaustion from her face. "She's just a bundle of joy to be with. She's so kind, gentle, and loving. I can't imagine why she would be angry or sad. But obviously"—her voice faltered—"something is wrong."

Peter looked at the large clock that hung on one side of the conference room. An hour had passed since he started the interview. He could see that the Hastings were exceedingly tired, and they were probably hungry as well. He was exhausted himself, and his head felt three times its normal size. He would finish up the interview later, after speaking with Naya.

"Maybe we should stop for now, so the two of you can get a cup of coffee or something," Peter suggested, putting down his pen next to Naya's chart on the table. "I'm sure this has been a long day for you. I do want you to know that without an evident reason for Naya's disturbances, it's going to take a while to figure out why Naya is suffering this way—and what we can do about it."

As tired as they must have been, the Hastings seemed reluctant to go too far from the vicinity of the emergency room. Mr. Hastings turned to his wife and gently brushed her cheek. "I think the doctor's right." He looked at Peter. "Where can we get that coffee—and maybe a bite to eat?"

"I'll take them down to the cafeteria," Sharon said, leading the couple toward the door of the conference room. "It isn't full service at night, but I think you'll be able to find something there."

Peter watched Naya's parents leave the room hand in hand. It was nice to see such a close-knit set of parents. They appeared to be warm and caring people. He could tell that they loved their daughter very much. While he was glad to have gotten apparently reliable information about his new patient, it left him with surprisingly little to go on.

He stretched his arms and legs and let out a silent yawn, turning his head to conceal it from anyone passing in the hallway. He gathered Naya's chart and walked back toward the on-call room. There was still a chance he could get some sleep before his shift in the ER began. He couldn't do much more about this case until he had a chance to talk with Naya.

{CHAPTER FOUR}

Thursday, Before Dawn

"Would you like something to drink?" the flight attendant asked the brunette sitting in the window seat.

"Coke, please, with lots of ice," agent Leia Bines replied as she pulled down her tray table.

Leia stretched in the economy-class seat, trying to get comfortable. The red eye from Los Angeles to New York was always rough; it was past midnight Pacific Time, and her destination was still hours away.

Leia thanked the gentleman sitting next to her as he passed along the can and cup. His eyes flitted from her face to her throat to her chest as he handed her the drink. Earlier, she'd noticed him looking at her legs. He was attractive enough, but Leia wasn't in the mood. She busied herself pouring the soda over the ice, which crackled and hissed.

"You visiting family?" the gentleman said.

"No, just business," Leia said with a pleasant smile, not quite meeting his eyes. She set her slim computer on the tray table and opened it, hoping he'd take the hint.

Leia had been summoned from her vacation in Hawaii to an urgent assignment in Newbury, Connecticut. She wasn't pleased to have her vacation cut short. Nor was she happy about the prospect of flying all the way from Hawaii to New York City and then driving to Newbury. Hawaii was supposed to have been a sanctuary. She had only recently returned from

Costa Rica after trying unsuccessfully to catch a high profile international kidnapping suspect.

"Welcome," her screen offered silently. She double-clicked on the file she had downloaded at the airport before boarding her flight: case number 3546. Leia knew she would have to go through the details of the case with a fine-tooth comb. She couldn't afford to be careless in any way. Her leg twitched again, reminding her that a few short days in a tropical paradise hadn't wiped out the effects of her most recent failure. She wasn't eager to take on another case so soon, only to find out that she had indeed lost her touch.

Over the next forty-five minutes, Leia learned about the ten-year-old girl who had mysteriously disappeared on her way home from school. There was no doubt that Janet was missing, but why? Many missing children were victims of kidnappings, but even more were runaways. In the two years that Leia had been in the CAC—the FBI special unit for crimes against children—she had come across many children trying to escape chaotic home environments. The Newbury police officer in charge of the case, one José Rodriguez, had interviewed the parents and neighbors and found no evidence of child abuse or neglect. He had organized a community search of the area around the victim's home. He had also located two suspects who appeared in the registry of sex offenders and was in the process of obtaining interviews with them. Leia was impressed—she had worked with more local police than she cared to remember, and few were as competent as Officer Rodriguez appeared to be.

Still, he had no real leads. What could have happened to a schoolgirl in a town like Newbury, Connecticut—a small university town where everybody knew practically everybody else? Leia just hoped the evidence hadn't disappeared with the victim.

She scrolled down to enlarge a picture of the missing girl. She was a beautiful Caucasian girl with wide blue eyes and short, blonde hair, wearing baggy pants and a purple T-shirt that read "Floating Heads." She didn't look any different to Leia than any other ten-year-old. So why had Leia been ordered to lead the search? Plenty of children went missing without interrupting a town sheriff's vacation, much less a federal agent's. There were also plenty of good agents in the eastern part of the country.

Who are you, Janet? she thought. Of course, if Leia's victims could answer such questions, she would be out of a job.

She tried not to think of the boy, but once again, she was in the old Ford police car, racing through the narrow, unpaved alleys of a village outside San José. The driver swerved around a corner, causing the car to shudder. Leia held on tightly to the door handle, hoping her local comrade's driving skills were as good as he'd bragged they were, even in the pitch darkness. As they skidded to a halt in front of the tin-roofed house, Leia leaped out of the car and dashed toward the door, her gun in one hand and a flashlight in the other. As the local officer tried to catch up, she kicked open the flimsy wooden door and ran through the small rooms, searching for the boy whose face had haunted her for the past three weeks—his liquid dark eyes, the angelic cheeks. He wasn't even four years old.

The smell of death overpowered her as she neared the back room, but she breathed it in to punish herself for what she now knew had happened. The kidnapper had panicked and fled early in the game, leaving the boy strapped to a metal cot to starve to death. Leia choked at the sight of his cherubic face—more than half-eaten by rats.

Miles above the sleeping country, Leia's hand tightened on her armrest. She couldn't afford to lose another child. She recalled her early investigations, when she had thought of herself as Leia Bines, Girl Detective: staking out a house to catch neighborhood vandals in the act, tracking a roommate's dog. How could she have anticipated the horrible weight of responsibility that accompanied protecting the most vulnerable members of the population?

During her seven years with the FBI, Leia had worked with a renowned forensic psychologist at the Behavioral Science Unit, memorizing the profiles of convicted felons in cases of missing children. She had learned the motives and methods of sociopaths through extensive interviews with convicted child molesters, discovering in the process that a number of them were repeat offenders who had fallen through the cracks in the system after their initial crimes.

Now, Leia was a well-known expert in her field, working out of the FBI office in San Francisco, the city of her childhood. When a difficult or prominent case arose, she was summoned, often to lead a Child Abduction Rapid Deployment team.

Leia set her watch to eastern time. She wondered if it would make more sense to sleep for a bit or read over Janet's information one more time. She knew it would be difficult to work with jet lag, given the huge time difference between Hawaii and the East Coast. Leia turned off her laptop and tucked the computer under the seat in front of her. She spread a blanket over her lap and tried to get some rest.

{CHAPTER FIVE}

Thursday

Peter was grateful that no more child-psych referrals had rolled into the ER in the wee hours of the morning. He dozed for about four hours; on waking, he had broken down and taken an antihistamine. Now it was nearly seven, and he felt almost normal as he left Strauss I and walked toward the ER to talk to Naya Hastings.

As he passed through the automatic doors to the ER, he noted how the early-morning sun seeping through the doors and windows gave the ER a whole different feeling than it had at night. The children's paintings and drawings, displayed with great pride on the walls, came to life as the sun hit the frames.

At the nurses' station, Peter saw the next shift signing in and the previous shift preparing to go home. Unfortunately for him, even though he had been the fellow on call the previous twenty-four hours, he was still obligated to stay for the rest of the day. He checked the board to make sure that Naya's name was still there. It was; they hadn't moved her out of room 105.

Mrs. Hastings was standing at the door of the room as Peter approached. She looked tired, but well groomed. He noticed that her eyes were the same pale blue as her scarf. Their round shape and her sharp features gave her the look of a bird.

"Good morning, Mrs. Hastings," Peter said, smiling.

"Good morning, doctor," Mrs. Hastings replied, her own smile a weary one.

"Is Naya inside?"

"Yes, she has found some company and is keeping herself occupied," Mrs. Hastings said, stepping away from the door.

Peter knocked gently before entering. Two girls sat next to each other at the small, circular table. A staff member supervised them from the corner. One of the girls was a blonde Caucasian girl, and the other a black-haired Indian girl with light brown skin. The Caucasian girl watched, fascinated, as the Indian girl drew a line figure with two crayons of different colors at the same time.

"I see double—" the blonde girl said, cutting her sentence short when she saw Peter.

"Good morning, girls," Peter said, grinning warmly. "My name is Dr. Gram. I'm here to see Naya." He looked at the blonde girl.

"I'm not Naya," the girl said, pointing to the Indian girl.

Surprised and a bit embarrassed, Peter looked at the black-haired girl, who continued to draw. Because the Hastings were white, he had assumed that Naya would be white as well. He realized that, weary as he had been the previous night, he had not asked Naya's parents about her prenatal and birth history. If he had, he would have known that the Hastings were not Naya's biological parents.

"Hi, Naya," he said sheepishly, looking now at the petite girl so engrossed in her drawing that she didn't bother to look up at him. She wore a pair of blue jeans and a bright pink, long-sleeved T-shirt. "I wanted to talk to you this morning—I didn't get a chance last night."

He looked again at the blonde girl, who stared at him intently. "I would like to speak to Naya alone," Peter said.

"My name is Melanie," she replied with disappointment in her voice. "You don't want to talk to me?" She rose reluctantly from her little chair, but then just stood next to Naya with her hand on the back of Naya's chair.

"Melanie, another doctor will be here soon to meet with you," Peter said gently. He indicated to the staff member that Melanie should be escorted from the room.

As the staff member led her toward the door, Melanie started to whine. "But I was watching her draw!"

"I promise you can come back and play with Naya once we're done talking," Peter said. "Thank you very much, Melanie, for being understanding."

"Sure," Melanie said snidely. She slammed the door behind her.

Peter stood next to Naya's chair. The small furniture in the room made him feel like a giant. "Is it all right if I sit next to you?" he asked, pulling the chair Melanie had just vacated toward him. She didn't respond. "How are you doing today?" The little wooden chair creaked in protest as he lowered his weight onto the small seat. "Can I see what you're drawing?" Peter tried to make eye contact.

Naya ignored him, but made no effort to hide her work.

"I like the colors you've chosen," Peter tried again. "I wonder what your favorite color is."

Naya continued to ignore him.

Peter sat silently, watching Naya complete the picture she was drawing. Its contents were typical for a child her age: a house, a tree, and a rainbow. But the level of detail was quite impressive; the house nearly resembled an architectural drawing, and the tree's leaves were meticulously detailed against the sky. The rainbow arched smoothly between the house and the tree. *She's going to be an amazing artist when she grows up*, Peter thought. *I've just got to keep her safe enough to make it there.*

After two minutes, he stood and shook his leg, which was beginning to fall asleep.

"Naya, finish up your drawing, and I'll be right back. I'm going to talk to your mother for a moment," Peter said.

He opened the door and stepped out into the hallway. Naya's mother walked hurriedly toward him.

"Is everything all right?" Mrs. Hastings asked anxiously.

Peter smiled ruefully. "It looks like Naya doesn't feel like talking to anybody right now."

"That's not like her," Mrs. Hastings said. "Maybe I should ask her to speak to you."

"It's okay. Anyway, I think it might be better if I could get some information from you that I missed last night, and Naya can keep herself occupied."

Mrs. Hastings nodded. "My husband stepped out for a moment. Should we wait for him?"

"He can join us when he returns," Peter said. He spoke briefly with one of the ER nurses, then led Mrs. Hastings to the conference room.

{CHAPTER SIX}

Thursday

Naya jumped when the door clicked closed, but she didn't look up. When she knew she was alone, she shifted her gaze from her drawing to the smoked-glass window in the door. She could see Peter walking away. She looked back to her picture and stared at the rainbow.

Naya was unhappy about her visit to the ER. She felt well rested after a few hours of sleep; however, that didn't mean she was ready to talk to anyone. All she wanted to do was go home. There wasn't anything wrong with her. She didn't understand why her parents had been so upset the night before. All she knew was that when they'd woken her up, she was already on her way to this dreadful place.

Naya quietly rose from her chair and went to the sink that stood in the corner of the room. She stood on her toes to turn on the faucet. She let the water run until it was warm, then gently washed her hands. The mirror that hung in front of her showed a girl with long, jet-black hair and big, brown eyes. Her cheekbones were even, her nose straight, the two halves of her face perfectly symmetrical.

Naya wondered if she looked like her real mother had looked when she was a girl.

There, my hands are clean again, she thought as she patted them dry with paper towel. The one thing she didn't like was other people touching her toys. But today, she was in a place where everybody touched everything. It made her hands feel dirty to touch things that so many other people had touched.

She went back to her seat and pulled out a second sheet of paper from beneath the picture she had just drawn. Naya liked to draw, and she was very good at it. She had started to draw at the age of three. Even at that young age, she had had excellent fine-motor control compared to other children. Now, at seven, she could draw as well as a twelve-year-old. She even had a favorite posture that she would assume every time she drew.

Naya sat perfectly straight in the chair, her right hand arched over the blank paper. She began to draw, and as she did, she remembered that she'd had a dream the previous night. She wondered why she hadn't remembered it before. She'd been standing at her bedroom window, looking at a group of white doves sitting on the balcony wall. They were talking to each other in whispers and stealing fleeting glances at her. She thought that if she got closer to them, she might be able to hear what they were saying.

Naya had found her green plastic stool and pulled it to the balcony door. Carefully, she climbed onto the stool and unlocked the top latch that kept the door from opening. She pushed the stool aside and turned the doorknob little by little, not wanting to startle the doves. They didn't seem bothered by her arrival; they continued to talk to each other in whispers that no longer seemed so soft.

As Naya approached them, the doves stopped chattering and looked at her simultaneously.

"Naya, thank you for coming," one of them said.

Naya stood motionless. "I heard you talking," she said.

"We were wondering if you'd like to join us," the dove said. "We're going away for good."

"Where are you going, and why should I come?" Naya asked curiously.

"We're going to a faraway place where everybody goes. We think you'll like it there."

"Maybe I like my bed better," Naya said. "Can I come back if I don't like it there?"

"Maybe ... but you have to decide, because we're leaving now," the dove said, and one by one, the birds began to fly away.

Naya shouted, "Wait! I do want to come." After all, the doves' chatter proved that this was just a dream; she could go and come back in a flash if she wanted to. Anything was possible in a dream. The third and fourth doves flew away as she tried to climb up onto the balcony ledge. But she couldn't get her footing on the wall. Frustrated, she tried harder. The only bird left now was the one who'd spoken to her, and the balcony wall seemed to grow taller and more slippery by the moment. Naya tried to dig her nails into the stone wall, only to feel pain shoot along her fingers. When the last dove lifted from the balcony ledge with a flapping of its wings, Naya sat on the ground and reached out toward the sky. Now she would never know what the nice place was like.

Naya finished the picture she was drawing. On the paper, six doves and a girl tried to fly away.

{CHAPTER SEVEN}

Thursday

"Did you get to eat anything this morning?" Peter asked Mrs. Hastings as they settled into chairs in the bright, chilly conference room.

"Fred went home to get some food for Naya," Mrs. Hastings said. "He'll get something for me as well." She smiled indulgently. "I didn't think Naya would like the hospital food."

"Are you all vegetarian?"

"No, only Naya. She never seemed to like the smell of meat. One of the few things I know about her biological mother is that she was vegetarian too. I've learned to cook Indian vegetarian food for Naya."

"So you adopted her?" Peter asked matter-of-factly, trying to mask his embarrassment at not having asked the question the previous night.

"Yes, when Naya was a year old. She's Indian—South Asian, not American Indian," Mrs. Hastings clarified.

"So she was a year old when she came to the U.S.?"

"A year and a half. We stayed in India to complete the adoption process."

"Why did you decide to adopt?"

"We couldn't have children of our own, so we decided to adopt. We learned about baby Naya through friends and decided to meet her during a visit to India. At that time, Naya was living at her maternal aunt's home in Bangalore."

"What about her parents?"

"We don't know who her biological father is, but her mother passed away when Naya was just a few months old."

"How did she die?"

"We don't know. The medical records were missing from the hospital, and Naya's aunt and uncle told us that the circumstances were unclear. We didn't really care, as Naya was the cutest brown-eyed baby we had ever seen. We fell in love with her instantly."

"Does she have any siblings?"

"Not that we know of."

"Is she in touch with any other members of her biological family?"

"Naya's uncle from her mother's side—the one I just mentioned—lives with his wife in New York City. Naya has always visited them for the Indian holidays and festivals. We want her to feel as connected with her culture as possible."

"Do you know if there is any psychiatric illness in the biological family?"

"Not that we know of. Is there something genetic we should be worried about?" Mrs. Hastings asked, her smooth brow furrowing.

"Not at this moment, but we'll have to rule out all possibilities," Peter replied. "Could I contact her uncle?"

"Of course, if you think it's necessary. I can give you his address and phone number."

Peter gave her the back of a prescription form to write on, then slipped the information into Naya's chart.

"Is there any family history that you know of for medical disorders like epilepsy, diabetes, or asthma?" Peter asked.

Mrs. Hastings shook her head. "We were told that her mother was physically healthy," she said. "No one seemed to know who her father was. What do you think could be wrong with Naya?"

"At this point, I can't be sure," Peter confessed. "I really have to speak to Naya before I can get a real idea of what might be wrong."

"But when can I take Naya home?" Mrs. Hastings asked, a sharp tone of worry entering her voice.

"I'll try again with Naya when we're finished here. It can be difficult figuring out what a seven-year-old is thinking—especially if she doesn't want to tell you," Peter said, smiling. "In the meantime," he continued, "can you tell me a little more about Naya's nightmares?"

"We started noticing the nightmares when she was six, but we've always thought of her as a restless sleeper—tossing and turning, and sometimes talking in her sleep. But when she turned six, she began shouting and screaming in her sleep."

"Does she look frightened?"

"She looks terrified. When I hold her, her heart is racing, and her head is hot and sweaty."

"Is she aware of your presence?"

"She doesn't seem to be."

"Has she ever woken up during a dream?"

"Never that I know of. Her eyes are often open, but I've learned that she's not really awake, because I've tried to talk to her, and she doesn't answer. Without waking up, she just seems to calm down after a period of time, and then she sleeps through the night—although she does appear very tired the next morning."

"Does she talk to you or Mr. Hastings about her dreams?"

"Not usually. Although recently she drew a picture, and when I asked her about it, she said it was her dream. She's quite an artist, you know," Mrs. Hastings said with pride.

"Yes," Peter said, "I saw one of her drawings this morning. At what point in her sleep cycle are these episodes occurring? Early? Late?"

"In the past, it would usually happen two to three hours after she went to bed—when we were still awake. But over the past few months, I've heard noises in the middle of the night and found her wandering around the house." Her eyes searched Peter's face. "Is this just something that happens with some children?"

"Sleepwalking? Yes, that can happen," Peter replied.

"Has she done anything like going out on the balcony before? Something dangerous?"

"No," Mrs. Hastings said. "That's why we brought her to the emergency room."

"You did the right thing, Mrs. Hastings," Peter reassured her. "I know that this can be an unpleasant experience for everyone involved."

Mrs. Hastings nodded. "Please," she said, "call me Jane."

"All right, Jane." Peter stood, and Mrs. Hastings followed his lead. "I'm going to see how Naya's doing."

"Yes, my husband is probably back and looking for me by now," Mrs. Hastings said.

As he held the conference room door for her, Peter gave an internal sigh of relief. These cases went so much more smoothly when the parents cooperated. Now, if he could just get Naya to talk to him, he might actually have a chance at solving this mystery.

{CHAPTER EIGHT}

Thursday

The cabin speakers crackled, and Leia awoke in a snap.

"Cabin crew, please prepare for landing," the flight attendant intoned.

Leia was used to sleeping at odd hours and waking quickly in a fully functional state. She had never needed a caffeine fix to get her going.

She stretched her cramped legs again and thought irritably that this case had better be something special. But Leia knew at the bottom of her heart that any missing child was a good reason for bringing her in on a job. After all, she had one of the best success rates in her field. In the past five years, she had found more children and led more CARD teams than the agents in the north- and southeastern regions put together. But she also knew well enough that every case did not have a happy ending.

At Gate 21, a stocky Hispanic man was waiting for her. He greeted her enthusiastically, with a smile and an outstretched hand. "Welcome to the East Coast, Agent Bines. I'm Detective José Rodriguez. Please call me José."

José Rodriguez was glad to see Leia Bines. He had followed her work over the past several years and knew that if anyone could put this case to bed, it was her. In person, she was even more beautiful than in the newspaper photos. Her lush, auburn hair bounced over her shoulders as they shook hands, and her smile made her peaches-and-cream complexion and sculpted features even more radiant.

"I hope your flight was okay," he said.

"It was fine, thank you," Leia replied. Her hazel eyes seemed to look straight through him.

Leia gently pulled her hand out of Detective Rodriguez's firm grip. He was a few inches shorter than she was; her low heels brought her to five-ten or so. She tried not to look at his receding hairline.

"I have a car waiting for us outside. Do you have other bags?" he asked, looking at Leia's carry-on luggage. She noticed that he also snuck a glance at her legs, and she tried not to grin.

"This is it," Leia said. She always traveled light.

"Then we'll be on our way to Newbury, if that's all right with you."

"Of course, Detective. Lead the way."

Leia followed him out of the airport and into the backseat of the waiting Lincoln Town Car. It was early morning here, and the sky was pink and gray over the airport. As the driver pulled away from the curb, Detective Rodriguez apologized for spoiling Leia's vacation.

She hoped he didn't notice her shivering beneath her light coat.

"The children come first, and vacations come later," she said firmly.

But if she really believed that, why was she longing right now to be walking the black-sand beach and watching the turtles at Punalu'u? Why did she so badly want to turn around and get on the first plane headed west?

{CHAPTER NINE}

Thursday

On his way back to room 105, Peter mulled potential causes for Naya's parasomnia. Sleepwalking and sleep terror disorders were not uncommon in children, but they were often frightening for the child and parents alike. Sleepwalking—known in the medical field as somnambulism—carried a high risk of injury, which was what concerned him most about Naya's case.

Peter wondered if it could be a sleep terror disorder. He had seen one such case in his outpatient practice. A twelve-year-old boy had presented with a history of screaming and shouting uncontrollably at the top of his lungs in the middle of the night, scaring the living daylights out of his sister, who slept in the room next to him. The episodes included profuse sweating and a dramatically increased heart rate. The boy said his heart would pound so hard, he thought it would explode. The boy's sister said he looked as though he'd seen a ghost and would often tease him about it.

Naya might also have a nightmare disorder—another disorder that could begin in childhood. Peter would also have to rule out a rare form of temporal-lobe epilepsy in which seizures often occurred at night. Naya would certainly have to have an EEG. But in any case, the first step in making a diagnosis was talking with the patient—if she would talk, that is.

Peter knocked gently on the door to room 105 and walked in. Naya looked up briefly from the drawing in front of her, but when she saw it was him, she went back to admiring her work.

"I've heard you're very good at drawing pictures," Peter said as he pulled up a little chair to the table and sat down in such a way that his eyes were level with Naya's.

"May I see what you drew?"

Naya turned her head slowly and looked right into Peter's eyes. She pushed her drawing toward him.

When he looked at the picture, Peter nearly gasped out loud. The drawing was stunningly detailed. It showed a dark-haired girl on a balcony looking up at six white birds lined up on the railing. Beyond the balcony, the sky was dark, and the trees appeared to be swaying in the wind. Peter wondered how Naya would be able to remember those details if she had been sleepwalking.

"Will you tell me about your picture?" Peter asked.

Naya pointed to the white birds. "They're going away," she said soberly.

"Where are they going?" Peter asked.

"I don't know—but they wanted me to go with them."

"Did you think you could go with them?"

"I could. They said so."

"Did you really *really* think you could go with them?" Peter asked once more.

"In the dream, I could."

"Did you know that when your parents found you, you were really trying to go with them? It didn't just happen in your dream." Peter watched Naya's face closely for her reaction.

She looked down at her hands where they lay on the table. "No," she said softly.

"It made them worried about you. That's why they brought you to the hospital," Peter said. "What you were trying to do was dangerous. Can you tell me why it was dangerous?"

Naya looked up at him again and shrugged.

"You could have fallen off the balcony!" Peter said, his tone communicating the seriousness of her action. "And what could have happened if you fell over the wall?"

"I could get hurt?" Naya replied, fishing for the answer Peter wanted to hear.

"Yes, you could break your bones and get badly hurt."

"My heart will stop beating, and I'll stop breathing," Naya said, her eyebrows lifting to disappear beneath the dark fringe of her bangs.

Peter found that Naya had an age-appropriate idea of death as a vague lack of body functioning. She didn't appear overly anxious, but he didn't want to scare her by discussing the topic further.

"Besides drawing, what else do you like to do?" he asked.

"I like to read, I like to play on the swings, and I like to watch TV," Naya replied.

"Are you a happy girl or a sad girl?" Peter asked.

"Happy. Well, I'm mostly happy, but I feel sad sometimes."

"Can you tell me one time you felt sad?"

"The day I left Noodle in the store."

"Who is Noodle?" Peter inquired.

"Noodle's my dog."

"What kind of dog is Noodle? Does he like to run and play?" Peter asked.

"Oh, he's not a real dog," Naya said. "He's only a toy dog."

"I think it's okay to feel sad if you lost your toy dog."

"Thank goodness I found Noodle when I went back to the store. I was very happy after that," Naya said, smiling broadly. She was clearly comforted by her story's happy ending.

"Now I'm going to ask you some difficult questions, Naya. You may or may not know the answers. It's okay for you to tell me you don't know the answer or that you don't want to talk about it."

Naya's expression turned more serious. She nodded.

"Some of the questions may sound a little silly, but I have to ask them anyway. Is that all right with you?" Peter asked.

"Yeah," Naya said.

"Have you ever felt sad for many days at a time—like for a whole week?"

"Uh-uh."

"Have you ever felt so sad that you felt that you didn't want to be alive anymore?"

"No," Naya replied. The serious look in her eyes conveyed to Peter that she understood the gravity of the question.

"Have you ever felt so happy that you felt like you had special powers—like a supergirl?"

"No," Naya said with a giggle. She rolled her eyes as if to say, *That is a silly question!*

"Have you ever felt like your mind was going so fast that you had to talk very fast to keep up?"

"No."

"Have you ever heard people talking to you, but when you looked around, nobody was there?"

"No."

"Have you ever felt you heard a voice outside your head—like a TV talking to you?"

"No."

"Sometimes people have bad dreams. Have you ever had bad dreams?"

Naya shifted her gaze from Peter and withdrew into silence.

"You don't have to talk about it now if you don't want to," Peter said, bending close until she looked at him again.

Naya nodded. "When am I going home?" she asked.

"I'm not sure yet. I'll have to talk to your mom and dad about that. We have to figure out how we can help you stay safe," Peter said with a reassuring smile. "I'm planning on talking with them in a few minutes. How does that sound?"

Naya nodded vaguely.

Peter stood up. His back ached, and he felt like a giant hovering over Naya in her small chair.

"I'm going to ask your new friend Melanie to come back inside and spend more time with you while I speak to your parents," Peter said in a comforting tone.

Peter exited the room and looked for Melanie, who was more than happy to go back in. But before he met with the Hastings, Peter needed to review Naya's case formulation and proposed treatment plan with the supervising attending on call. Only after that could he discuss his recommendations with the Hastings.

{CHAPTER TEN}

Thursday

It took more than two hours for Leia and Detective Rodriguez to reach Newbury from the airport, and as the city gave way to suburbs and then small towns scattered between tracts of farmland, the detective peppered Leia with questions about her past cases. She was flattered by the depth of his knowledge of her career. She could tell by his questions that he was real police—dedicated to his cause on the force.

"Can I ask you a personal question?" the detective asked.

"Sure," Leia said without hesitation, while simultaneously bracing herself to rebuff him.

"What got you into this particular line of work? I mean, it hasn't taken you very long to get where you're now. Did you have this in mind when you started out?"

Leia paused, surprised both by the question and by her impulse to answer honestly, rather than roll out the usual platitudes about it being her duty to protect the vulnerable from predators.

"Well, Detective," she said finally, "if you really want to know … I grew up in San Francisco, in a house on Valencia Street in the Mission District. My family lived next door to another family that was like a mirror of ours. They had a daughter—Rosalia—who was my age, and a son my brother's age. My father is of Mexican descent, and so was theirs. Their mother was a gringa, and so was mine."

Outside the car window, Leia glimpsed the orderly rows of an orchard. Figures on ladders pulled apples from the trees to fill their white shoulder bags.

"The summer when Rosalia and I were nine years old," she continued, "we were playing on the sidewalk outside her house, and I went inside, just for a couple of minutes. When I came back out, I saw two boys taking her, dragging her into a car. They were wearing red caps and red bandanas. They were Norteños, and they thought Rosalia's brother had joined the Sureños, their rival gang. So they took Rosalia to teach him a lesson. And before the FBI could find her, they'd killed her and thrown her body from an overpass onto the James Lick Freeway.

"So, that, Detective, is why I do what I do."

Detective Rodriguez hadn't looked away, not even for a moment, as Leia told her story. Most people looked away, even seasoned police. She was really starting to respect the guy.

"So, Detective Rodriguez, how were you lucky enough to be assigned this case?" Leia asked.

"I'm part of the community-policing project in Newbury."

Leia looked at him curiously. "What is that, exactly?"

"It's a new program that integrates the services of various agencies, such as law-enforcement officials, juvenile-justice workers, domestic-violence counselors, mental-health professionals, and child-welfare and school agencies."

"That's some program," Leia said. She had not heard of such a program before.

"The program has two goals, basically," Detective Rodriguez continued. "On one hand, to better understand the relationship between a child's exposure to violence and the symptoms of traumatic stress disorders. On the other hand, to find ways to help kids and families exposed to violence. The various agencies work with the traumatized children in 'a psychologically minded and developmentally appropriate manner,' as the official spiel goes."

"It sounds like a good program." Leia was impressed by what she'd heard. "So you probably know already if any other children have been reported missing before or since Janet disappeared."

"None in this geographical area," Detective Rodriguez said. "Right now, Janet is classified as a missing child."

Finally, Leia could hold back no longer. "Do you have any idea why I was ordered to take this case ASAP if it's only a missing child? Surely the northeastern CARD team could have handled it alone?" Leia could contain her puzzlement no longer, and her expression conveyed her confusion.

"No one told you?" Detective Rodriguez asked. "I assume you know who Senator Thomas Bailey is."

"The presidential candidate? Of course I know who he is!" Leia exclaimed.

"Did you know that Senator Bailey has a fifty-acre horse ranch in Newbury?"

"No, I wasn't aware of that fact."

"One of the CARD team agents found a schoolbag on his property the day before yesterday. It's Janet's."

"Things are beginning to make more sense now," Leia said. She was there to keep headlines like "Missing child found on presidential candidate's ranch" from the front page of the *New York Times*. Such a scandal would be devastating to the senator's campaign. Bailey wanted this case resolved quickly, and by the best agents.

"So what do we know about Janet's family? Any sign of abuse or instability?"

"Everything points to a stable nuclear family. Both parents live in the home and, from all accounts, have a good relationship with each other and their daughter. We have no reason to suspect any physical or emotional abuse."

"Does she have other siblings?"

"No, she's an only child."

"Is there any history of mental illness in any of the family members?"

"Not to our knowledge."

"So they found her schoolbag. What was in it?"

"A math textbook, a notebook, a book from the school library, and a pencil case. Just normal school materials."

"Were they able to dust the bag for prints?"

"They've only gotten a couple so far. One is Janet's thumb and the other is only a partial. They're still working on it; we'll know if they find anything else later today."

Detective Rodriguez's mobile phone jingled, and Leia recognized the ringtone as U2's "One." He unsnapped the leather case strapped to his belt and flipped the phone open.

"Rodriguez," he said, and as he listened to the voice on the other end of the line, he turned away from Leia and rubbed his forehead. "Okay," he said. "We'll be there in fifteen."

Leia watched him place his phone back in its case. She could tell he didn't want to look at her, and when he finally did, she could see that he was upset.

"They found a body," he said grimly.

Leia's stomach turned to cold stone. "Janet?"

"Don't know, but we won't be going to the precinct first," Detective Rodriguez said, tapping the driver's shoulder.

They would have to turn around and head back south to the previous exit, then drive west two miles past Senator Bailey's ranch. Leia stared silently out the window and tried to prepare herself for the worst possible outcome. It was too soon. She clasped her hands together to hide their shaking.

Detective Rodriguez was preparing for the worst himself. In his few short years on the force, he'd had to tell parents that their children were dead, but never like this. At least once a summer, some college freshman drank too much and drove off the road or got ahold of a gun and blew his own head off. But this was most likely murder, and homicides involving children, he knew, fueled the kind of public outrage that could hamper an investigation—an unfortunate circumstance when all he wanted to do was solve the case.

{CHAPTER ELEVEN}

Thursday

At nine AM, Peter sat in the hospital coffee shop, wolfing down a bagel with lots of cream cheese. He was thinking that it was almost too good to be true that he had a few moments to himself when he heard someone paging him over the loudspeakers. He stuffed the last few bites of the bagel into his mouth and hurried out into the hallway, looking for the nearest in-house telephone.

It was Sharon who had paged him.

"Dr. Gram, the Hastings' insurance agent wants to talk to you," she said. "They're giving me a hard time with Naya's authorization for an inpatient stay."

"Damn it," Peter muttered. It wasn't the first time he'd had to go toe-to-toe with insurance representatives. If it were up to them, children at risk for psychosis would be sent home daily. "Do you have a contact number?"

Sharon gave him the contact number and told him to ask for Penelope Rolling.

"She'll probably play dumb, but I've already given her all the details of the case," she added. "Besides, I know you know what to do. From what I hear, nobody wrangles with those people like you do, Peter."

"Oh, those old rumors," Peter said dismissively. "I start them myself, you know. Anyway, I'll meet you in the peds ER in a few minutes. Thanks, Sharon," Peter said and hung up the telephone.

Peter's head was pounding. He only took antihistamines as a last resort, since they tended to back up his sinuses, but he couldn't walk around all day dripping mucus onto his patients. And now he would be forced to rationalize to an uneducated insurance clerk why Naya needed to be hospitalized. He had already spent thirty minutes going over the details of the case with the supervising Child and Adolescent Psychiatry attending. Now he had to go over the entire process all over again—this time, with somebody who probably lacked even the faintest idea of what a childhood psychiatric illness was. With the advent of managed medical care, mental-health treatment had become an endless discussion about the need for care with a web of people who were not qualified to make such decisions in the first place.

Peter went to the back of the ER nursing station, where the insurance pre-authorization phones were located. He sat down, dialed the 800 number, and navigated the arduous automated answering system with a growing sense of annoyance. Finally, a phone rang at the other end of the line.

"This is Penelope Rolling at the preauthorization unit speaking. How may I help you?"

"This is Dr. Gram from Newbury Peds, calling in reference to Naya Hastings," Peter said, trying to make his voice as pleasant as possible. Approaching the matter with anger wouldn't help his situation.

"One moment, please, while I pull up her file." After a brief pause, Penelope continued, "Dr. Gram, could you tell us what your formulation of this case is at this point in time? We don't think this patient requires acute inpatient care." Penelope spoke in a soft, melodious voice.

Peter clenched his teeth. He could feel his blood heating to a boil.

"What do you mean," he said slowly, "she doesn't need hospitalization? We have a seven-year-old girl who tried jumping off a second-story balcony yesterday. We don't know whether she's sleepwalking, psychotic, epileptic, or all of the above at this point in time."

Authorization for inpatient care had been refused many times before; every doctor on the inpatient unit had felt the sting of cheap insurance companies. It made Peter want to embellish the facts to get the authorization, but he resisted the temptation—a tough call. Only recently, a Newbury teenager had been discharged from the ER when the request for inpatient hospitalization was denied, and he had committed suicide later that night. The event had shaken the whole pediatric department. Peter sensed its shadow and took a deep breath.

"Is the patient suicidal at this time?" Penelope asked calmly.

"No, she's not. My concern is that when she's aslee—"

"Is she hearing any voices currently?" Penelope interrupted.

Peter wished he could reach through the phone and get his hands around the woman's neck. "No," he said flatly.

"Is she in any danger to herself at this point in time?"

"While she's sleeping, she's a danger to herself. It's the episodes of somnambulism that concern me a great deal."

"But is she in danger right now?" Penelope asked.

"Not at this very second," Peter said angrily, unable to keep his temper in check any longer, "because it happens to be nine thirty in the morning, and she's not asleep! I'm not going to let this happen! Listen, I want a doc-to-doc review." He wasn't taking no for an answer.

"At what number can the doctor reach you?" Penelope inquired evenly. Peter wondered if she were even a living, breathing creature.

Peter squinted to read the faded numbers printed above the dialing pad and recited them into the phone.

"We will get back to you soon. Thank you for your cooperation," Penelope said.

Peter slammed the receiver down, but it didn't make him feel any better. He swiveled around in the chair, letting the backrest slam into the desk as he did so.

He saw Sharon approaching the nurses' station and waved to get her attention.

"I can't believe the audacity of these insurance companies," Peter said angrily when Sharon joined him at the phones. "I think I was talking to a robot."

"I know," Sharon said in her soft, nasal voice, stroking the fingernails of one hand with the other without seeming aware of the gesture. "All in pursuit of the almighty dollar. They can't afford to think about real people. Did you ask for a doc-to-doc?"

"Oh, you bet. That's why I'm glued to this seat!" Peter ranted. "I can't wait to get this over with."

Sharon was equally familiar with this scenario. They had both spent endless hours haggling with patients' insurance companies.

"Why it is so much more difficult to get authorization for mental health versus physical health?" Peter wondered aloud.

The telephone rang, and Peter swung around in his chair to grab the phone.

"Hi, Dr. Gram. This is Dr. Brian Foley, calling you from Mandolin Managed Care—how can I help you today?"

Mandolin Managed Care was a "behavioral managed care" company— a company that managed mental-health care for major medical health-insurance companies. Their existence made the process of mental-health care authorization a nightmare mitigated by layers of reviewers who assessed the need for a particular type of service. In Peter's experience, he most often needed to speak to a physician. A child's mental health was nothing to play around with.

"Please tell me, Dr. Foley, that you know at least something about this case."

"I do, Dr. Gram. If you could just tell me what you plan to do during the hospitalization stay ..."

Peter sighed with relief.

"Well, we're not sure if this event was caused by a somnambulism problem or a first-break psychotic episode. In either case, the child's sleep behavior has worsened over the past several weeks. It could be dangerous at this point to send her back home without a complete workup and observation period.

"We would like to do an EEG," Peter continued, "to rule out any underlying seizure disorder. We would also like to schedule an MRI to make sure she has no organic processes evolving."

"Okay," said Dr. Foley. He sounded bored.

"We would like to observe her sleep behavior on the inpatient unit to see if she displays any dangerous behaviors to herself or others before we send her back into the community. At this point in time, I'm not sure she's safe without round-the-clock supervision."

"I can authorize two days of hospital stay to do this workup, and then you'll need to call me for further authorization," Dr. Foley said.

"We need at least three days," Peter said, "as I can schedule only one test a day. The next available day for an MRI is three days from today." Peter tried to bargain without allowing frustration to creep into his voice.

"Then I'll speak to you in three days. A reviewer will call to set up a time for our conversation."

"Thank you," Peter said. "I'll speak to you then."

Peter hung up and swung around to smile at Sharon. "We did it!" he exclaimed, feeling as if he had just won a battle.

"Congratulations!" Sharon said with a smile on her face. "Would you like me to tell the Hastings that we want Naya to stay on the inpatient unit?"

"Leave that to me," Peter said quickly. He feared that Sharon might botch it up with her typically insensitive approach.

"That's fine," Sharon said, regaining her reserve. She left the room, her posture stiff and straight. Now she'd have some free time this morning to paint new designs on her pretty long fingernails, Peter thought unkindly as he made his way to room 105.

First, he would discuss the matter with Naya's parents, and then he would help them tell Naya that she wouldn't be going home quite yet.

{CHAPTER TWELVE}

Thursday

"Suction, please," Dr. Everson Hunter said to the surgical nurse standing next to him.

She inserted a clear tube into the hole in the boy's abdomen and sucked away the fluids hampering Dr. Hunter's suturing. He finished sewing the abdominal muscle together with a sense of accomplishment.

"Good job, everyone," Everson said, stepping back from the boy's body. They had spent seven hours rejoining veins and arteries, then closing multiple stab injuries in the twenty-year-old college kid.

He'll live, Everson thought to himself. Now all that was left was suturing the layers of skin together at each injury site. "You can finish up," he instructed the second-year surgical resident.

As Everson pulled off his surgical gloves, the team in the OR applauded. Latex-free gloves muffled the sound. Everson took a bow and left the operating theater for the scrubbing sinks, and then the men's locker room. Finished with his last case for the morning, he would change into a fresh pair of scrubs before making surgical rounds. He whistled in the locker room, then smiled and nodded good morning to a group of residents on their way out. It was a good day. He drummed a beat with his fingers on the metal door of his locker, adding an accompaniment to the tune playing in his head.

Inside the locker was a slender, full-length mirror. Everson looked into it as he massaged his bald scalp, then ran his hands over his smoothly shaven face. He flexed his arm muscles and watched as they bulged, quivering with energy. In the mirror, his dark brown skin glistened with sweat. Satisfied with what he saw, he kicked off his sneakers and stripped down to his underwear. He squirted on some of his favorite cologne and quickly donned a clean pair of scrubs.

As he darted out of the locker room and headed toward the surgical wards, Everson glanced down at his watch and realized that, going this way, he would be a few minutes late. He backtracked, deciding to cut through the pediatric ER instead.

As a seasoned surgeon, Everson knew the ins and outs of Newbury Pediatric Hospital. Striding through the pediatric ER, he saw a familiar figure standing in the middle of the hallway up ahead.

"What's up, bad boy?" Everson teased in his slight Jamaican accent. Peter was far from a bad boy. He slapped his young friend on the back.

"Hey, man," Peter said. "I'm pretty swamped over here."

"Lots of crazy kids out there, huh? That's why I always told you surgery's the way to go."

"I'm all about the mind, my friend," Peter quipped, tapping his temple with a finger. "You go ahead and take the body. Hey, you look like you're on the run. What happened—you kill someone or something?" he joked.

"Yeah, yeah." Everson grinned. "On the contrary: I gave this dude his life back." He was still high—the instant gratification of a successful surgery was irreplaceable.

"How's Evelyn?" Peter asked. "I sure enjoyed dinner last week. That girlfriend of yours can cook!"

"She's fine. Every time she sees you, she can't stop talking afterward about how calm you are," Everson said.

"Anything's calm compared to your hotheaded BS, huh?" Peter said with a grin.

"Nothing wrong with a little passion," Everson said with good humor. "Hey, if you're lucky, maybe someday you'll find a woman who appreciates your good qualities. Well, one besides my girlfriend, of course."

Peter rolled his eyes and sighed. "Yeah, yeah," he said. "You just want me to join you in your sad, whipped state. What you forget is that you're what, like, almost two decades older than I am? I've got plenty of time to catch up, friend."

Everson laughed. "It's true. But, if nothing else, I just think you could stand to get some action once in a while."

Peter didn't bother to dignify this with a response. These days, he was pretty used to the joshing of the hospital staff. When would they understand that he was busy enough already without having to fit in romantic dinners and long walks on the beach? Besides, Peter had his reasons for staying single … and most of the hospital staff didn't know the half of it.

Everson changed the subject as he started to walk away. "Are you working out later?" he asked over one shoulder. He was going to be late in spite of his shortcut.

"Yeah. See you then," Peter called as Everson dashed around the corner.

Everson was happy to have bumped into Peter. Given that they were both so busy, it was rare that they met during working hours.

On the sixth floor, which was the postoperative surgical floor, Everson sprinted from the elevator toward a group of interns and surgical residents.

"Let's get going," he said.

They stopped chatting immediately and fell on his heels; he liked the way it felt. None of them wanted to look bad in the eyes of the best surgeon in the hospital.

{CHAPTER THIRTEEN}

Thursday

The Town Car turned sharply onto a bumpy gravel road. Leia braced herself against the door's armrest. As the road wound up a hill, her mind flashed to the dark streets of the village outside San José. She gave herself a mental shake. She needed to have a clear head now.

At the top of the hill, the ground leveled out, and she could see two police cruisers and an ambulance with its lights rolling. The car came to a halt and was immediately engulfed in a cloud of dust.

"Looks like the gang's all here," Detective Rodriguez commented as he swung open the door.

Leia thanked the driver as she followed the detective out of the car. Her palms were moist, and the cool autumn breeze brushed them, making her shiver. The air at the crime scene smelled deceptively earthy and fresh.

All the other vehicles were empty. Leia followed the detective across a broad, grassy area and toward a line of red maple trees interspersed with oaks. The colors seemed fantastic to Leia, a city girl: brilliant green grass, azure sky, blood-red leaves, black tree trunks. She felt as though she'd stepped into a child's picture. They walked through the trees and into a more thickly wooded area. The terrain sloped downward as they continued, and Leia caught a glimpse up ahead of a tall, gray rock towering between the trees and interspersed tall grass. Leia and the detective finally reached the yellow perimeter of tape that secured the crime scene. Leia ducked under the tape and followed the detective to the group of three uniformed officers and an EMT.

"Well, guys, I'm going to head back then," the EMT said. The police officers waved good-bye as he trekked back toward the woods.

"Hey, José," said the burliest of the three officers, shaking hands with Detective Rodriguez. "Thanks for getting here so quick."

"No problem," José said. "Lieutenant Steven Andrew, this is Agent Leia Bines from the FBI."

Leia shook hands with the lieutenant over his substantial paunch.

José turned to Leia. "And this is Officer Jeremy Meyers and Officer Tony Masta."

Leia shook their hands. "How do you do, officers?"

"This is terrible," Officer Masta said. "I've never seen anything like it, and I hope I never do again."

"Well, I'd better get started, then," Leia said, more to herself than anyone else.

José and Lieutenant Andrew followed Leia as she walked toward the huge rock. The heels of her pumps sank into the damp earth; she should have worn boots.

"They call it Elephant Rock," Lieutenant Andrew said as he drew closer to Leia, panting a little from the exertion.

"It does look like an elephant." Leia stopped a few yards from the huge outcropping, which stood about fifteen feet high and a hundred feet long. The color was a perfect elephant gray. As she approached the rock, the smell of decomposing flesh began to fill the air. Leia pressed her forearm against her nose and mouth. A few feet in front of Elephant Rock lay a black plastic sheet covering a tiny form—far too small to be the body of a ten-year-old girl. Maybe it wasn't Janet. Maybe there was still time.

From the pocket of her suede jacket, Leia took a pair of surgical gloves and pulled them on.

"Have you gotten an ID yet, Lieutenant?" she asked. She walked toward the form on the ground and squatted.

"Oh, we know who it is," Lieutenant Andrew said as Leia reached for the edge of the black plastic sheet. "But I have to warn you—"

Leia lifted the sheet and found herself staring into the beautiful blue eyes of Janet Troy. Her head was tipped back on the ground, and her blonde hair was brushed back from her face, as though the killer had wanted her to see the stars. Her lips were slightly parted.

"—it's only the head."

Leia dropped the plastic sheet and took a quick breath. "Okay," she said, composing herself and steeling her nerves for another view. She pulled the plastic cover away again. She wrinkled her nose as the smell of decomposing flesh intensified.

Janet's head had been severed from her torso at the lower neck. Suddenly, Leia was playing a whole new ball game.

Leia looked up at Elephant Rock. The killer had placed the head directly in front of the landmark, dead center, as if in front of an altar. But where was the rest of the body? She studied the ground around the head for signs of digging. She turned to look at the trees and bushes that spread out from the foot of the boulder. When she looked back at Janet's face, a fly had settled in the corner of the child's eye.

Leia pulled the sheet over Janet's head and stood up. She turned to José and Lieutenant Andrew, who both were only one or two shades of green away from losing their breakfast.

"What about the rest of the body?" Leia asked Lieutenant Andrew.

"We're not sure," the lieutenant said, running his hands over his patchy crew cut. "I called a forensic squad. They should be down here any minute." He had turned away from the scene and was moving imperceptibly—and probably unconsciously—away from the head.

Leia felt for him. There had probably never been such a gruesome incident in his jurisdiction. Small university towns weren't prone to violent cases.

"Did you know Janet?" Leia asked.

"Of course. Her dad is the night manager at the grocery store not even a mile from my house. Our families go to the same church. Now I'm going to have to go break the news to her parents that not only is their daughter never coming home, but some son of a bitch has cut off her head!" He stuck his thumbs into his eyes, as though he were struggling to keep from crying.

Leia put her hand on the lieutenant's beefy forearm. His uniform shirt was crisp with starch. "Listen, Lieutenant Andrew," she said, and she squeezed his forearm until he met her eyes. "I understand how difficult this whole thing must be for you, but I need you to do two things for me."

He nodded.

"I need you to bring in a dog squad as quickly as possible. If there are any other body parts in the vicinity, we need to find them. I also need a forensic pathologist and an entomologist over here as quickly as possible. We have to estimate the time of the death before the evidence decomposes any more than it already has. Now, I can make a few calls myself, but I wanted to check with you first to make sure I wouldn't be stepping on your toes."

"Please, be my guest," the lieutenant said with relief in his voice.

"And I need you to think hard about who might be capable of doing something like this. Have any of your officers had strange arrests over the past six months … anything you heard them talking about in the squad room, anything they came to you with? Has anyone you know—friends, acquaintances, neighbors, friends of friends—been acting strangely? If you think of anything at all, no matter how small, I want you to tell me, okay?"

He nodded. Leia gave his forearm a final squeeze, and he trudged back toward the woods to summon the dog squad.

"Are we currently on the senator's property, by chance?" Leia asked José.

"No, his property ends about a mile east of here," José said. "This part belongs to the state."

"He'll be relieved about that, I'm sure," Leia said wryly.

"True," José said, "but we're still going to be all over him and his staff. In fact, if you're all right here, I'm going to take Jeremy and Tony over there right now and get started compiling a list of people to interview. If you need anything at all, call my cell phone." He gave her his and Lieutenant Andrew's numbers, and she programmed them into her phone.

José began to walk back in the direction of the parked cars, then stopped and turned back toward Leia.

"This has turned into a real nightmare," he said. "But if that's how it has to be, I'm glad you're here, Agent Bines."

Leia smiled tightly. She almost couldn't bear his gratitude, especially when she had so much left to prove. She began walking away from Elephant Rock, through the trees. She had a long day ahead of her.

{CHAPTER FOURTEEN}

Thursday

When Peter returned to room 105, the Hastings and Naya had finished their breakfast, and Naya was watching *The Little Mermaid* on television.

"How are you this morning, Mr. and Mrs. Hastings?" Peter asked, shaking their hands.

"Good to see you, Doctor," Mr. Hastings said warmly.

"And, Naya, how are you?"

"Hi, Dr. Gram," Naya said, smiling and waving. Peter could tell she was excited by the break from her daily routine.

"Naya, I need to speak to your mom and dad in private for a few minutes. Then I'll want to talk with you, if that's okay."

Naya nodded, suddenly serious.

"You can sit outside with Sharon, who is one of our social workers. She'll be glad to play with you for a few minutes," Peter said.

"Okay," Naya said without a fuss. She jumped off the purple couch, and Peter directed her to the nursing station, where Sharon sat filing her nails.

Peter closed the door and sat on a tall stool across from the Hastings. He paused, a bit nervous to tell them about the management plan that he had devised. He knew they wouldn't be pleased.

"To begin with," he said, "my priority is Naya's safety. While I don't think she's in any serious danger, I and the attending physician would like to keep Naya in the hospital for a few days, so that we can run a few tests and rule out the more serious disorders that might be causing Naya's problem."

Jane Hastings's face paled as Peter spoke. She clasped her hands tightly in her lap. "What kind of tests?" she asked calmly. Her husband frowned next to her on the couch. She reached over and took one of his hands.

"An EEG and an MRI." Peter shared his reasons for ordering the tests, then added, "We would also like to be able to observe Naya while she sleeps. This kind of supervision will give us some clues as to what might be causing the nightmares and sleepwalking ... and it will keep Naya safe, which I think is all of our highest priority."

"How many days?" Mr. Hastings questioned gruffly.

"We have a three-day authorization from the insurance company. I think we can complete all the tests within that time frame."

Mr. Hastings sighed heavily and looked at his wife, whose eyes were now welling up with tears. "How can we argue with that?"

"But how can we just leave her here?" Mrs. Hastings said, a few tears spilling down her cheeks. Her husband put his arm around her shoulders. "How will we tell her?"

"As soon as you're ready," Peter said gently, "I'll bring Naya back, and I'll help you explain the plan to her."

"Where will she be staying?" Mrs. Hastings inquired, taking a Kleenex from her purse and dabbing at her eyes.

"The hospital's child psychiatry unit is housed in a separate building called Strauss I. It's close by. As soon as we've had a talk with Naya, I'll get the admissions process rolling and have the nurse take you over, so you can see what it's like." Peter stood up. He stuck his head out of the room and signaled to Sharon to send Naya back.

"Naya, your parents and I have something to tell you," he said to the approaching girl.

Naya paused just inside the door, her body stiffening, as though she might turn and run. Then her mother held out her arms, and Naya went into them, squeezing in between her parents on the couch.

"Naya, do you remember why you're here in the hospital?" Peter asked.

Naya nodded.

"Well, your parents and I are worried that a sickness might be making you have bad dreams. We want you to stay in the hospital for a few days, so that we can do some tests to see if you're sick."

Naya looked at her mother, her small, smooth brow knitted together under her bangs. "I have to sleep here?"

Jane Hastings nodded.

"You'll be staying in a building called Strauss I, Naya. You get there from here by walking through a long, long hallway. Other children will be staying there too." He paused and studied Naya's worried expression. "So what do you think about our plan?" he asked.

Naya sat silently between her parents, looking from one to the other, as though gauging how difficult it might be to argue her way out of the decision.

"I know it's not how you would really like to spend your time, Naya," Peter added gently, "but we want to make sure you're well before we send you home."

Naya looked at the floor and shrugged.

"Mr. and Mrs. Hastings, I'll need you to fill out some paperwork in the admissions office," Peter said. "Then I'll have a nurse walk you over to Strauss I."

Mr. and Mrs. Hastings began gathering their belongings from around the room.

"You can take your drawings too, Naya," Peter said, pointing to the loose sheets lying on the little table.

Naya gathered the papers and tucked them under her arm. She avoided looking at Peter, clearly upset about what he was doing to her.

"I'll meet you at Strauss I in an hour or so to complete the admission process. We can talk more then about what's going to happen next," Peter said, walking out of the room toward the nursing station. His nose was beginning to run again, and the back of his throat felt scratchy. He blew his nose loudly, then began documenting everything that had transpired since he was first called to see Naya. The consultation note was going to take him a good hour to write.

{CHAPTER FIFTEEN}

Thursday

Leia and the other officers fanned out over the large area around Janet's remains. She would survey the land between Elephant Rock and the senator's ranch. She headed east from Elephant Rock and found herself wading through shrubs and trees. After walking about a half mile, she found herself out of the woods and in a field of silage corn that had already been harvested. She continued to trek through the field in the direction of the ranch.

In the distance, Leia could see a short, wooden fence demarcating the senator's property and the end of the cornfield. She scouted the fence for openings and found a division near a small, clear brook. She stuck a piece of straw into the water and found it was only about ankle deep. Anybody could enter or exit the ranch right here.

Leia gazed across the senator's vast property; it appeared almost infinite. Only by squinting could she make out some structures in the distance. She presumed that they were either the senator's house or his stables. She took the map Detective Rodriguez had given her from the pocket of her jacket. On it, he had marked a red circle where Janet's book bag had been found. Leia estimated that the point was approximately midway between the structures and the brook.

Leia decided to see for herself where the bag had been found. But she wouldn't trek all that way on foot—especially not in heels. She turned around and retraced her steps back to Elephant Rock. She would drive to the senator's and visit the site that way. As she reentered the woods, she heard the high whine and bark of the canine unit. The closer she got to them, the more fervently they barked. They must have found something.

"What's going on?" Leia yelled out to the officers standing a few yards away, holding tightly to the leashes of two muscular German shepherds.

"We've found another body part," the taller officer called. "It looks like an arm."

Leia crouched down to get a closer look at the cylindrical mass of gray-ish flesh. It was about nine inches long. She pushed it gently with her gloved fingers. "Part of an arm, anyway," she said, squinting up at the officer. "Okay, have another officer mark this site, and then keep looking. Can you split up?"

The taller officer nodded. As the men and their dogs disappeared into the trees, Leia took out her cell phone and called José.

"It's Leia," she said. "The dogs found something. It looks like an upper arm, from the shoulder to the elbow."

She could almost hear José wince. "What the hell am I going to tell the paper? Who does something like this?"

"I can tell you exactly who does something like this—but I'll have to do it later. Right now, I think we need more people down here. If there are two pieces of the body in the area, I have a feeling they're all here. And with pieces this small, we've got a lot more hunting to do."

"Call the lieutenant," José said. "He'll get you more people."

Leia phoned Lieutenant Andrew, who brought stakes and police tape to mark the newest site.

"Of course, I'll get you more people," he said when Leia made her request shortly after his arrival.

"One more favor?"

"Name it."

"Can you get a chopper to take an aerial photograph of this entire geo-graphical area?" Leia asked. "I need a better idea of the lay of the land and how someone might get here from the surrounding area. I don't think Janet was killed or dismembered here. I haven't seen a drop of fresh blood anywhere yet."

The lieutenant pulled his cell phone from the holder on his belt.
"And Lieutenant?"
He paused and looked up at Leia.
"I know you don't want to, but you have to tell the family. Don't let them hear this on the radio or see it on TV. I'll go with you if you like."
Lieutenant Andrew nodded. "I appreciate the offer, Agent Bines," he said gruffly.

*   *   *   *

Baxter and Juniper were the finest canines in their graduating class. In addition to their extensive instruction at the K9 institute, they had trained at the Body Farm, where they had had great success locating decomposing tissue, even when it was covered by a few feet of soil. Their sinuses were filled now with the scent of Janet's body. The woods were filled with tantalizing tendrils of that same smell. Baxter and Juniper just had to follow them.

It was Juniper who found the limbless torso.

On the eastern side of Elephant Rock, Baxter found the distal phalange of a right index finger. It was a much harder find, given the size of the body part. Baxter was highly gifted when it came to the game of Smell-and-Find.

As the dogs led their handlers in ever-widening circles around Elephant Rock, they discovered more and more pieces of flesh and bone, and a body began to take shape—the body of Janet Troy.

*   *   *   *

The lieutenant drove slowly up the driveway. In his twenty-two years as a police officer, he had never shirked his duty. But this task made him want to run away, leave town, leave the country—anything to avoid telling Catherine and Herbert Troy what he had come to tell them.

He stood in front of their door for a long time, his heart heavy inside his chest. As he lifted his finger toward the bell, the door opened, and Herbert stood in front of him, haggard and weary eyed.

"Come in, Steven," Herbert said.

The lieutenant looked away from his friend's face as tears filled his eyes. Herbert led him into the living room, where Catherine Troy sat shriveled on the sofa. Catherine burst into tears as soon as she saw him.

"It's Janet," Lieutenant Andrew blurted out over the sound of Catherine's sobs. "We've found her, and I'm ... I'm so, so sorry ..." He began to sob himself. "She's dead. Janet's dead."

Herbert sank down next to his wife with his head in his hands. A howl of pain erupted behind his trembling fingers.

"We'll find who did it," the lieutenant said as he wiped his own tears. "I'll find who did it." He said it over and over again, although he doubted the Troys could even hear him. The words became a chant in his mind—a mantra.

{CHAPTER SIXTEEN}

Thursday

Peter completed his consultation at the ER and headed back to the child-psychiatry unit. Since it was a beautiful, crisp autumn day, and he felt it had been too long since he had seen sunlight, he took the longer, outdoor route, leaving through the front entrance of the peds ER.

The unit was located inside Strauss I, a handsome colonial redbrick building that had been acquired and renovated by the hospital. The unit was separate from the medical and surgical parts of the hospital, and it had its own entrance and parking lot.

Peter climbed the steps to the sliding doors and flashed his ID in front of the scanner that hung next to the entrance. The glass doors sprang open, allowing him to enter the rectangular waiting room. The room was large enough to hold ten to fifteen people at a time. Comfortable matching sofas were arranged invitingly around the room, and a table in one corner held a number of magazines.

Beyond the waiting room, Suzie, the day receptionist, sat at her desk, the telephone at her ear. Peter waved to her as he passed, and Suzie smiled and waved back.

Peter scanned his ID card at a set of thick metal doors. He heard the magnetic lock open with a click. He entered a corridor lined with offices. At the end of the hallway and to the right was a second, smaller waiting area, where one of the unit social workers was meeting with a family. To his left was a second set of metal doors that led to the children's living quarters. Before scanning his ID, Peter looked through the glass window in the middle of the door to make sure there wasn't a child standing on the other side. He went through the door, checking to see that it had closed securely behind him.

Unlike any other ward in the hospital, Strauss I was a locked unit. Only faculty and authorized staff were allowed to come and go as needed. All other visitors had to get a temporary ID card that authorized them to enter and exit once only. Each time they visited the unit, they had to get renewed permission.

The building was T-shaped, with the living space for the children located on the stem of the T and administrative offices located on the arms. Peter walked down the long, empty hallway. He could hear the chatter of voices in a room farther along. It was ten in the morning, and all the children were in school.

Peter went through the first door on his right, which led to the nurses' station and its attached conference room.

As in any unit, the nurses' station saw the most action. In the child-psych unit, the station was the place where staff from various disciplines congregated and exchanged information. The heart of the nurses' station was the massive, wheeled chart rack, which contained vital information on all the unit's patients.

"Good morning, everybody," Peter said loudly as he entered the nurses' station.

In response, he heard various calls of "Good morning to you" and various grunts from the staff members. As a result of his on-call duties, Peter had missed morning rounds, at which a representative of each discipline and the physicians discussed the events of the past twenty-four hours. The fellows were always a part of this meeting and were expected to talk about their cases.

"Is everybody ready to go to work?" Peter heard Dorothy Fisher ask. Dorothy was the Sterling Professor in child and adolescent psychiatry at the university. She directed the unit. She ended rounds each morning with the same question, and the fellows always answered the same way.

"Yes, we are," the fellows chimed together.

The fellowship program chose four child and adolescent psychiatry fellows who rotated on the unit for a year during their two-year program in the hospital. The first years were in charge of managing the psychiatric care of all the patients on the pediatric unit. Peter, a first-year fellow, was partnered with co-fellow Sheetal Patel. Sheetal covered Peter's patients when he was away from the unit, and the two of them shared an office in the outpatient clinic. The other two fellows, Eric Scott and Pamela Weathers, were teamed together. Peter was thankful he hadn't been paired with Eric, who never seemed to stop talking. Since their fellowship had begun in July, Peter and Sheetal had become quite good friends.

The unit had a maximum census of twelve inpatients during any given day. Each of the fellows was in charge of three patients from the unit as a part of their rotation. They were responsible for other patients in the day-treatment program and outpatient clinic as well, and they also covered the ER and off-hours of the inpatient unit in a rotating call schedule—the shift Peter had just completed. Now he would work a full day before going home.

The unit team was rounded out by two unit social workers, the unit psychologist, and the school principal and her crew of teachers. Matt Goldman, the director of nursing, seemed to live on the unit. He supervised the nurses and the mental-health associates, also known as MHAs, who worked directly with the children. Rarely was Peter there when Matt wasn't. If an outsider had asked who really ran the unit, any of the staff would have said, "Matt, of course."

Before doing anything else, Peter checked with Matt to make sure Naya's room was ready.

"We're all set," Matt said, looking up from the log of medications dispensed during the morning shift.

"Did I tell you that she's going to need sleep observation for the night?" Peter asked.

Matt sighed. "You might have to reevaluate one of your other patients, then," Matt said, frowning. He was always operating with an acute shortage of trained staff members.

"Maybe Timothy can go without sleep observation, since he hasn't had a disturbance all week," Peter said.

"Just put in the physician's order, and I'll get to it soon," Matt replied.

Peter was catching up on his patients with Sheetal in the conference room when the phone rang, and Matt called to him.

"It was Suzie," Matt said. "Naya and her family are in the waiting room."

As Peter left the nurses' station, he told Matt, "We'll be in the family room for about fifteen minutes, doing paperwork. Are you available for the tour?"

Matt sighed again and looked at the paperwork in front of him. "Sure," he said. "Why not?"

Peter gave him the thumbs-up and exited through the blue metal doors, making sure they closed tightly behind him.

{CHAPTER SEVENTEEN}

Thursday

As the day progressed, the number of law-enforcement professionals milling around Elephant Rock increased. Detective Rodriguez had created a special task force, some of the members of which were busy photographing the area and logging the dogs' grisly finds—which continued at an alarming rate.

The state's leading forensic pathologist, Dr. Jason Kelly, had arrived and was examining and cataloging the body pieces that had been recovered so far. Dr. Kelly had taught for many years at the Department of Forensic Pathology at the University of Sheffield in the UK. He had come to New England on a special project during which he was to train and work with the Newbury and Danbury police departments. He was a short, bald Englishman with the fingers of an artist and the eyes of a hawk.

Leia had retrieved her own notebook and colored pencils from the car. She found it useful to document as much as she could for herself; drawing the scene gave her a feel for the different ways a person might approach it. She leaned on the hood of the Town Car and traced out a rough sketch of Elephant Rock with a gray pencil, then drew an X where each body part had been found so far. She heard gravel popping beneath the tires of a car on the road, and then, before she knew it, a dark, unmarked squad car was speeding around the corner, headed straight for her. Leia stepped back reflexively, and the car came to a halt a few feet from where she had stood.

Leia's irritation evaporated when she spotted who was in the driver's seat.

The door swung open, and a tall woman with a briefcase and a smooth, blonde chignon stepped out with a big smile on her face.

Leia stuffed her notebook and pencils back into her bag and walked to meet one of the few people in the world she truly admired. They embraced tightly.

"Carroll," Leia said, "it's been much too long!"

Dr. Carroll Prize, a friend of Leia's from college, was New York City's renowned forensic entomologist. Carroll and Leia had seen each other only occasionally since working on a particularly difficult case together four years before.

"Thanks for coming so quickly," Leia said. "I know you're in demand in these parts."

"Yes, well … there's only one of my kind on the East Coast," Carroll said jokingly with a smirk.

"Ah, yes," Leia said, with a tinge of sarcasm, although she knew Carroll was right. Out of the handful of forensic entomologists that existed in the world, Carroll was the best. Her addition to this team could make the investigation.

"So what do we have so far?" Carroll asked, sobering.

"Come and see for yourself," Leia said. She took Carroll's arm and led her toward the crime scene, briefing her along the way. In the woods, they ran into Dr. Kelly, who was crouched over the torso of the corpse.

"Carroll," Dr. Kelly said, smiling good-naturedly, "we've got to stop meeting like this." He sobered when he turned back to the body in front of him. "This is an ugly business we've got here today."

Carroll reached into the pocket of her elegant black pants suit and pulled out a pair of latex gloves. "What's your estimate on the time?" she asked.

"We're way past rigor mortis, so you'll have to answer that question."

"What happens after rigor mortis?" Leia asked.

"Well," Dr. Kelly explained, "rigor mortis occurs in a few hours after a person has died. Chemical reactions cause the muscle fibers to contract, then remain contracted until they begin to break down themselves, which happens after seventy-two hours. After that, we can't use rigor mortis to determine the time of death with any certainty." He looked at Carroll through his clear plastic goggles. "That's where Dr. Prize comes in."

Leia noticed that there were no bruises or other marks on the child's torso.

"We should be able to get pretty close to the time of actual death," Carroll said, taking a pair of goggles from her briefcase and sliding them on over her coiffure. She crouched next to Janet's arm and lifted it gently with a pencil she had taken from her pocket.

Dr. Kelly squinted up at Leia. "One point to particularly note," he said, "is that the body has been dismembered in a very systematic way. This killer is no hacker."

"What do you mean?" asked Leia.

"A person who decides to dismember a body usually does so with a saw or an ax. There's really no other way—unless you very deliberately take the body apart at the joints, which is what this person did. Perhaps what's most unusual here is that *every* body part I've seen so far has been dismembered at the joint."

Dr. Kelly invited them to examine how the killer had removed the ball of the shoulder joint from its socket. Then he stood and motioned for them to follow him to a roped-off bush several yards away, under which the killer had placed Janet's right upper arm.

"Imagine that the victim was a puppet whose joints were connected by string," Dr. Kelly continued. "The portion of the corpse I've seen here today is laid out as though those strings have been snipped, and the puppet pulled apart."

"What was used to do this? Can you tell?" asked Leia.

"Yes—our killer used a very sharp instrument, and he or she was proficient at this kind of work. Notice that there are no overlapping cuts or jagged edges on the skin. Each cut was done in one sweep."

"Was that the way she was killed?" Leia wondered aloud.

"Most probably," Dr. Kelly said. "I think she bled to death, as there are no other marks on her head, neck, or arms. She was most likely dismembered somewhere else and laid out here afterward. I haven't seen a drop of blood yet."

Leia's brain was racing. She flipped open her phone and dialed Lieutenant Andrew.

"Where would I get some fluorescent flags?" she asked him. "The bigger, the better. I want to mark each one of Janet's body parts with them to see if they'll show up on the aerial image."

"I'll have a couple of guys bring some down," Lieutenant Andrew said.

"And Lieutenant, maybe I've already asked you this, but has anything like this ever happened before in Newbury or anyplace nearby—anything even remotely similar?"

"Agent Bines," the lieutenant said, "I've been on the Newbury police force for twenty-two years, and I can guarantee you that I've never seen anything like this."

"Thanks, Lieutenant."

"I'll get you those flags."

Leia closed her phone and slid it back into her pocket. She rejoined Carroll and Dr. Kelly, who had walked back over to the torso.

"What is it, Leia?" Carroll asked. "You've got that look in your eyes— the one that tells me your body is here, but your mind is orbiting Pluto."

"Well, obviously, this killer had something very specific in mind when he killed Janet Troy. But did he have Janet Troy in mind, or did she just happen to cross his path at the wrong time?"

"I'll let you answer those questions, my friend," Carroll said. "Right now, I'm interested in maggots. Dr. Kelly, may I flip the body?"

"Of course, Dr. Prize," Dr. Kelly said, standing and giving a short bow in Carroll's direction.

Leia stood like an eager pupil, watching Carroll as she carefully turned Janet's torso. She then took a forceps and a magnifying glass from her briefcase and examined Janet's back.

"You see these smooth maggots?" Carroll asked, grasping one of the squirming insects with her forceps and holding it up toward Leia and Dr. Kelly. Leia instinctively took a step back.

"Oh, yeah, I see them," Leia said a little faintly. "Not so close, please."

"They're purely corpse feeders," Carroll said. "They belong to the blow-fly family Calliphoridae. The adult blowfly is metallic blue or green and resembles a common housefly. The adults invade the corpse within the first twenty-four hours and lay eggs in all available orifices and openings.

"The baby flies that hatch from the eggs, like this one"—she gestured with the maggot again—"go through various developmental stages called instars, during which they shed their skin. I'll collect a number of the mag-gots at various stages and take them back to my lab.

"In the lab," Carroll continued, "we simulate the temperature condi-tions that have been present here in this very spot during the past few weeks, and we cultivate more eggs on a liver specimen. Then we'll calcu-late the time it takes to go through a whole cycle from egg to adult blow-fly, compare what we have in the lab with what we found here, calculate the development rate, and determine the time of death."

"How long is that going to take?" Leia asked with real concern. Time was of the essence here. What if they had a brand-new serial killer on their hands—one who was looking to continue his budding career?

"I'll give it a Priority One when I get back to the lab … but, off the record, from what I'm seeing here, these young adults are skittering around the corpse like hyperactive spiders."

"So?"

"They still can't fly. They're waiting for their wings to expand, which usually happens about six to ten days after the third instar becomes a pupa."

"Which means?" Leia pestered.

"The body has been here for about nine to ten days," Carroll concluded.

"Good Lord," Leia said. "That means there's a good possibility she was murdered on the same day she was reported missing." Leia's heart sank. While it was better for Janet that the killer hadn't kept her alive and pro-longed her suffering, it was worse for those left living who had to find her killer—and fast. Leia and Carroll's eyes met over the torso of Janet Troy's corpse.

"It looks like this murderer kills for the thrill of it," Carroll said, and Leia nodded curtly. She did not relish telling Lieutenant Andrew and Detective Rodriguez that a serial killer was most likely still at large in their community.

{CHAPTER EIGHTEEN}

Thursday

Naya was afraid. She didn't want to stay in this hospital. She thought it seemed different from the other, regular hospital, even though she had never stayed in any sort of hospital before. This hospital didn't seem at all like the hospital her classmate had described after having her tonsils removed. Besides, Naya didn't even feel sick.

She and her parents stood at the reception desk, talking to Suzie and waiting for Dr. Gram, whom Naya soon saw coming through the door. At least she knew who he was. She wouldn't mind talking to him again.

"Hello again," Dr. Gram said to her.

Naya smiled. She tried to say, "Hi," but it came out as a whisper.

"Dr. Gram will take you into the unit itself," Suzie said to Naya's parents, "but feel free to ask me questions at any time."

"Are you ready?" Peter asked all of them.

Naya could tell he was trying to sound excited so that she would feel excited too, but all she felt was the fear that had been lying deep in her stomach rise through her body and get stuck in her throat. As if he felt her panic, Dr. Gram squatted so that he could look into Naya's eyes. His steady gaze made her feel a little better.

"First, we'll see the room where you'll be staying," he said.

"Can my mom and dad stay in the room too?" Naya asked.

"No, they can't," Dr. Gram said in a soft voice, "but they can visit you every day."

"Who else is in this hospital? Will I be all alone?"

"There are ten more children on the unit," Dr. Gram said. "This unit is named after the doctor who worked here with kids just like you many years ago."

"What about my clothes and my toothbrush? I need them," Naya said in a squeaky voice.

"Your parents will bring them when they come to visit you later this evening," Dr. Gram said. He looked at Naya's parents.

"Yes, honey," Naya's mother said, stepping forward to stroke Naya's hair. "We'll run home and get your things and come right back."

Naya grabbed ahold of her mother's hand and squeezed the familiar slender fingers. She didn't want to let go. Her father rested his hand on her head, and she wanted to burst into tears. But she wouldn't. She would be brave.

"There are lots of toys on the unit," Dr. Gram said, "but if you have a special toy at home, you can ask your parents to bring it in—that's fine too."

Naya nodded and whispered the name into her mother's ear.

"Okay, let's go inside," Dr. Gram said.

Naya walked between her parents as they followed Dr. Gram. They passed through a set of heavy blue doors and into a hallway painted in bright colors. On the walls hung many drawings made by children. Then they went through a second set of heavy blue doors. Naya hadn't seen one other child yet, and she began to wonder if Dr. Gram had lied to her about the other children.

As though he had read her mind, Dr. Gram turned to Naya just then and said, "All the other kids are at school."

"We go to school here?" The idea of a hospital having a school delighted Naya. It made the hospital seem like a regular place. But then she remembered something, and she felt the smile sag on her face. She looked up at her father. "But what about my friends, Daddy?" She knew her voice was what her parents called "whiny," but they didn't tell her to change it this time.

"You'll make new friends here, Naya," Dr. Gram said, "and you'll get to do lots of fun things with them."

They reached the end of the hallway, and Dr. Gram turned right, into an area with more couches and chairs.

"Let's stop here in the family room for a few minutes to complete some more paperwork," he said to Naya's parents. He crouched in front of Naya. Again, she noted his kind blue eyes. "In the meantime, Naya, if you want, I can ask my friend Matt, who is also our nurse, to show you your room."

"Okay," Naya said.

She sat between her parents in the bright room on a long couch that sat beneath a large window. She looked around and noticed a shelf holding numerous toys and stuffed animals. On one wall hung a large chalkboard. She saw a picture of a sunflower drawn by one of the other children. She was beginning to gradually feel at ease; the hospital seemed like a friendly place.

Dr. Gram returned with Matt, who had spiky hair and wore a blue smock, white pants, and funny shoes that looked as if they belonged to an elf. Naya liked him immediately and even took his hand as they walked out of the room. When she turned back to wave, she saw that Dr. Gram was smiling, but her parents still looked worried. They all waved back.

When Naya and Matt returned, Naya's parents were signing papers on the coffee table.

"I like my room," Naya said to Dr. Gram with a smile.

"I thought you would," Dr. Gram said, smiling back at her. "I think we're just about finished here. Do you want to show your parents around?"

Naya jumped up and down with excitement. "Come on, Mommy. Let me show you my room!"

As they walked into the children's living quarters, Matt told Naya's parents about each area, with Naya adding what she remembered from her own tour.

"So you're an expert already, Naya," Dr. Gram chuckled.

They stopped at the school, where the children Naya had just met waved to her. She waved back. She had never stayed over in a place with so many other children.

Finally, they reached Naya's room. She liked it as much as she had the first time she'd seen it. The walls were painted three different shades of yellow and decorated with framed cartoons. Matt had called the room "a double," meaning that two children could share it, so there were two desks and chairs, two wall shelves, and two beds. Naya showed her mother the one she had picked out, near the window.

Naya thought her mother might cry when they said good-bye, and she was right.

"It's okay, Mommy," she said, patting her mother on the back. "I'll be home soon. Right now, Matt's going to take me to school. Right, Matt?"

Matt looked as if he wanted to laugh. "Right, Naya," he said.

Naya wiggled out of her mother's embrace and gave her father a long, hard hug too. Then she took Matt's hand, and they walked down the hallway toward the classroom.

{CHAPTER NINETEEN}

Thursday

It was well past noon, and the team at the crime scene had found, photographed, and flagged every part of Janet Troy's body. The police department helicopter had arrived, landing at the edge of the field that Leia had explored earlier.

Leia approached Lieutenant Andrew, who was standing near Elephant Rock and talking with the aerial photographer.

"I'd like to go up with them, Lieutenant, if it's all right with you," Leia said.

"Of course," Lieutenant Andrew said. "Come with me, and I'll introduce you to the pilot."

Soon enough, Leia was strapping herself in behind the pilot's seat. The pilot handed her and the photographer each a set of insulated radio headphones to muffle the sound of the engine. The pilot started the propeller, then spoke into the mouthpiece of his own headset to make sure that Leia and the photographer could hear him clearly.

Then they were in the air, hovering over the woods and Elephant Rock. Leia could already see many of the markers that the police officers had placed, although some were obscured by foliage. However, as they gained altitude, Leia could easily guess where the other markers would be based on the disturbing pattern she saw. She knew that the photographer would have no difficulty identifying what needed to be captured with his digital camera.

Leia instructed the pilot to turn east and fly over the senator's ranch. Within a few seconds, they were flying over the fence that Leia had found earlier. She looked out to see how far the ranch extended. The east end of the property abutted the southwest end of Willow Lake. The pilot circled around, turning back west toward Elephant Rock.

When she returned to the woods, Leia found that José had returned from the senator's ranch. He and Lieutenant Andrew were discussing how best to move Janet's body to the medical examiner's lab, so that Dr. Kelly could complete his autopsy, determine the exact cause of death, and search for any evidence left on the body by the killer.

"You won't believe what I saw from the air," Leia said, breathlessly interrupting them. "Imagine that Elephant Rock represents the head of a person, okay?"

The men nodded indulgently.

"Then draw a line to represent the body, lines to represent the arms, the legs, the fingers, the toes. What do you have?"

"Uh," José said, "a very large stick figure?"

"Exactly," Leia said.

"What do you mean?" José asked.

"That's what I saw from the air. If you connect the dots—all the flags we placed this morning—you have the image of a giant stick figure."

"What the hell kind of sick game is this?" Lieutenant Andrew asked bitterly.

It seemed he'd aged since coming back from his sad visit with Janet's parents. For the first time, Leia noticed the bruised-looking bags beneath his eyes, the lines etched on his brow. "Why would someone kill a little girl in the first place? Then to spread her body out like that …" The lieutenant shook his head with disgust. "Well, I just can't even get past the first part of the question, to tell you the truth." He rubbed his eyes with his thumbs.

"I asked the photographer to print out a copy of what we saw from up there," Leia said, walking away. "I'll see if it's ready."

The photographer had downloaded the photos to his laptop and whizzed out a few prints for Leia with his portable inkjet printer. She hurried back to José and the lieutenant and found that Carroll had joined them.

"What do you see here?" Leia asked all of them, holding out the picture that showed the most markers.

"It's a message meant for the heavens only," Carroll observed with her typical keen insight.

"Exactly," Leia said. "This girl's death held some symbolic value for the killer. It wasn't a random killing, but a well-planned and executed ritual."

"What do you think it symbolizes?" asked José.

"That's what we have to figure out," Leia replied.

"It seems to me," Carroll said, "that the killer wanted the body to be seen, so he had to stretch it out, make it huge. Maybe that's the reason she was cut apart at every joint."

"But why here?" asked the lieutenant plaintively, still coming to grips with the fact that such a gruesome incident had happened within his jurisdiction.

"I think the killer is very familiar with this area and chose this location specifically for the feeling of comfort it offers him," Leia commented. "I suspect that the killer is local … someone who has lived here for at least several years, if not most of his life."

She turned to José. "Is it possible to find out how long each one of the senator's employees has lived in the area?"

"Of course," José said.

"And I'm going to want to interview the senator and his wife myself. Can you arrange that?"

"Got it," José said.

"Leia, I'm going to get these samples back to the lab," said Carroll. "I'll be in touch."

The two women embraced. Leia, José, and Lieutenant Andrew watched Carroll walk up toward the road.

"You must be hungry," José said to Leia, looking at his watch.

"Maybe we can grab something to eat on our way to the senator's house," Leia said. "Lieutenant, please call me if anything new develops here." Lieutenant Andrew nodded.

"We'll have the driver take us back to the precinct office first," José said. "We'll need my squad car to drive out to the senator's ranch."

Just as Leia and José got into the backseat of the Town Car, a van from the local television station pulled up.

"Damn … the media are arriving," José said. "Drive, please," he said to the driver.

"We need to play this close to the chest," Leia said, thinking aloud. She dialed Lieutenant Andrew. "We don't want any of the details of this murder in the press or on TV—none of it," she warned. "Keep the media away from the scene, and release only the bare minimum to the public. A child has been killed, the killer is unknown, and the details have to remain under wraps for the sake of the investigation. Warn the public to keep their children in their sight at all times and to report any suspicious behavior. Encourage anyone who saw Janet Troy the day she disappeared to come forward. Make sure you brief all your staff, Lieutenant."

"Do you think we have a serial killer on the loose?" asked José when Leia had hung up the telephone.

"Have you seen or heard of any other murders with this signature?"

"We'll have to look in our database back at the precinct office," José said. "But I've never heard of anything like it."

{CHAPTER TWENTY}

Thursday

Senator Thomas Bailey sat in the spacious office of his country estate, reading a bill and frowning. When he realized he'd read the same sentence several times, he gave up, swiveled his chair around, and stared out the window. He was truly sorry for Janet Troy and her family. But it was also unfortunate for him that Janet's bag had been found on his property. The timing of this tragedy wasn't good for him.

The past month the senator and his wife, Beth, had been very busy entertaining wealthy donors to raise campaign funds. Many of these donors were also potential buyers for the horses that were bred on the ranch. Needless to say, Senator Bailey needed this investigation to be concluded quietly and quickly, and Lieutenant Andrew had assured him that it would be. Still, Senator Bailey had contacted the FBI director personally and asked him to send his best agent to clean up the mess.

He had been visiting the ranch the day the girl disappeared, and now he was trapped here when he should have been in Washington DC, drumming up votes for the bill he was cosponsoring and increasing support for his presidential bid. Instead, he had spent the morning comforting his wife and his staff as police officers invaded his home.

The senator called Mary, the house matron, into his office.

"Two more guests will be arriving soon—a police detective and an agent from the FBI," he said when Mary walked in. "I expect they'll join in the questioning after they're finished with me." He paused. "Have the other officers spoken to you yet?"

Mary shook her head. The senator could see how nervous she was about the investigation; her lips were pressed into a thin, anxious line.

"They will ask you to account for everyone's whereabouts during the past several weeks."

"Yes, sir," Mary replied.

"Now, I don't want you to worry, Mary," the senator said, "because I'll take care of everything. You don't have to know anything other than your immediate responsibilities for running the house and for managing the staff members who report to you."

Mary managed to look relieved, although the senator could still see intermittent flashes of fear behind her eyes. Unfortunately, she was going to be a real liability.

"Has Mrs. Bailey been interviewed yet?" the senator asked.

"I don't think so, sir."

"Do you know what she's doing right now?"

"She's locked in her study, planning for the weekend," Mary said.

"Good," the senator said. "Why don't we let her finish what she's doing. You know how she hates to be interrupted."

"Yes, sir."

*   *   *   *

Leia rang the bell, then waited with José on the front porch of Senator Bailey's twenty-room mansion until the door was pulled open by a trim, middle-aged woman dressed in a dark green skirt suit.

"Detective Rodriguez? Agent Bines?" she said. "I'm Mary, Senator Bailey's house matron." They shook hands with her as she ushered them into the two-story foyer. To the right of the foyer, a grand staircase swept up to the next level.

"Please wait here," Mary said. "Senator Bailey will be with you in just a moment."

The two of them looked around as they stood silently. Leia noticed a few handsomely carved statues and paintings, probably Caribbean in origin.

Shoes tapped on the floor behind them. Turning, they saw the senator, dressed in a blue pin-striped suit, approaching them from the end of the hallway. It was apparent to Leia from his lean form and powerful stride that the senator was physically fit. But his worried face and graying hair made him look a decade older than Leia knew he was.

"It's a pleasure to meet you, Agent Bines." The senator welcomed Leia with a firm handshake. "And Detective Rodriguez, good to see you again. We can talk in my office. This way, please."

A strong smell of rosewood greeted Leia as she entered the senator's office. She breathed deeply. Not many people could afford rosewood these days.

"Senator, I apologize in advance if you've already answered these questions for Detective Rodriguez this morning."

"It's all right, Agent Bines. Please, go ahead."

"As you know," Leia said, "we've found the body of the girl whose book bag was recovered on your property."

The senator nodded gravely. "This has been such a misfortune for that child and her family," he said, and Leia noted the sincerity in his voice. "I'll do everything I can to help you with this case."

"Do you have any reason to believe that anybody who lives or works here could have been involved in the murder in any way?" Leia asked. She watched the senator's face closely as he answered.

"Not to my knowledge," he said, seeming to meet Leia's eyes without actually gazing into them, "and I've known the majority of my staff personally for many years."

"How long have you owned this property?" Leia looked casually around the office as she continued her questioning. She noted the shelves were well stocked with books and small objets d'art.

"We purchased this ranch about thirty years ago, and have since used it as our home. My wife, Beth, is here year-round, and I'm here on weekends and during Senate recesses."

"Has there been any unusual activity on your ranch recently?"

"We've had many guests visiting in the past months. It's been a busy time for all of us."

"Well, I'm certainly sorry to trouble you, but we're going to need a list of your staff and guests for the past thirty days. When do you think you might have that for us?"

"I can have my administrative assistant get it to you by tomorrow afternoon."

"Great," Leia said. "As you know, Detective Rodriguez and his officers have already begun interviewing your staff. We'll be continuing that process for at least the next couple of days, if not longer."

"What about the independent contractors you mentioned earlier—the ones who help with the maintenance of the ranch?" José asked. "How do we contact them?"

"I'll add those contact numbers to the list," the senator said.

"Anybody in particular you think might be of interest to us?" asked Leia.

The senator rubbed his chin. "Not that I can think of," he said.

"Can you show us where the girl's bag was found?" José asked.

"Sure. Let me take you for a drive," the senator said, grabbing the keys on his desk.

Once they were on their way, bouncing along a dirt track in a Range Rover, the senator told Leia about the history of the ranch. The Carson family, who were also in the horse-breeding business, had previously owned the ranch. Apparently, they had foreclosed because of a stroke of bad business luck.

Finally, the senator bumped to a halt and killed the engine.

"This is where the dogs found the bag." He pointed at the ground nearby. "As soon as I saw what was inside it, I called the police," he added.

"Dogs?" Leia asked.

"We have four Dobermans on the ranch. I try to walk with them every morning. We go all over the ranch."

"Where are they at night?"

"In a kennel, back up by the horse barns."

"How far is your property line to the west?" Leia asked.

"Not too far from here, where it runs up against the southwest end of Willow Lake. There's also a neighboring ranch down there," the senator said, gesturing west.

"Can we walk down there?" asked José.

"Sure. It's not too far," the senator replied, leading the group.

"Do you know your neighbors?" questioned Leia.

"I know the McLeans'; their ranch borders ours and most of Willow Lake. Rob and Linda McLean are friendly; they have no kids. They breed and show pedigree dogs professionally. Next to the McLean property is an apple orchard owned by Mr. Deed. I've never met him but I think his property takes you right into town."

"Do you know if these properties are fenced?" José asked.

"Yes, ours is and I believe the others are fenced too," the senator said.

Just then, they passed an opening in the senator's fence.

"Are there many openings in the fence like this?" asked Leia, thinking of the opening she had spotted on the senator's property near Elephant Rock.

"We leave breaks in the fences between properties to allow wild deer and other animals to pass through without getting stuck as they migrate toward the lake in the summer," the senator said.

Leia looked in the direction he was gazing and could see Willow Lake—just a glint of water through the trees.

"Looks like somebody could pretty easily walk through here at night unnoticed," José commented.

"Yes, they could," the senator said. "As you can see, these are very large properties."

"Well, Senator, we've taken up enough of your time," Leia said.

As the group walked back to the house from the Range Rover, the senator asked almost tentatively, "So, do you have good leads on this case, Agent Bines—any evidence to go on?"

"Unfortunately, Senator Bailey, I can't discuss the details of the case, even with you. You, of course, understand the importance of discretion in matters like these."

"Of course," the senator said.

{CHAPTER TWENTY-ONE}

Thursday

Peter had lunch at a taco stand in the hospital gardens. Naya and her parents were still on his mind. The separation of a child from her parents was difficult for him to watch, especially when the family was closely knit. Some children's parents—especially those of the kids approaching twelve, the age cutoff for the pediatric psych unit—seemed relieved to leave their children behind, but Peter acknowledged how much stress a mentally ill child could cause for everyone else in the family.

Mrs. Hastings had wondered what sorts of children would be on the unit with Naya, and Peter had explained the range of disorders, from attention deficit hyperactivity disorder or oppositional defiant disorder to mood disorders like depression or bipolar disorder.

"Are these other children dangerous?" Mr. Hastings had asked.

"Most of them aren't," Peter said, "especially when under close supervision."

He explained the three special observation statuses, which included one-to-one observation, direct observation, and sleep observation. One-to-one observation was the most intense form of observation, wherein a staff member was present with the child at all times, within an arm's length—or closer, if specified. This type of observation was reserved for the most acutely ill children—those who posed an imminent threat or danger to themselves or others. The previous month, Peter had had a patient on one-to-one, an eleven-year-old boy who seemed determined to harm and even kill himself.

Direct observation involved a staff member who not only monitored the child but documented the child's activities every fifteen minutes. The staff member could leave the child alone, but only under special emergency circumstances. Most often, children who tended to act out or act impulsively were placed under direct observation.

Sleep observation was used at night to monitor children like Naya, who had a possible sleep disorder or concern for nighttime safety.

"We'll keep a close eye on Naya and keep her safe at all times," Peter had reassured Mr. and Mrs. Hastings.

Peter held one last form in his hand. "This is a form that you have to sign acknowledging that you have heard what I'm going to tell you about our manual restraint and seclusion policy," he said with some hesitancy. This part of the hospitalization was especially difficult to explain to the parents of any child, especially if the child did not have any overtly aggressive behaviors.

"What do you mean by that?" Mrs. Hastings asked with a frown.

"Sometimes, when a child is behaviorally out of control and poses a danger to themselves or others, the staff will have to do one of two interventions." Peter went on to explain, "If the child is violently out of control, staff will manually restrain him or her, which means they will hold the child on the floor by the arms and legs for up to fifteen minutes to keep them from injuring themselves or others. A child of any age can be manually restrained. If such an intervention was used, then you as the parent will be notified."

"And what is the second intervention?" Mrs. Hastings asked nervously.

Peter outlined the procedure known as "locked seclusion." This was a procedure where the child was put in the Quiet Room. The intention was to help the child regain control. The walls of the Quiet Room were padded with a special soft material, and the room was empty except for a video camera attached to an upper corner of the room to monitor the child. The video feed could be viewed on a small monitor outside the room. On occasions, the door of the room needed to be closed and locked.

If that were to happen, the child was in locked seclusion. Only children more than nine years of age were allowed by state regulations to be placed in locked seclusion. The child could be in locked seclusion for a maximum of thirty minutes at a time. Both types of intervention required rigorous documentation.

"These procedures can be initiated only by a physician," Peter said reassuringly, "and besides, I don't think any of this will apply to Naya, since she is under nine and has no such behavioral issues. Still, I'm required to inform you of these policies."

Peter handing over the last form to Mr. Hastings, who read it and—with obvious reluctance—signed it.

When Peter returned to the unit after lunch, he decided to find Naya and get her compulsory physical examination—a requirement for admission—out of the way. Naya was in the dining room, lining up with the other children after lunch.

"Good afternoon, Dr. Gram!" shouted the youngsters in an off-pitch chorus when they saw Peter standing in the doorway.

"Good afternoon to all of you," Peter said, and he walked down the line with his hand out, so that the children who wanted to could give him a high five or two as he passed.

Naya was at the end of the line. Peter stopped next to her and bent close to tell her he needed to meet with her for a little while to do a medical checkup. He told the MHA staff that she would be back for the next class.

Naya stepped off the line and walked away with Peter toward the examination room, located next to the nurses' station. As he passed by the station, Peter asked one of the nurses to assist him.

As Peter and Naya approached the examination room, Peter said, "Do you know what a medical checkup is?"

"To make sure my heart is still working," Naya said seriously.

"Yes, and to make sure there's nothing wrong with your body that might be causing you to have bad dreams at night."

"Naya, this is Jennifer," Peter said, gesturing to the woman who had just joined them in the hall. "She's a nurse, and she's going to help us with the examination."

Peter unlocked the door, and the three of them stepped into a small room that smelled of rubbing alcohol and metal. There was an examination table on one side of the room and a sink on the other.

"I need you to hop up here, please," Peter said, tapping the examination table.

Naya leaped onto the table with no difficulty and sat facing him, legs dangling. Peter conducted a quick visual examination, noting that she didn't have any abnormal features that might indicate that she had a genetic syndrome. He then checked her ears, nose, and throat to make sure she didn't have any upper respiratory tract infections.

"I need you to lie down for a minute, please," Peter instructed Naya. "I'm going to press your tummy, and I want you to tell me if you have any pain."

Naya complied with his instructions and squirmed as he palpated her abdomen; she was ticklish, like so many of Peter's patients. He picked up a stethoscope and listened to her heartbeat.

"Do you want to hear your heart?" he asked and, when she nodded, handed her the listening end of the stethoscope while holding the other on her chest.

Naya put the ends of the stethoscope in her ears. "They sound like drums," she said with such sincerity that Peter wanted to laugh out loud.

"Now," he said, suppressing his smile, "I need you to do a couple of things for me. They may seem a little silly, but I need to make sure that the rest of your body is working properly."

Peter made the brief neurological examination fun by having Naya hop on one foot and then the other. He showed her how to tandem walk with her arms stretched out. He asked her to touch his finger, then her nose, and made the task more difficult by moving his finger from side to side. Naya completed all tasks with ease.

"You're a very bright and healthy girl," Peter complimented Naya as he wrapped up the examination.

"Then why am I here?" Naya asked innocently.

"We need to figure out why you were walking around in your room while you were asleep," Peter explained.

"But I don't remember that," Naya said, pouting.

"That's okay. No one remembers what they do while they're asleep. If they did, it wouldn't be called sleepwalking," Peter said, trying to comfort her.

"Does this happen to other little girls?" Naya asked. "Or am I the only one?"

Peter could tell she didn't want to be the only one.

"Yes, of course others have this problem," he said. "We see lots of kids who walk and talk in their sleep."

"But do all of them come here?"

"No, only the ones who might hurt themselves by accident."

"Like me," Naya said softly.

"Yes, like you. You nearly climbed over the wall of your balcony. That was very dangerous," Peter reiterated. "You're here so we can keep you safe. Now, tomorrow morning, you're going to have another examination to make sure you're well and healthy," Peter said, trying to explain in the best way he could that she was going for an MRI.

"Will it hurt?" Naya asked fearfully.

"No, it won't hurt. All you have to do is lie down still, and a big machine will take pictures of your head like a big camera. The machine will be a bit noisy, but it's nothing to be afraid of."

"Can I see the pictures after the big camera takes them?"

"Sure you can, after it's done."

"Will you be there?" Naya asked Peter in a soft voice.

"Of course," Peter said with a reassuring smile.

They said good-bye to Jennifer, and Peter led Naya out of the examination room. He was pleased with the way she seemed to be bonding with him. Her cooperation would make it much easier for him to get to the bottom of the problem.

As they walked down the hallway back toward the classrooms, Naya reached up and slipped her small hand into his.

"After the camera takes pictures of your head, you're going to have another test called an EEG." Peter explained to Naya what she could expect during the procedure. She began to giggle as he described the wires that would be attached to her head.

"I'll look funny," she said, "like an alien."

They reached the classroom, and Peter gave Naya's hand a squeeze, then let go. Her expression went suddenly serious.

"Dr. Gram?"

"Yes, Naya?"

"Is it scary here at night?"

Peter crouched down and looked calmly into Naya's eyes. "A staff member is going to watch over you while you sleep, so you don't have to worry. You'll be safe, and I'll check on you often."

Naya nodded.

"Now have a good afternoon at school," Peter said.

A bit later, as Peter sat entering Naya's admitting orders into the computer, he heard an overhead page: "Dr. Gram, report to the courtyard, stat."

Stat? Must be something serious. He rose quickly and looked at Matt, who was sitting next to him at the nurses' station.

"It sounds like I might need your help," he said.

Matt was unimpressed by the urgency of the page. He barely looked at Peter. "I'll be there in a moment," he said.

Peter rushed to the courtyard to find a huge commotion. Some of the children were screaming and crying while three staff members held Timothy down on the ground. Peter rushed to them, asking what had happened.

"I'm not sure what triggered it," one of the staff members said.

"Timothy, if you calm down, then we can talk about it," Peter said close against Timothy's ear, over Timothy's screams.

"Fuck you! Fuck you all!" Timothy yelled at the top of his lungs.

It still shocked Peter to hear profanity from a seven-year-old boy. He watched Timothy struggle violently. One staff member held his legs in a special hold at the knees, while two others held each arm. The boy's usually pale, freckled skin was flushed pink with rage.

"Let's carry him to the seclusion room," Peter said to the MHAs. It was dangerous to continuously restrain Timothy while he was this agitated; Timothy was big and strong for his age. The psychotropic medications he had taken over the years had caused him to gain weight.

As the teacher gathered the other children, trying to get them out of the courtyard, Peter noticed Naya standing in a corner, looking very frightened. Unfortunately, he couldn't speak to her that moment, as he needed to take care of the crisis first.

Matt appeared at his elbow. "So what do you think, doc?" Matt said. "Thorazine?"

"Twenty-five milligrams IM," Peter said.

Once Naya and the other children had left the area, Peter and the other staff carried the wiggling, squirming, cursing Timothy to the seclusion room. Matt met them there with a syringe.

Peter instructed the others to roll Timothy over, so that Matt could give him the medicine intramuscularly in the buttocks. Timothy screamed in agony and continued to curse.

Thorazine was a medication used occasionally for patients on the inpatient unit. One of the oldest antipsychotic medications on the market, it had the power to calm down a severely agitated child quickly, even in small doses. Only after the child was calm could a rational conversation be conducted in a useful manner.

Timothy was a boy who became extremely angry for what seemed to the adults around him the littlest of reasons. Most often, his reaction was out of proportion to the stimulus. He was diagnosed as having attention deficit hyperactivity disorder and a mood disorder. Doctors didn't diagnose mental illnesses like bipolar disorder at such a young age, as the symptoms were undifferentiated. Timothy had been exposed to cocaine in utero and placed in numerous foster homes since birth. There were allegations of physical abuse during these placements that were never proven. He was on the unit now after trying to stab his foster parents' son in the face with a pencil a week before.

Even after the injection of Thorazine, Timothy continued to struggle. Peter noted that the staff was tiring out. They looked at him imploringly, silently warning that they wouldn't be able to restrain him for much longer. Unfortunately for Peter, Timothy was less than nine years of age and couldn't be put in locked seclusion. Peter instructed the staff to let Timothy go and to exit the seclusion room, leaving him alone with Timothy. Peter stood against the closed door, and Timothy lay sprawled on the floor in front of him. Peter hoped the drug would take effect before Timothy realized no one was holding him any longer.

Timothy rolled back and forth on the floor, still shouting and screaming, but he didn't try to hit Peter or really even seem to notice that he was there. Finally, he did notice. He stood up and began trying to push Peter away from the door. Peter knew that the only way he could remove himself from the struggle was to move away from the door, but if he did so, Timothy would run out of the seclusion room and could continue to pose a threat to the other patients and staff.

Peter needed an alternate strategy. He signaled to Matt, who was standing outside, to lock the seclusion-room door, so that Peter could step away from it and remove himself from the power struggle with Timothy. After all, a child locked in the seclusion room with a doctor wasn't technically in locked seclusion, because he wasn't alone.

"Get away from me," Timothy wailed as Peter moved away from the door.

Then Timothy started to cry. "I want to go! I want to go!"

"Where do you want to go?" Peter asked in a soft voice.

"I want my mommy, I want my mommy." Timothy's crying became uncontrollable. He lay down on his face on the floor and bawled. Tears wet the padded floor, and mucus poured from his nose. His eyelids and cheeks were mottled and swollen.

"We can talk about it," Peter soothed, "but first you have to calm down." He knelt on the floor next to Timothy and gently stroked the boy's back. Peter's touch seemed to break a dam in the boy. Timothy began to cry even louder—in pain now rather than anger, his guard completely down. Peter knew this kind of crying could be cathartic for a child, but as he continued to rub Timothy's back, a feeling of sadness over-whelmed him. It was very painful to see a child in such emotional agony. He tried to separate from Timothy and block out his own emotions, so that he could remain objective. As if in sympathy, his own nose began to run, and he wiped it on his sleeve.

After a few minutes, Timothy gradually began to calm down. His skin began to turn white between his freckles once again.

"Can we sit for a moment in the corner?" Peter asked him quietly.

Timothy nodded and moved with Peter to the corner of the room. Peter stood up and signaled to Matt that he could unlock the door.

Peter wasn't sure which mommy Timothy had been referring to. His biological mother had been in and out of his life every few years until recently, when her parental rights had been terminated. He had been in so many foster homes and had so many foster mothers. His relationships with adults were so chaotic that his sense of self and others was profoundly fragile.

"Which mommy are you asking for?" Peter asked.

"I don't know," Timothy said, wiping his tears. "I liked Miss Pauline." He sniffled. Miss Pauline's home was his most recent and longest foster placement. He had formed attachments to Miss Pauline and her son, but ultimately, a sibling was something he couldn't tolerate. He wanted Miss Pauline all to himself. It was in a moment of jealousy that he had tried to stab her son, the incident that in turn led to his current hospitalization.

Timothy let out a small yawn. Peter could see that the medication was beginning to take effect. Confident that Timothy was in complete control of himself, Peter escorted him back to his room. Timothy plopped down on his bed and fell immediately asleep.

Peter walked out of Timothy's room and went to the nurses' station. He was now officially exhausted.

"Matt," he said slumping down in a chair, "I'm going to check in with Naya and then call it a day."

Matt looked at him with sympathy. "Okay, Doc," Matt said. "Take it easy."

Peter took a deep breath and heaved himself out of the chair. He peeked inside Naya's room, where she was sitting by herself on the bed.

"Is school out for the day?" Peter asked, even though he knew the answer.

Naya nodded.

Peter gave her a comforting smile. "Can I sit next to you?" he asked.

Naya nodded again and slid over a little, making room for him to join her.

Peter sat down and picked up the little stuffed bear that lay on the bed. "Is this Noodle?" he asked.

Naya shook her head. "I told you, Noodle's a dog. Anyway, he's at home. That isn't even my bear. It's the hospital's bear."

Peter held the bear out to Naya. "But he still needs a friend, don't you think?"

Naya stared at the bear for a moment, then took it from Peter and cuddled it in her arms.

"I know what you saw today must have scared you."

"Yeah," Naya said softly. "Is that what's going to happen to me?" She asked the question as though resigned to her fate.

"No," Peter reassured her. "I promise that won't happen to you." He patted her on her hand. "You'll be safe here."

"I'm scared," Naya said with a quiver in her voice.

"No, Naya, you don't have to be. Like I said before, there will be a staff member sitting right next to your door while you sleep. I'll be back in the morning, and the first thing I'll do is check in on you."

"All right," Naya said.

Peter patted Naya on the shoulder, then left her room and went to gather his belongings from the fellows' office. He would meet Everson at the gym for a short workout, then go home and get some rest.

{CHAPTER TWENTY-TWO}

Thursday

By the time José and Leia left the senator's ranch, it was almost four in the afternoon, and the immense weight of jet lag was slowly crushing Leia.

"Could we get a cup of coffee?" she asked José. Maybe the caffeine would help her stay awake—at least until she could get to her motel room.

"Sure," José replied, and just minutes later, they were pulling into the parking lot of Café Eclipse, a small gourmet coffee shop in the heart of Newbury.

The double espresso helped clear Leia's head.

"The Holiday Inn where you'll be staying is just a few blocks from here," José said. "You look about ready to crash."

"Does the Holiday Inn have a swimming pool?" Leia asked with a smirk on her face.

"Yes, of course. I did my homework, Agent Bines," José said with a warm smile.

Leia considered swimming the ultimate form of relaxation. She could spend hours swimming laps.

José took a sip of his cappuccino. "So, what do you make of our meeting with the senator?" he asked Leia.

"I think he's very nervous about the whole thing."

"Do you think he might have anything to do with the murder?"

"I suspect he's worried that somebody who works on the ranch might be involved."

"Then why call you in?"

"I'm not sure," Leia said. "He's a cautious man. Maybe he wanted to make sure he wasn't the one to blow the whistle on this person. He wants someone else to discover what he already knows."

"After I drop you at your hotel, I'll go back to the ranch and continue to supervise the questioning of the staff."

"See if you can get a list of all the vendors who make regular deliveries to the ranch," Leia added. "Hey, thanks for the coffee. Now I'll be able to stay awake at least long enough to go over some of the stuff we've gathered today." She stifled a yawn.

José drove her to the Holiday Inn. He pointed out the unmarked squad car he'd had delivered for her. "It has a GPS navigation system, so that you can get around town on your own if you need to."

"Aren't you thoughtful, Detective."

"But if you like, I'll still pick you up in the morning to take you over to the precinct to look through the database. Eight o'clock?"

"How about seven? We have a lot of ground to cover," Leia replied.

José carried Leia's luggage to the front desk and left her there to check in.

Once Leia was in her room alone with her belongings stowed neatly in the dresser and closet, she began to shake all over. She sat down on the bed. *It's the coffee,* she told herself, although she knew it wasn't true. She was shaking because she was scared—scared that she wouldn't be able to crack the case. What real evidence did she have, after all? None. A little girl had been killed in the most gruesome fashion imaginable, and not one person could be linked to the crime.

Okay, Bines, she thought, *get it together. You've worked with less than this.*

She sat down at the desk and stared at the aerial photograph. She took a black marker from her bag and connected the visible markers.

There's a message in this picture, Leia said to herself. *And I'm going to find out what it is.*

{CHAPTER TWENTY-THREE}

Thursday

Peter's health club was located within a few minutes of the hospital, which made it a convenient favorite among the hospital staff. Peter parked his bright red Jeep Grand Cherokee next to Everson's blue BMW convertible.

He found Everson in the free-weight area, standing in front of a floor-to-ceiling, wall-to wall-mirror. Peter smiled to himself. It was true that his friend was a bit vain.

Everson, who was holding a barbell weighted with a hundred pounds over his head, grinned when he saw Peter approaching him from behind. He pumped the barbell up and down, working his shoulder muscles.

"Give me a hand," he said, huffing. "I need to do two more reps."

"Man, oh man," Peter said. "You sure can lift weights for an old guy."

Peter stood behind Everson, put his hands under Everson's elbows, and pushed up as Everson tried to lift the bar once again. "One, two," he said as Everson completed his shoulder routine.

"That was rough," Everson said as he flexed his shoulder muscles and looked in the mirror. "I'll spot you if you want to try a couple."

"I have to warm up," Peter said, but then he gauged his level of exhaustion and found it high. "On second thought," he said, "I think I'll just do a half hour of cardio, then head home."

Everson studied his face. "What happened to you? Looks like you had a rough day."

"I was on call last night. The ER was crammed with kids, and I ended up admitting one with some truly bizarre symptoms."

Everson looked at him inquiringly. Peter knew his friend loved hearing stories of Peter's psych cases.

"This girl," Peter said, "had a dream that felt so real to her, she was ready to jump off her balcony. Not only that, but she drew a picture of the dream that sort of made the hair on the back of my neck stand up. She's seven years old, but the detail in that picture ... man, I don't know."

"Scary, man," Everson said. "Good thing she didn't actually jump."

"Yep," Peter said, "but it wasn't for lack of trying. If that ledge had been lower, or the railing less difficult to climb ..." He suppressed a shudder thinking of Naya's little body lying on the sidewalk beneath the balcony. "The problem is, we don't know why she did it."

"Brain tumor?"

"I don't think so, but we're doing an MRI and an EEG tomorrow. Then there's this other kid, Timothy, who scared the hell out of everyone on the unit this afternoon."

Peter described Timothy's case.

"That's rough," Everson said. "I don't know why you'd want to specialize over there, man. I couldn't take it. I just cut 'em open and sew 'em back together. I don't have to talk to them too much, which is okay with me."

Peter looked at his sweat-drenched friend and marveled for the millionth time at how different they were.

"I should be done in a half hour too," Everson continued, looking at his watch.

"You got here early," Peter said.

"That's the privilege of being the chief," Everson gloated. "Hey, how about we go to the cabin tomorrow and chill out?"

"I'll see what I can do," Peter answered. Everson loved Peter's uncle's cabin on Willow Lake. During medical school, Peter, Everson, and some of their other friends used the cabin often to fish and get away from the stresses of school, the hospital, and the university crowd. Everson was the only one of the old gang who still liked going there with him.

"If being chief is so great, what's bothering you?" Peter asked, knowing that Everson's request for downtime indicated the need for a break.

"Work's all right," Everson said. "It's Evelyn. She's all up in my face all the time about one thing or another. Nothing's ever right with her. She's always worrying about something."

"Maybe you need to be more patient with her. She's stuck with you longer than anyone else."

"I know, I know," Everson said.

Peter loved and admired his friend, but he didn't know how Evelyn—or any woman, for that matter—could put up with Everson's idiosyncrasies and difficult work schedule. He trivialized things that other people found important, which Peter had seen lead to frequent quarrels.

"Okay, man," Peter said, "I'll see you in thirty."

Peter joined the rest of the head bobbers on the elliptical machines while Everson continued his shoulder presses. Before they knew it, the two men were both done and entering the men's locker room, where they were greeted by a well-built man dressed in shorts and a T-shirt. He was putting a fresh load of towels on the linen shelf. It was Arcus, a part-time club employee. Peter didn't know him very well, but he knew Everson hung out with Arcus occasionally. Everson had mentioned that they had "partied" together. Peter had never been much of a partier.

"Towel, Doc?" Arcus asked Everson.

"Yes, Arcus," Everson said.

"Dr. Gram?"

"Sure, thanks," Peter said. Arcus hung around and chatted about his day job and an article he'd read in *Time* magazine about aliens. Peter toweled off and changed into a pair of jeans and a sweatshirt. He threw the damp towel into the laundry hamper in the corner and picked up his gym bag.

Everson was stripping down, preparing to shower.

"Let me know if you can go to the cabin tomorrow, right?" Everson reminded Peter.

"I'll catch up with you at the hospital tomorrow," Peter said, combing his springy hair down with his fingers.

"All right, see ya," Everson said and sauntered off toward the showers.

Peter's shoulders slumped as he left the gym. He was beginning to fade and couldn't wait to get home.

*   *   *   *

Everson took a long, hot shower. He whistled as he patted himself dry, the sound echoing through the now-empty locker room. He wrapped a towel around his waist, then went to the sinks and stood admiring himself in the mirror. No wonder Evelyn couldn't resist him.

Then, behind him, Everson saw someone come around the corner. Damn, he'd hoped Arcus would've left already.

Arcus had changed into street clothes—a pair of jeans and a hooded sweatshirt. He was tall enough—nearly as tall as Everson—and his black hair was distinguished by a speckling of gray. Arcus would have been good-looking except for his long, crooked nose, Everson thought. And he needed to shave off that thin mustache that ran across his upper lip.

"Whassup, my boy?" Everson asked Arcus.

"You tell me," Arcus replied in a gruff voice.

"Not bad, could be better."

"I can help you with that," Arcus said, walking closer.

"Yeah," Everson said, "I'd like some, but I don't have any money with me, man."

"You're good for it, right, Doc?" Arcus said. "How much do you want?"

"I could use a little more today, but I'm telling you, I really can't afford it."

"Don't worry, man—I'll spot you."

Everson hesitated. He'd sworn he was going to quit, and he really didn't have the money. "Oh, what the hell—give me two packs," he said.

"That's what I thought," Arcus said, slipping his hands into his jean pockets. "Here, this is your special for today." He handed a little plastic bag to Everson.

"Thanks," Everson said, concealing the bag completely in his left palm. "You're the man."

"What about Dr. Gram? Is he a friend in need?"

Everson snorted out a laugh. "Peter?" he said. "Don't go there, my boy. You won't be expanding your clientele in that direction. Hey, how's everything been going since—"

"Hey, let's not talk about that." Arcus gave Everson a pained scowl.

While Everson dressed, Arcus began folding a laundry bag full of clean towels and stacking them on the shelves. Everson liked Arcus all right as a person, but he'd been wishing lately that the man would just disappear and take Everson's taste for his wares with him. He certainly regretted getting Arcus the job at the club, where he now saw him on almost a daily basis.

Everson had met Arcus a year before, at the hospital during a surgical consultation, and Arcus had mentioned that he was looking for a part-time job a few hours a week. It had seemed convenient at first, knowing where to find his dealer whenever he needed a little taste, and Arcus had picked up a few more clients at the health club. But now Everson's taste was getting ahead of his paycheck, and he knew Arcus would only rely on credit for so long.

{CHAPTER TWENTY-FOUR}

Thursday Evening

Shortly after Dr. Gram left Naya's room, her parents appeared for visiting hours, as promised. They brought her pajamas, clothes for the next few days, and Noodle. Naya watched as the evening nurse marked her initials on her belongings with a permanent marker and logged them in a record that was put in her chart, so they wouldn't get lost or mixed with the other children's.

Naya was feeling a bit more comfortable on the unit, but she still had many questions.

"Why are the other kids taking medicine, and I'm not?" Naya asked her mother, feeling a little disappointed. When everyone else got pills in paper cups, it seemed cool.

Naya's mother looked surprised. "Well," she said haltingly, "some kids may need medicine if they are not feeling well, and others may not. You just happen to be one of the kids who feels fine."

Naya was satisfied with the answer. She told her parents about having witnessed the boy who had become angry and lost control. She watched as her parents tried to hide their fear and worry from her.

It was nearing dinnertime, and visiting hours were coming to end. Naya could tell that her parents didn't want to leave her there, and it made her feel braver. She wished them a good night and headed to the dining room with the rest of the children. Anyway, she would see them soon. Her mother had promised that she would be there first thing in the morning in preparation for the MRI and EEG.

As Naya stood in line for dinner, someone nudged her in the back. She turned around and saw a pale girl with brown, curly hair who was the same height as she was. She had seen this girl in the playroom with a woman whom Naya assumed was the other little girl's mother.

"What's your name?" the girl asked.

"Naya."

"My name's Sasha," the girl said with a friendly smile.

"Hi," Naya said politely.

"Can I be your friend?"

"Uh, yeah, sure," Naya said, moving up in line toward the dietary staff.

"We can sit together at that table," Sasha said, pointing out to one of the six round dining tables.

Naya was given a prepared meal containing mashed potatoes, beans, and grilled chicken.

"I'm vegetarian," she told the staff.

"Oh! I'm sorry, dear," a woman apologized. "Here, this is your tray." Instead of the chicken dinner, the new tray contained yellow rice, beans, and a cup of mixed fruit. Naya was satisfied with what she saw there.

Sasha followed Naya to the table with a tray of her own. Near the door, an adult supervised the children, reminding Naya of the way teachers supervised the lunchroom at school to keep the children from fighting and goofing around.

"Do you like beans?" Sasha asked Naya, scrunching up her nose.

"Yep, I do."

"I don't. Do you want some of mine?" Sasha pointed to the beans on her plate.

"Nah, I have enough," Naya said.

"Sasha, you have to eat all your food if you want those positive points," an adult sitting at the next table said. "How else will you get that prize you wanted?"

"But I don't want to eat beans," Sasha whined with her lower lip poked out.

"Sasha, you like beans. You eat them all the time," the adult said.

A naughty smile appeared on Sasha's face.

"And if you continue to whine, you'll get negative points," the adult warned.

Naya observed the interaction. She hadn't heard about the points and prizes yet. She wondered what she could win.

"Oh, well," Sasha sighed, "I guess I'll eat them."

Naya couldn't understand why Sasha would say she didn't like beans when she really did. But in any case, she wasn't going to ask.

Once the two girls were done eating, Sasha showed Naya what to do with her tray.

"It's quiet time now," they heard one of the staff members announcing. "Go on into your rooms."

"Can I show Naya my toys?" Sasha asked loudly.

"Not now, and watch your tone of voice, please," said the adult who was directing the children out of the dining room and back into the hallway leading to the bedrooms.

"This is my room," Sasha said, running into a room two doors down and across the hall from Naya's. Naya couldn't see into Sasha's room, but she heard a rhythmic, springy sound that was very familiar. Someone was jumping on the bed.

Then a petite, round-faced Asian woman came down the hall and went into Sasha's room. Naya heard the woman tell Sasha that it was time to sit or lie down. The sound of jumping continued. The woman said that if Sasha didn't stop, she would earn negative points, and the sound stopped. Soon, the woman appeared in the doorway of Naya's room, where Naya was sitting on the bed.

"Hi, I'm Nancy," she said, smiling. "I'll be sitting by your door tonight, just to make sure you're safe while you sleep. What's your name, sweetie?"

"Naya."

"Naya, I'm going to help you get ready for bed, and then, if you'd like, we can read a story together."

Nancy helped Naya get into her pajamas and showed her to the common bathroom that the girls shared. Naya waited for her turn and completed her bedtime ritual of brushing her teeth and washing her face. Her parents had raised Naya to be an independent little girl. She noticed that some of the other children who were much older than her needed a lot more assistance.

Once Naya had finished using the bathroom, she went back to her room. Nancy had pulled up a chair and sat just outside the door in the hallway.

It was close to seven o'clock; the children were expected to be asleep by eight o'clock at the latest. Nancy went into Naya's room and sat at the foot of her bed. She had two fairy-tale books in her hand. Naya chose *Snow White and the Seven Dwarfs*, which Nancy read in a gentle, soothing voice. Naya fell asleep before Snow White had even bitten the poisoned apple.

*　　*　　*　　*

Naya opened her eyes to bright sunshine. She sat up in a large field covered with tall, green grass. The field was surrounded by lots of trees rustling in a gentle breeze that blew from the direction of the sun. She looked all around for other people, but all she could see was a few birds flying away and butterflies frolicking in the breeze. She had never been alone in a place like this. She began to feel scared but weirdly calm at the same time. She scanned the ring of trees once again and saw something there, in the distance.

It was something big, tall, and gray, and it was swaying to and fro. She couldn't tell what it was, but it was moving toward her through the trees. She began to walk toward what she thought must be some kind of animal. Yes! It was!

"Dummy, it's an elephant," Naya said to herself. "But what's an elephant doing out here in a field? I guess elephants do eat grass." She remembered this bit of trivia from a visit to the zoo. "And there's lots of it here."

Naya continued to walk toward the elephant. She heard a humming sound that got louder and louder. Was the elephant humming? Then Naya noticed a dent in the long grass, just before she nearly trampled something lying there. Naya froze, and her heart beat faster. It was a person—a girl. The girl was humming a song.

"Um, hello?" Naya said.

The humming stopped, and the girl called out, "Who's there?"

Naya stepped closer and saw that it was a young white girl with beautiful blonde hair. She was older than Naya, but not yet a teenager. The girl was looking up into the sky.

Naya walked over so that the girl could see her. "Hello," she said again. "I'm Naya. Who are you?"

"My name is Janet," the girl replied.

"What are you doing here?" Naya asked.

"I'm taking my elephant for a walk. He's hungry, because he didn't eat dinner yesterday."

"Then why are you lying in the grass?"

"I can't get up. I need to be tied back together. Do you have some string?"

"What do you mean?" Naya asked, puzzled.

"Look, my body isn't joined together like yours. Come closer, and I'll show you."

Naya moved closer. She saw that Janet wore a white, long-sleeved shirt and a plaid, woolen skirt.

"You have to bend down," Janet instructed.

Naya knelt next to Janet, who lay extraordinarily still, only moving her eyes and mouth as she spoke. It was as if she were playing Freeze Tag or Simon Says.

"Look at my neck," Janet said, rolling her eyeballs down.

Naya squinted and saw what Janet was talking about. There was a gap between her neck and her body. It was as though someone had sliced through Janet's neck, then placed her head just above her body.

Naya held her breath. She'd never seen anything like this before. She studied the gap for a few more moments, then stood to look at the rest of Janet's body, which was riddled with many more gaps everywhere—even between her fingers.

Naya's breath began coming in short, noisy bursts.

"Don't be scared," Janet said with a peaceful smile. "All I need for you to do is to get some string and help put me back together."

"What happened to you?" Naya gasped.

"I don't know exactly how this happened, but I think somebody did it to me."

"Who did it?"

"I think it was the big bad man," Janet said sadly.

"Will he do it to me too?" Naya asked, terrified.

"No, he won't."

"How do you know?"

"Because Jerry is protecting us."

"Who's Jerry?"

"Jerry's my elephant."

"That elephant?" Naya asked, pointing toward the mammoth animal that was now standing not far from them.

"Yes," Janet said, looking at Jerry with a soft smile.

Naya's heart was still pounding, but she began to feel that other sense of calm at the same time. She knew she had to help Janet. She just wasn't sure how.

"You can ask the doctor to help me," Janet said, as though she had read Naya's thoughts.

"You mean the one who's helping me—Dr. Gram?"

"Yes, him," Janet replied.

"Do you think he'll understand if I tell him about you?"

"He's the only one who will understand," reaffirmed Janet.

"I like him," Naya said. "I'll tell him about you when I see him today."

"But before you go," Janet said, "could you lie down next to me and tell me a story?"

"Oh, yes! I remember a story I just heard," Naya said, excited to tell the story of Snow White.

Naya lay down next to Janet and recited the story. The golden sunshine warmed her skin, and the gentle breeze cooled it. She began to feel sleepy and found her eyelids so heavy, she could no longer keep them up.

Meeting Janet was surely the strangest thing that had ever happened to her. She began to think that maybe this was only a dream.

{CHAPTER TWENTY-FIVE}

Friday

Peter woke up early, glad that Friday had finally come. *Only another eight hours of work before the weekend!* He wasn't on call this weekend and had decided to go into New York City to see a bargain matinee on Broadway.

Peter roamed into the kitchen of his one-bedroom apartment. It was still dark outside, but dawn would break soon. Peter decided to go to the hospital early. Naya's MRI was scheduled for the morning, just after rounds. If he could finish some of his work, he would be able to accompany Naya to the MRI lab.

It was seven thirty when Peter stepped onto the unit, buzzing past the blue doors and walking to the nurses' station, which was empty. Peter peeked into the medication-dispensation room and saw Matt preparing the children's medications for the eight o'clock doses.

"How was your night?" Matt asked Peter when he returned to the nurses' station and found Peter entering data into the computer.

"I slept like a baby."

"You look well rested. Why are you here so early?"

"I'm just finishing some of the work for Sasha and Timothy before morning report," Peter explained.

At morning report, the physicians got together with the rest of the staff team. The outgoing shift of nurses signed off on the events that had occurred the previous evening, and the fellows narrated a clinical update of their patients and the events in the past twenty-four hours. Then the team agreed on a treatment plan for each child.

One by one, the other fellows trickled into the nurses' station and sat around a large, circular table located in the center of the area. Dorothy Fisher came in last, and the charge nurse for the previous shift read out a summary of events, one child at a time. Just as the nurse began to talk about Naya, Matt joined the meeting, having just finished dispensing the morning medicines to the children.

"Naya Hastings," the nurse read out from the notes that Nancy, the MHA, had written down during her shift. "Naya went to bed at around eight thirty and was asleep by nine fifteen. At around one AM, she got out of bed and stood in the center of the room. I went in and asked her if everything was all right. Naya wasn't responsive, and she stood talking to herself. I couldn't understand what she was talking about. It appeared that she was having a conversation with somebody. She was standing with her eyes wide open. She was nonresponsive to my presence and to the waving of my hand in front of her face. I did not want to touch or shake her for fear of startling her. I stood by the door and watched her for the next hour as she stood in this one location before returning to bed. Toward the end of the episode, she lay down on the floor and narrated part of a story that I had read to her just before she fell asleep. After that time, she got back into bed and slept without any further incident. She woke this morning with some recollection of the event. She appeared a little anxious when I asked her if she had a bad dream, and she did not want to talk to me about it."

Peter was stunned. He had never encountered a child with such symptoms. What was unusual was the period of time the episode had lasted. But it wasn't unheard of for people to perform complex maneuvers during their sleep.

"Can you tell us more about the case, Peter?" Dorothy asked him.

Peter presented an abbreviated version of Naya's case for the rest of the team. He mentioned that Naya was scheduled for an MRI in the morning, followed by an EEG later that afternoon.

"What's your differential diagnosis?" Dorothy continued.

"My first thought would be a sleep-related disorder, though I would like to rule out any medical condition or other psychotic process," Peter replied self-consciously. He wished he had more to present.

"Has Naya ever had any other hallucinatory experiences?"

"She denies any so far, but I can't be sure. She could be concealing that fact."

"What about any family history of such experiences, or any other psychiatric history?"

Peter went on to tell them that Naya had been adopted, and that he needed to contact Naya's one available relative to get more information about her biological family.

"I think that is an important piece of information," Dorothy said. "We don't know if she has any underlying familial illness that might be presenting itself in an unusual way."

"Sure, I'll look into that after I finish with the MRI this morning," Peter said, nodding. He remembered that the contact information for Naya's uncle was in her chart.

After discussing Naya's case, the team breezed through the rest of the cases in the context of limited time. Once the rounds ended, the fellows disbanded and went off to their offices to continue with their day.

Peter headed to Naya's room. She was sitting at the desk with her back to the door. He knocked gently on the open door, and Naya turned around and acknowledged him with a smile. As he approached the desk, he could see that she was drawing.

"I see you've been keeping yourself busy this morning," Peter said, hovering over Naya, trying to see what she was drawing. Just at that moment, he heard a familiar overhead page from the front desk calling for him.

"I think your mother's here," Peter told Naya, walking back to the door.

"I need to finish my picture," Naya said, ignoring his announcement.

"You can finish it after we come back from the examination you're having this morning," Peter said, gesturing for her to come with him.

Naya scowled but hopped off the chair and joined Peter at the door. She was neatly dressed and looked well rested. She stuck out her hand toward Peter, expecting him to take it, which he did. The two of them walked hand in hand to the waiting room.

Once she saw her mother, Naya dropped Peter's hand and ran to her. Peter was happy to see them hug each other so warmly. Many of the children he had treated in the past had uncaring parents—or no parents at all.

Peter escorted Naya and her mother through the tunnel that connected Strauss I to the main medical hospital. The MRI lab was situated in the radiology department on the third floor of the hospital. The clerk there told Peter that Naya's turn was coming up any minute, and that he could wait with them until her name was called.

Peter went back and sat next to Mrs. Hastings while Naya stood browsing through a magazine a few feet away.

"How was Naya last night?" Mrs. Hastings asked Peter with some anxiety.

"She had an episode last night," Peter replied and explained what had happened.

"What do you think it was?"

"I'm not sure yet, but we're doing everything we can to find out," Peter reassured Mrs. Hastings. "I do want to let you know that I'm going to be contacting Naya's uncle. Did you get a chance to tell him I might be calling?"

"Yes," Mrs. Hastings said. "I talked with Mr. Iyengar last night to tell him about Naya. He's expecting your call."

"And how do you pronounce his first name?" Peter asked, wanting to be culturally sensitive and avoid making a fool of himself when talking to the man.

"His first name is Munish," Mrs. Hastings said, spelling it out.

"Munish Iyengar," Peter recited aloud to himself.

Naya overheard Peter say her uncle's name. "Are you going to talk to my Munish uncle?" she asked excitedly, approaching her mother.

"Yes, maybe a little later today," Peter said.

"Can I speak to him?"

"Sure you can," Peter said with a wink.

The clerk called Naya's name.

"It's time to go now," Peter said and walked with them to the MRI lab. Naya held her mother's hand firmly, her mouth a straight, tight line. She was obviously frightened. Peter was glad that her mother had come to be with her this morning. It was more the exception than the rule.

{CHAPTER TWENTY-SIX}

Friday

When Leia and José arrived at the precinct office the next morning, sipping coffee, Lieutenant Andrew was already there. Leia could tell he was determined to solve the case as swiftly as possible. He had probably even sworn to the Troys that he would find out who killed their daughter.

"Good morning, José. Morning, Agent Bines," the lieutenant welcomed them.

"Please, call me Leia," Leia said, greeting him with a handshake and following him into his office.

Lieutenant Andrew filled them in with what he had found so far in the national crime databases: a disappointing nothing. No crime with this kind of distinctive fingerprint had come up. But the records had only been digitized back to 1975. "There's one more place we can look," he said. "There are files in the basement of all the unsolved murders that occurred prior to 1975." He stood up behind his desk. "Are you game?"

"Lead the way," Leia said.

"Sure!" José said with vigor. "Let's not waste any time."

Lieutenant Andrew led them to the section of the basement reserved for record storage. They wove through the rows of tall shelves until the lieutenant stopped in front of a shelf labeled Unsolved Murder Cases in faded permanent marker.

The case folders were stored in large file boxes. Each box contained cases for approximately a ten-year period. Leia could tell by the layer of dust that this section had not been touched for a long time. The lieutenant dropped the boxes on the floor, kicking up clouds of dust.

José and Leia gathered a box each and lugged them to nearby desks. Each box had a label that recorded the time period. Lieutenant Andrew had 1950 to 1959, Leia 1940 to 1949, and José 1960 to 1974. Each of the boxes contained fifty to sixty folders that included all investigative reports and photographs of the case. The three of them began to go through the folders one by one.

"Did you find out anything of interest at the senator's house yesterday?" asked Lieutenant Andrew as he leafed through a folder.

"Not really," Leia said. "The one thing we know is that the killer knows the geographical area well," replied Leia. "That makes me think it might be someone who works at the ranch. By the way, José, what did you learn last night when you went back?"

"The regular staff looks clean, but I still have to get ahold of the contractors who work for the senator and have access to the ranch," José said with a brisk shrug. "Any one of them could be suspects."

It didn't take long to screen the folders and set a few aside. They selected files described homicide cases in which children were the victims. Most of the cases were gunshot murders that didn't have any relevance to the current case.

"You got to take a look at this," José called out, laying out a folder on the desk.

Lieutenant Andrew and Leia rushed to José's desk. He had found a newspaper clipping that read, "Body found at Elephant Rock" in big, bold letters.

"I don't believe this," huffed Lieutenant Andrew. "Are you telling me this isn't the first time?"

"I knew we'd find a similar case," Leia said confidently as she browsed through the rest of the folder, which included photographs of the crime scene and other well-documented details.

The case was about Debbie Sanders, a twelve-year-old girl reported missing about a week before she was found dead. Surprisingly, the body had been found in the same location as the current case and had been mutilated in the same manner. There had been no evidence of sexual molestation or rape. The case had never been solved, and no leads uncovered.

"How long ago did this happen?" asked Lieutenant Andrew.

"In 1967," José read out. "The time of death was estimated to be in the first two weeks of October."

"As you can see, the body was severed at every joint and spread out," commented Leia. "Too bad we don't have an aerial photograph."

"But look," José said, turning over some of the detective notes. On a single piece of paper was a sticklike figure of a person with a few lines scribbled under that looked like, *most probable pattern of display.*

The lieutenant held his head in his hands. "A serial killer on the loose. In Newbury. Unbelievable."

José concurred with the lieutenant. However, Leia had doubts that this was the work of a serial. She did believe that the two murders had been committed by the same individual. It appeared to be the work of an unusual killer. It was unlikely to be a copycat after so many years, especially as copycat killings were copies of publicly renowned cases. This case had long been forgotten.

Both José and Lieutenant Andrew were perplexed by Leia's observation. "Why don't you think the two killings were perpetuated by a serial killer?" José asked with curiosity.

Leia smiled and said, "You could be right, but given the time span and the way the body was laid out, I don't think it is. I believe we're most likely dealing with a ritual killer."

"What's the difference?" Lieutenant Andrew asked, obviously embarrassed.

Leia smiled. "A serial killer is someone who commits three or more murders over an extended period of time. Usually, the killer torments his victims and kills them slowly. He is a sadistic killer whose interest wanes after the kill. No self-respecting serial would have put forth the effort to display the body parts in such an artistic manner."

"Why, then, after so many years?" the lieutenant wondered aloud.

"Thirty-seven, to be exact!" exclaimed José.

The three of them intensified their search through the remaining boxes, looking for similar cases. After spending a good hour and a half on the endeavor, they were both disappointed and glad to turn up nothing else of interest.

"I'll continue to look around here," said Lieutenant Andrew.

Leia and José left the precinct. Leia decided that she needed some time alone to think about the case. It was almost time for lunch, and her hotel room seemed like a quiet place for her to put her mind to this challenge.

{CHAPTER TWENTY-SEVEN}

Friday

Naya walked out of the MRI lab with her mother on one side and Dr. Gram on the other. She was glad the test was over, although the technician had been friendly and the machine's humming and clicking had only frightened her a little bit. It was almost noon, and she was hungry. Her tummy rumbled.

Dr. Gram must have heard it. "You can have lunch soon," he said, looking at his watch. "The other kids will be eating soon too. And remember, after lunch, you'll be going for the other test we talked about."

"The EEG," Naya recounted. "Can my mom eat with me?" she asked.

"Not today, honey," Naya's mother said even before Dr. Gram could say a word. "I have to run to the bank from here, but I'll come by to see you during visiting hours."

"So my mother won't be with me for my next test?" Naya asked with some anxiety.

"I believe your father will be with you in the afternoon," Dr. Gram said quickly. Naya could tell he didn't want her to worry.

"That's right," Naya's mother confirmed. "Daddy will be here in the afternoon."

"And if you like, I'll sit with you while you eat your lunch," Dr. Gram told Naya.

As they walked down the hall, a tall, dark-skinned man approached, going the other way. He was wearing a baggy blue uniform. He looked at

Naya and smiled. His teeth were very white. But she was not feeling friendly just then, and she looked away, toward the wall.

"Dr. Gram," the man said.

"Dr. Hunter," Dr. Gram said in a voice that sounded as though he were laughing. Naya looked over in time to see them slap a high five as they passed each other.

They walked back through the hospital tunnel, but Naya didn't enjoy it this time. She turned her head away when her mother kissed her good-bye.

In the dining room, the other children were almost at the end of their meal and some were already lining up for their next class. Naya picked up the tray that the staff had set aside for her and sat down with Dr. Gram at one of the tables.

"How did you sleep last night?" Dr. Gram asked.

"Fine," Naya said as she munched away at her sandwich.

"Did you sleep well?"

"Yes, I think so—but I also had a dream," she said softly, shifting her gaze away from Dr. Gram's kind eyes to her plate.

"Sometimes dreams can be hard to talk about," Dr. Gram said.

"I can show you a picture about my dream."

"The one you were drawing in the morning before you left the room?" Naya nodded.

"We can take a look after you finish eating," Dr. Gram reassured her.

After lunch, Naya led Dr. Gram to her room.

"Can I sit here?" Dr. Gram asked before sitting on her bed.

"Uh-huh," Naya said. She sat in the chair at the desk that was located at the foot of her bed.

Dr. Gram leaned over to look at what Naya had drawn, but she covered the paper with her arm.

"I'm not done yet," she said, picking up a crayon to draw.

Dr. Gram waited patiently while she finished the picture.

"Here," Naya said, standing up from the chair and handing the sheet of paper to him.

She watched as he looked at the disjointed figure with yellow hair lying in the grass. Next to that was a second figure with black hair. In the background, she had drawn the elephant, Jerry.

"Can you tell me more about what you've drawn?" Dr. Gram asked Naya gently.

"This is the girl I spoke to, and this is her elephant," Naya said, pointing to them.

"And who is this?"

"That's me!" Naya replied with a smile.

"What happened to the girl?" Dr. Gram asked, noticing that Naya had drawn the girl a little differently than she had drawn herself.

"She wants to stitch her body back together—she asked me for some string."

"Is there something wrong with her body?" Dr. Gram asked.

"Her body is cut into pieces," Naya said, trying her best to explain what she was thinking.

"How did that happen?" Dr. Gram looked worried.

Naya shrugged.

"You said this is her elephant. Is it her pet?" Peter asked.

"Yes, Jerry is her pet. She said he would protect us."

"Protect you from what?" Now Dr. Gram was frowning heavily.

"From the big, bad man," Naya said softly.

"The big, bad man?" Dr. Gram repeated.

"Yes."

"Does this girl have a name?"

"She told me her name—but I forgot."

"You can always tell me when you remember," Dr. Gram said, staring at the picture. It seemed to have upset him. "Is she a happy or sad girl?"

"I don't know," Naya said. She pouted, noticing that she'd forgotten to draw the girl's mouth.

"What about you?"

"I'm a happy girl," Naya said, pointing to the big smile she had drawn on the face of the figure that represented her.

"Naya, you've done such a wonderful job today talking about your thoughts and feelings," Dr. Gram said, and his praise made Naya smile. "You can keep your pictures in your room, and even hang them up on the wall if you want."

"Okeydoke!" she said, taking the drawing out of his hand and placing it on the desk. Maybe she would put it on the wall next to her picture of the doves from her other dream.

"You can stay in your room for a few minutes now," Dr. Gram said. "Your next class will be starting in ten minutes. I'll ask one of the staff to take you there."

"Okay," Naya said, pulling out a few more blank sheets of paper from the desk drawer and settling in her chair.

{CHAPTER TWENTY-EIGHT}

Friday

Peter left Naya's room thinking about the drawing. It had almost made him sick to hear Naya talk about how a girl's body had been cut apart. How would Naya know about such things, especially with such protective parents? Something just wasn't adding up. He went to the nurses' station and sat down next to Matt, who was eating his lunch and reading a newspaper."

"You eat yet?" Matt asked Peter.

"No, I'll go get something pretty soon," he said distractedly.

"Did you hear about what happened?"

"What happened?"

"You know that little girl who disappeared? They found her body at Elephant Rock," Matt told Peter, handing him the front page.

Peter grabbed the paper and read the bold headline: "Murder at Elephant Rock," he read aloud.

His eyes widened with astonishment as he looked at the picture of the blond-haired, blue-eyed ten-year-old named Janet Troy. She looked just like the girl in Naya's drawing.

"Is this the first time you've heard this story?" he asked Matt nervously.

"Hot off the press," Matt replied. "What's wrong? Your face just turned all red."

"By any chance, could any of the kids have seen this?" Peter asked, handing the paper back to Matt.

"Are you kidding me? This stuff isn't appropriate for our unit."

"I know. I'll be back in a second." Peter dashed back to Naya's room. He wanted to catch her before she went to her next class. Naya was just walking out of her room with an MHA. She stopped when she saw Peter hurrying down the hall toward her.

"Naya," he said, "is it all right with you if I borrowed the picture you showed me just a few minutes ago?"

"Sure," Naya said, pointing to her room. "It's on the desk."

"Thank you, Naya," Peter said. "I'll see you later."

Peter rushed back to the nurses' station and held the picture out to Matt.

"And?" Matt said, looking first at the picture and then at Peter.

"This is a picture that Naya drew of the dream she had last night. As you can see, it's a picture of a girl who's been cut up, just like the one in the news."

"Okay?"

"The elephant, I think, represents Elephant Rock."

"Wow, Dr. Gram," he said, "you're reading way too much into the picture. Remember, the kids in here are all nuts." Matt turned back to his lunch.

"That's what you think," Peter said, deflated but still defiant. "I'm going to get some lunch."

"Maybe she does need some medication!" Matt called out as Peter walked away. "Or … maybe you do!"

Peter rolled up the picture as he headed off the unit. The one thing he had not told Matt was that Naya's picture looked a lot like Elephant Rock—something Matt wouldn't have known, because there was no picture of Elephant Rock in the newspaper. But Peter had been there many times before.

Peter found himself reminiscing about being ten years old and playing around Elephant Rock. Elephant Rock had been his favorite hideaway. Climbing to the top gave him immense pleasure and a sense of power. In his mind, from the top of Elephant Rock, he could see the whole world.

Back then, he spent a lot of time with his aunt Beth, who was his mother's sister and his godmother.

Peter remembered the difficult times when he took refuge at Elephant Rock. His parents had been struggling through their marriage, and his mother had sent him to live with Aunt Beth and Uncle Thomas on the ranch. He had explored every corner of the ranch, and over time, he came to know the area like the back of his hand.

"Hi, Peter." Peter heard his name as he stood motionless at the cafeteria salad bar. He surfaced from the depths of his thoughts and turned to see Sheetal Patel, his partnering psychiatric fellow, who had apparently come to the hospital cafeteria to grab some lunch too.

Peter slid his tray over on the salad counter, making some room for hers. Sheetal was a tall, wide-hipped South Indian woman with flowing, black hair. Her fair, wheatish complexion was complemented by the few brown freckles on her long, straight nose.

"I'll bet you're glad it's Friday," Sheetal said with a wide, shiny smile.

"I am," Peter said, helping himself to some salad.

"I saw your new admission playing on the unit. Did you tell me she was Indian?" Sheetal picked up a plate.

"I thought I mentioned it during rounds."

"Do you know where she's from?"

"I don't remember, but now that I think of it, she might be from Bangalore. That's where you're from, right?" Peter knew that Bangalore was one of the largest cities in India and that it was one of the leading cities these days for IT businesses and telemarketing outsourced from U.S. companies. Sheetal had given him the impression that Bangalore had been a hip place to grow up.

The two of them paid for their healthy lunch and sat chatting about their cases at a table outside. Sheetal talked about a little Russian boy who, like Timothy, had been exposed to cocaine in utero and placed into the foster-care system at birth. At the age of three, an older boy at one of the foster homes had sexually abused him so severely that the hospital had to perform reconstructive surgery to repair his rectum. Now he understandably struggled with issues of control—especially concerning withholding his feces. At times, he used his feces as a weapon to fend of anybody who angered him.

"I guess I'll stay out of his way," laughed Peter. He told Sheetal about the strange coincidence he had run into concerning Naya's case.

"Do you know anything about her biological family?" asked Sheetal.

"No, but I have a number for her maternal uncle. I was planning on calling him this afternoon."

"Maybe one of her parents was schizophrenic," Sheetal commented.

"Do you think it could be some form of psychosis?"

Sheetal paused for a moment, her fork hovering in the air. "Only at night? I doubt it."

They both knew that psychosis was a symptom represented by out-of-reality experiences, such as auditory or visual hallucinations; delusions that were fixed; false beliefs; or disorganization of thought. Naya didn't have any of those symptoms while she was awake.

Back on the unit, Peter dialed the number Jane Hastings had given him for Mr. Iyengar. After the fourth ring, a woman with an Indian accent answered.

"Can I speak to Mr. Iyengar, please?" Peter asked the woman.

"May I know who is calling?" the voice on the other end asked somewhat suspiciously.

Peter introduced himself and stated that he was calling about Naya. He didn't want to give too many details, as he wasn't sure who he was talking to.

"May I know who I'm speaking to?" Peter queried.

"This is Naya's aunt, Mrs. Iyengar. Jane called to tell us of her hospitalization. We were sad to hear."

Peter had gotten written consent for exchange of information from Mrs. Hastings beforehand, so he spoke briefly with Mrs. Iyengar about the events that had led to Naya's hospitalization.

"Do you know much about Naya's biological parents?" he asked.

"I'm afraid I don't," Mrs. Iyengar said. "It really would be better if you talked to my husband. Unfortunately, he isn't at home today. He'll be arriving home from a business trip later tonight."

Damn, Peter thought. He felt it was extremely important to get this information as soon as possible. Naya's background had implications for her course of treatment, especially given the present pressure from the insurance company to get her out of the hospital.

"Would it be all right if I came to see Mr. Iyengar at home tomorrow?" he asked hesitantly. "I'm coming into the city for other reasons, and it won't be out of my way."

Peter looked over at Sheetal, who was sitting next to him at the nurses' station. She was shaking her head at his unusual request.

"I don't think that should be a problem," Mrs. Iyengar said, although Peter didn't think she sounded too happy about his request. "What time would you like to come?"

Peter calculated how much time he'd need to still make the matinee. "How about ten thirty in the morning?" he said.

"Okay … he'll be expecting you," Mrs. Iyengar said.

Peter verified their address, then tapped it and their telephone number into his PDA. He hung up the phone and looked at Sheetal, who was still shaking her head.

"That's desperation," she said with a smile. But she was only teasing him. Peter knew that, like him, she would go out of her way to help a child, even if it meant making a home visit during her free time.

"Anyway, I'll be in the neighborhood," Peter said trying to account for his actions.

"You don't need to rationalize," Sheetal said, grinning.

At that moment, the phone rang. Peter picked it up to find that it was Penelope Rolling, the insurance agent, calling for a clinical update on Naya.

"This is Dr. Gram speaking," Peter said, disgruntled. He had already had a doc-to-doc. Why was she bothering him again?

Dutifully, he recited the events of the previous night. He told Penelope Rolling that the MRI had been done this morning, and that he was expecting the results by the end of the day—or even the following week, given that the weekend was coming. "She's also scheduled for an EEG this afternoon," he added.

"Is she suicidal or homicidal?" Penelope Rolling asked him flatly.

Peter felt his temper rising again. "We think she might have some psychotic symptoms, but we're not sure as of yet," he snapped. He repressed what little guilt he felt for playing up Naya's symptoms.

"We can authorize Naya's stay over the weekend, but we will need an update on Monday in order for us to authorize more time than that."

"Thank you," Peter said and hung up the phone. He rubbed his forehead, which ached dully from tension and his cold. He still had to call Timothy and Sasha's insurance companies as well.

"I'll see you later," Sheetal said.

Peter swiveled toward her in his chair. "Say, would you be able to cover for me if I left a little early today? Around three?"

"Sure," Sheetal said. Peter knew she understood that he would do the same for her. "Oh, and if I don't see you before you leave, enjoy the play."

Peter updated Timothy and Sasha's insurance authorization, which meant another forty-five minutes on the phone. Then he headed back to the children's living quarters. He wanted to ask Naya for something.

He spotted Naya and Sasha playing together in a corner with some dolls and plastic cutlery. When he approached them, interrupting their play, Sasha ran toward him with her arms open wide, shouting, "You're the best doctor!"

Peter stretched out his hand, stopping her from getting too close to him.

"You need to remember your boundaries," Peter reminded her. "First of all, if you want a hug, you need to ask for one."

"Can I have a hug?" Sasha squealed with excitement.

"Sure," Peter said, and complied. A number of the children on the unit lacked appropriate boundaries and needed to be reminded of them during almost every interaction.

Naya watched Sasha as she came back to the corner. "Dr. Gram is my doctor too," she told Sasha, as though pleased that they had Peter in common.

"No, he's not yours! You're lying!" Sasha yelled angrily.

Peter watched Naya recoil in fear. She looked at Peter for help.

"I'm the doctor for both of you," Peter said, "and for Timothy as well." This kind of rivalry was common among the children on the unit.

"Will you see me first today?" Sasha implored.

"No," Peter said. "I'll be seeing neither of you today. I'm leaving a little early, so I'll see the two of you on Monday." Peter watched Sasha, hoping she wouldn't have another fit.

To his surprise, she accepted the decision without a fuss. "Okay. Bye-bye," she told Peter, shutting him out.

"Naya," Peter said. "Could I talk with you for a minute before I leave?"

Peter took Naya a few feet away from Sasha and told her that he had spoken to her aunt, and that her uncle wasn't at home. He would let her speak to them on Monday after her uncle returned home. He didn't tell her that he was planning to visit them over the weekend.

"Can I keep the picture you gave me earlier?" he asked. "I'll bring it back to you on Monday." Peter knew that Naya would agree, but he still felt he needed her permission.

Naya consented, then bade Peter good-bye and returned to playing with Sasha.

Peter fetched the picture from Naya's desk. He looked at his watch. It was almost two thirty. He went to the nurses' station and informed Matt that he was leaving early, and that Dr. Patel was covering for him. On his way out, he stopped by the MRI lab to check the results of Naya's test. The good news was that there were no abnormal findings—no white-matter lesion or brain tumor. The bad news was that Peter still didn't have an explanation for Naya's symptoms. He predicted that the EEG she was scheduled to have that afternoon wouldn't show any abnormalities in electrical brain activity either. He stared at the picture as he walked to his car. Was Naya psychotic, or was there something else going on that Peter couldn't understand?

{CHAPTER TWENTY-NINE}

Friday Afternoon

Leia sat on the floor in her motel room with the contents of the 1967 case folder scattered in front of her. She had scrutinized every aspect of the case to the last detail and only came up with more questions. What message did the killer intend to deliver by displaying the bodies in such a way, and for whom was it intended?

One other oddity about the 1967 case was the presence of animal bones buried in various locations at the site in specific patterns. There was a possibility of finding something similar now that could lead to desperately needed clues.

Leia felt she might have missed something important that could answer these questions. She decided to venture out to Elephant Rock right away. She called Detective Rodriguez but got his voice mail, so she left a message for him to meet her there. She gathered the strewn documents together neatly and put them back into the folder. She strapped on her firearm, a Sig Sauer P230 SL and threw on her leather jacket.

Leia found the unmarked squad car José had left parked for her and programmed the GPS system. It wasn't long before she was cruising out of town, toward Elephant Rock.

＊   ＊   ＊   ＊

Peter took the shortest route to Elephant Rock, navigating the familiar unpaved back roads he had discovered while driving around the ranch many years before. He wanted to avoid any police traffic that might still be patrolling the area. If the police were still at the scene, he would just come back another time.

At the dead end, he came to a grinding halt. He waited for the plume of dust to settle, then got out of the car and trekked into the woods, walking north. He went as quietly as he could, listening for the sounds of police officers patrolling the woods. After a few minutes, Peter noticed that no birds were singing … and got the distinct feeling that someone was watching him. He shook off the feeling as paranoia and continued on.

It took about fifteen minutes to reach the south side of Elephant Rock. As he walked toward it, Peter couldn't help but smile. He reached out and laid his hand against the freckled granite, warm from the sun. He had always thought of the landmark as a big, benevolent beast. He patted its haunch and began to climb, careful not to slip on the leaves that covered every horizontal surface this time of the year. Once he reached the flat top of the giant rock, he walked a few feet forward until he was looking out over the entire northern landscape.

When he was young, Peter had stood in this very spot and imagined he could see the whole world. It had made him feel powerful and safe. He had come to Elephant Rock filled with sorrow, confusion, and anger; here, the birdsong, the wind in the leaves, and the feel of the sun had cleansed his being. He realized that it had been years since he had stood in this spot.

Now, looking out on the woods, he saw streams of yellow police tape woven through the trees like a spider's web, along with large red fluorescent flags placed at various points on the ground. He began to climb down the north side of the rock, jumping down the last few feet and landing with a thud. He ducked under the yellow police tape and walked across the clearing, passing a matted-down place in the grass. Peter shuddered, thinking of poor Janet Troy.

At the edge of the clearing, Peter turned around. He pulled Naya's picture out of his pocket. The elephant in the picture obviously represented Elephant Rock. The clearing in the picture, like the clearing where Peter now stood, was ringed with trees clothed in bright leaves. The head of the blonde girl in the picture was located, relatively speaking, just where Peter had noticed the matted section of grass. Peter's head reeled. A seven-year-old girl like Naya would never have ventured down this way, and Peter didn't imagine her parents were too keen on hiking or walking in the woods. The eerie silence of the woods seemed to ring in his ears, and a chill ran down his spine. The feeling of being watched intensified.

"Don't move," a stern female voice said from behind him.

Peter froze, his heart racing with fear. He realized then how foolish it had been to come to a crime scene that had just been cleared.

"I have a gun," the woman said, "and it's pointed at your head. I want you to put your hands on your head and turn around slowly."

"Okay, okay," Peter blurted. "Just don't shoot."

Still holding Naya's picture, he put both hands on his head, turned slowly around, and came face-to-face with a woman in a brown suede jacket and khaki pants. She was standing less than five feet away from him, pointing a gun at his chest. *How did she get that close to me without my hearing her?* Peter wondered. Even as he stared down the barrel of her gun, he found himself focusing on how beautiful she was, with lovely, full lips and a shimmer of reddish hair.

"Who are you, and what are you doing here?" the woman asked Peter.

"My name is Peter Gram—Dr. Peter Gram," Peter said nervously.

"What are you doing here?" the woman repeated.

"I read about the murder in the paper, and I needed to investigate something for myself."

"Investigate what?" the woman asked him.

Peter sputtered, "I don't know how to explain it … I mean, it's going to sound crazy."

"Try me," the woman said.

"Who are you? Are you going to kill me?" He heard the hysterical edge to his own voice and thought he saw the ghost of a smile flit across the woman's face. She lowered the gun a bit, but he still didn't like where it was pointing—in fact, getting shot in the chest might be preferable.

"I'm an FBI agent," she said.

"You are?"

She nodded once, emphatically. "Janet Troy is my case."

"Okay, well." Peter licked his dry lips. "Do you see the picture I'm holding?" he asked.

"What about it?"

"A seven-year-old patient of mine drew it from a dream she had last night. It looks just like this crime scene."

"Okay, enough," the woman said. "I want you to lie on the ground with your face down and your hands behind your back,"

"As long as you promise to put that gun away," Peter said, lowering himself to the ground with his nose in the dirt and his hands behind his back. He felt the agent grab Naya's picture from his hands. Then he felt the cold contact of metal snapping around his right wrist, and then his left.

"Hey, that's not necessary. I'm no threat to you!" Peter said angrily. He sniffled hard. Not only was he facedown in the dirt, but his nose was beginning to run.

"That's the only way I could put my gun down," the woman answered harshly. "You can turn around now and sit up if you like."

Peter rolled over in the leaves awkwardly, finally propping himself in a sitting position. The FBI agent was looking at Naya's drawing.

"Is this some kind of a joke?" she demanded, waving the picture at Peter.

"No, it isn't," Peter snapped back.

"You said you were a doctor—a surgeon, I suppose."

"What are you talking about? Why would I be a surgeon? And I'm not, anyway. I'm a child psychiatrist. The child who drew that picture is currently hospitalized on our inpatient unit. The elephant represents Elephant Rock, and I think the disjointed figure is the victim."

"And who is the other figure?" the agent asked, looking at the picture.

"The patient," Peter said.

"And how did you know to connect the elephant in this picture with Elephant Rock?"

"I read about the murder in the newspaper this morning, after my patient had told me about her dream. I couldn't help but see the connection between the two. I realized she had drawn a picture of this place—without ever having been here."

"Couldn't she have seen it in the newspaper?"

"There was no picture in the paper," Peter recalled.

"So how did you know her drawing looked like Elephant Rock?"

"I'm very familiar with this area," Peter said, instantly realizing that it was probably not the best thing to say.

"I think the killer knows this area very well too," the agent observed dryly.

"I think I'm not going to say much more right now," he said and sat silently looking at the agent. He wished he didn't find her so damned attractive.

"I'm going to call for backup," the agent said, taking a few steps away from him.

Peter watched her make a call on her cell phone.

"Another officer is almost here," the agent remarked.

Suddenly, to the east, they heard the sound of feet sliding on gravel.

"You stay here," the agent instructed Peter—as if he had a choice.

Peter watched her pull out her gun and run into the woods. He hoped whoever it was didn't find him sitting there all by himself with handcuffs on. "Damn," he muttered, "I should have stayed in the hospital."

Five minutes later, the agent had not returned. In the distance, toward the main road, Peter heard a car approaching. A few minutes later, someone ran toward him through the trees. It was José Rodriguez. Peter had never been happier to see a familiar face.

"Detective Rodriguez," he sighed. "Thank goodness."

"Dr. Gram!" José said with surprise. "What the hell is going on? Agent Bines said she'd apprehended someone poking around in the woods."

"It's a long story," Peter mumbled.

"Where's Agent Bines?" asked José. Just then, Agent Bines emerged from the trees to the east, pulling twigs from her hair.

"This is Agent Leia Bines," Detective Rodriguez said. "I'd like to introduce you to Dr. Peter Gram, whom I've worked with many times through the community-policing project."

"Oh, we've met," Agent Bines said gruffly.

"Can you please tell her to take these cuffs off?" Peter asked José.

Agent Bines turned her back on Peter. "Give me one reason to believe I haven't caught our killer," she said to José.

"You mean Peter?" José asked incredulously. "Respectfully, Agent Bines—Leia—Dr. Gram is the farthest thing from a murder suspect I can think of."

"You're sure you can trust him?" Agent Bines said.

"Yes, I'll vouch for him," Detective Rodriguez said. "Besides, if he's the murder suspect, who were you just chasing through the woods?"

Agent Bines removed Peter's handcuffs, and Peter stood, rubbing his wrists.

"Leia Bines," the agent said and held out her hand to Peter. She was smiling slightly. "I apologize for cuffing you, Dr. Gram. But this is a murder investigation, after all."

Peter shook her hand, trying not to notice how smooth her long fingers felt in his grip. He knew he still had a lot of explaining to do.

"You see, I grew up around here," Peter said, pointing toward the ranch.

"You mean on Senator Bailey's ranch?" Leia clarified.

"Yes, he's my uncle—his wife is my mother's sister," Peter told them. "I used to play around here when I was a kid. I know all the ins and outs of this place."

Agent Bines handed Naya's picture back to him.

"So, your patient's name is Naya," she commented.

"Yes," Peter said, looking at the girlish script in which Naya had signed her name. "Naya has been having strange experiences at night, and we're unable to say exactly what they are. I was trying to determine if there was any connection between her dream and this incident."

"You mean something paranormal?" Agent Bines asked. The corners of her mouth tightened a little. Was she laughing at him?

"That's one way to look at it," Peter said.

"How did you get here?" Detective Rodriguez asked. "I didn't see your car up on the road."

"I'm parked on the other side of Elephant Rock. I climbed over it. There are many ways to get in and out of here. I can draw you a map if you'd like."

"That would be helpful," Agent Bines said, looking in the direction from where she had heard another visitor.

"Did you find anything out there?" Peter inquired.

"No, but I think there was somebody else watching us," Leia told José.

"I'm going to look around some more," José said, walking away from Peter and Leia.

"You're free to go, Dr. Gram. Here's my number—just in case you need to reach me." Leia scribbled her cell number on a piece of paper and handed it to Peter. "I'd like you to come down to the precinct office and look at a map of the area with me. I could use someone who knows this area well."

Peter stuffed the piece of paper into his pocket. "Okay," he said. "I'll, um, give you a call to set something up. I'll be in the city tomorrow, but I'll contact you when I get back."

"I appreciate it," Agent Bines said, holding his gaze.

Finally, Peter looked away. "I'll have to climb back over the rock to get back to my car," he said.

"I'll come with you," Agent Bines said, indicating that he should take the lead.

They trekked back across the clearing toward Elephant Rock.

"What are these markers?" Peter asked the agent as they passed a few of them.

"I'll tell you this, but you have to promise to keep the information confidential. Janet Troy's body was dismembered. Those are points where the body parts were found. If you draw a line through each of those points, you get a stick figure—just like the one your patient has drawn."

"You must be kidding," Peter said in disbelief.

Just as they reached the top of the rock, Peter looked down once more, trying to connect the flags as Agent Bines had suggested.

"You need to be much higher to see all of it," Leia told Peter with her hand toward the sky. "I have an aerial photo if you want to take a look."

"There's my car," Peter said. He looked back over his shoulder at Agent Bines and caught that slight smile on her face once more. She waved, and Peter climbed down to his car.

{CHAPTER THIRTY}

Friday

The slaaf stopped and bent over, panting. What a close call—he should have been more careful. Luckily, the young, female agent had not seen him. He sat under a tree, regaining his energy. His plans had not panned out exactly as intended. He wasn't sure whether his task had been completed, as there were so many interruptions by these people. It was no longer safe to finish burying the body parts.

Around noon, the slaaf had felt compelled to return to Elephant Rock and finish his duty. He needed to make sure that Anansi was no longer targeting him. He had left his job a little earlier than usual. He didn't drive, but rather took the bus to the far end of town and then spent the next few hours walking to Elephant Rock.

When the slaaf had neared the woods, he had cautiously passed the police ribbons to the point where he had rested the girl's head. He was disappointed that his decoy to Anansi was no longer there. He wasn't sure if Anansi had seen it. He didn't know what to do next.

The slaaf had stood pondering the consequences of his failure when he heard footsteps coming toward him in the woods. He hurried to hide behind a large tree a few feet from Elephant Rock and watched with fear. He wasn't sure if it was Anansi, come to express anger and disappointment. To his surprise, he saw a tall, familiar white man standing at the top of the rock. The slaaf almost laughed aloud. He was absolutely sure that wasn't Anansi. But what was Peter doing here?

He watched in disbelief as Peter descended from the top of the rock. He followed a few yards back, along the treeline, hidden by the cover of brush and trees, as Peter crossed the clearing. Peter held up a piece of paper and stared at Elephant Rock. Suddenly, the slaaf saw a woman holding a gun approach Peter from behind. He crouched down immediately and watched them talk, but was unable to hear what they said from so far away.

He moved silently toward them and stood behind a tree only a few yards away. Why was the paper Peter holding so important? He wished he could get a look at it. He didn't want anything around that might lead the cops to him.

Peter and the woman were talking about a little girl's drawing. The woman with the gun seemed to think Peter had killed the girl the cops had found at Elephant Rock. The slaaf couldn't hear their conversation clearly. He strained his ears and extended his torso as far as he could. Unfortunately, his foot slipped on the gravel incline, causing him to slide backward. He knew he had blown his cover and had to move fast. He whirled when the woman moved swiftly in his direction. He ran as fast as he could through the woods, not even turning back to see if the woman was following him.

Now the slaaf was exhausted and out of breath. But he knew the woods better than this woman—probably better than anyone. After spending two minutes mustering some strength, he jogged farther into the woods. He knew a place to hide until dark. He found the low outcropping of rock and lay down beneath it, then pulled loose leaves in around him.

The slaaf stared at the backs of his hands. His skin appeared intact except for slight aberrations on both hands. He was not yet coming apart. Perhaps Anansi had been appeased at last. *Thank you, Anansi—thank you for hearing my prayers.* The slaaf lay on the ground, staring at the darkening sky with relief. He listened but heard no signs that anyone had followed him there. He was relieved to have escaped; getting caught could have been a real disaster. He closed his eyes and let his head rest on the ground, but his mind was still racing. Even though he had thanked Anansi, the god had tricked him before. As soon as the slaaf let his guard down, Anansi would appear again, as demanding as ever.

Anansi, Anansi, Anansi ... the name ran endlessly in his head like a drumbeat, underlying everything he did. He wished he had never heard of Anansi, and then it would be as if Anansi never existed. But Anansi did exist, and he was very powerful. The slaaf had devoted his life to Anansi, offered himself as Anansi's servant for all eternity.

He thought of his life before Anansi. Before Anansi, he had been a boy instead of a slaaf. How simple it had seemed, growing up in his parents' home in the small, coastal town. His father had worked in the local restaurant as a cook, and his mother sold vegetables at the local market. His father worked mostly in the evenings and his mother during the day. They were a happy family, and he enjoyed being their only child. His father had often spoken of Anansi and liked to scare his son with embellished stories.

But the boy always felt closer to his mother than his father, who at times had too much to drink and yelled at him and his mother. The boy went to the local school, which wasn't too far from his home. Every day, his mother would drop him off on her way to the vegetable market, and during their short walk, she would encourage him to study hard at school. She made him believe that getting good grades would lead to a better life.

After school was over at three o'clock, the boy would come back home by himself. He would call out to his father, who was often just getting ready for the evening shift at work, and fix himself a snack. Once he had done his homework, he would go out to play with his friends.

One hot summer afternoon when the boy was five years old, he returned home after playing with his friends, wanting to quench his thirst. He went to the kitchen and poured himself a cold cup of water from the clay pot. He drank it quickly, put the cup down on the table, and turned to run outside again and rejoin the game ... but as he did so, he saw his father pacing restlessly around the bedroom. He appeared to be searching for something.

The boy stood in the bedroom doorway, hoping to help his father find whatever he was looking for. Suddenly, his father rushed toward him, screaming, "Where is it? What did you do with the small bag of white powder that was beside the bed?"

"I don't know what you're talking about," the boy answered with terror in his voice.

"You had better not lie to me!" the boy's father bellowed. He grabbed the boy by his shirt and pulled him in close. His eyes were mad, like those of an animal in a trap. His breath was hot and smelled of coffee. "If you lie to me, Anansi will eat you alive. He will come at night while you're sleeping and rip you limb from limb."

The boy's mother arrived home just then. She pulled his father away and screamed in his face, "I took it! I took the powder! I won't have it in my house anymore."

At that, the boy's father stormed out of the house. The boy clutched his mother's arm and sobbed. He had never seen either of his parents that way before. His mother comforted him by stroking his hair and wiping his tears.

"Why was he so angry with me?" the boy asked.

"He wasn't angry with you, son," his mother said. "Your father can be moody and silly sometimes." She took him in her arms and began to hum a song, as though he were small again. "He can be a good man too. You have to be patient with him."

The next morning, he found his father sleeping next to his mother in their bed, and things over the next few days returned to normal. Over the next year, the boy forgot about the episode. Then, one day, when he was six years old, he came home at noon from school. There was a political rally planned, and the principal had let out all the classes early.

The boy walked home, carrying the one book that he had taken to school with him. He smelled the fresh ocean breeze blowing across his face. It took him no more than fifteen minutes to reach the gate of his family's two-room shack. He opened the gate and walked across a small garden of tomatoes that his mother had planted. He called out to his father, but there was no answer. He walked to the back of the shack to see if his father was working in the yard, but he wasn't, so the boy went inside.

He could smell the rich aroma of curry that his mother had made for lunch before she left to work that morning. His father wasn't in the larger room that served as their living area and kitchen. The boy put his book down on the floor and walked toward the bedroom. The door was closed. Just as he was about to push it open, he heard some strange sounds coming from the other side. He pushed the door open gently, only a small bit, so he could look inside the room.

On his parents' bed, he saw his father gyrating and writhing over another person—a woman who was lighter skinned than his mother. The boy stood watching in shock as they rocked rhythmically together. All of a sudden, the woman began to scream and struggle, pushing at the boy's father with her hands. His father grunted, grasped the woman's throat, and squeezed it as he continued to pound himself on top of her. Within moments, the woman lying under him was still and silent. The boy's father then yelled out in a triumphant scream and turned toward the boy, looking him right in the eye. His father's eyes were bloodshot, and sweat dripped from his face.

Terrified, the boy ran out of the house all the way to the beach, where he collapsed on the warm sand.

The boy didn't know how long he lay there. The next thing he knew, the sun had set, and it was getting dark. The tide was almost touching him. He pulled himself to his feet and slowly walked back home. His mother was standing outside in the yard, waiting for him. She was worried, but relieved to see him back. "Where were you?" she asked him.

"I went for a walk because school finished early."

The boy was quiet for the rest of the evening. He looked around the house and saw no evidence of any other woman having ever been there. After supper, his mother tucked him into his bed in the living area. She commented that he didn't look very good and that he needed to get some rest, after which she turned off the light and went to the other room to sleep.

The boy lay in bed, thinking about what he had seen. It was as if a savage beast had taken over his father. Would the beast still be there when his father returned home that night? Would his father kill the boy's mother next? Time passed slowly as he waited for the sound of his father's footsteps.

It was close to midnight and the boy was half-asleep when he awoke to the sensation of warm air blowing on his face. He opened his eyes to find his father peering down at him. His father's breath reeked of local rum. "You awake?" his father asked, slurring as he spoke.

The boy was silent. He felt himself tremble with fear. He watched his father stand there mumbling to himself. Then the man bent forward and whispered in his ear, "You blood clot, if you ever tell your mother about today, Anansi will cut you up into little pieces and have you for dinner. You hear me, you little bastard? You hear me? Believe me, Anansi will kill you … and if he doesn't, I will."

The boy nodded and watched his father retreat into the room where his mother slept. His whole body was trembling. He waited for the bedroom door to shut and the light go out. He pulled the light covers over his head and began to cry. He cried himself to sleep that night.

The next day, everyone but the boy acted the same as they always had. His father acted as if the events from the previous day had never occurred, and his mother, unaware of those events, carried on as usual. But the boy could think of nothing else for many months.

Days passed, and then months passed, and the boy thought about the incident less and less. But he didn't forget about Anansi. The boy needed to keep a lookout for him. The trickster was unpredictable: he could be kind, or he could be cruel. He lived in the sky and looked down at everyone from his home there. He saw everything. In the boy's mind, Anansi had bloodshot eyes and a small mouth filled with sharp teeth. He was most definitely someone you didn't want to mess with.

{CHAPTER THIRTY-ONE}

Friday Evening

Leia and José decided to scout around Elephant Rock with the hope of finding whoever had been sneaking around. Leia located the place where the person had probably been standing when he'd slipped on the gravel. They might even be able to get a partial footprint from the site. José called the night-shift officer at the precinct and had him round up a team to see if they could get a print. Then he got some tape from his car and began roping off the area.

In the meantime, Leia wandered into the woods in the direction the person had probably run.

"Hey," José said, "if you'll wait a minute, I'll go with you."

But Leia became absorbed in her hunt for broken branches and bent grass that marked the person's trail, and she followed these signs deeper and deeper into the woods. He was most likely far gone by now, but she didn't want to leave any loose ends only to discover that she could have apprehended the killer.

Thirty minutes later, it was getting dark, and it occurred to Leia that she probably shouldn't have wandered off alone; the time change had left her expecting sunset a few hours later. José was probably looking for her. She called his name loudly, and the sound echoed through the trees. She heard his faint reply.

"This way!" she shouted. "Southeast!" She would wait for him here, so that they didn't miss each other in the woods. Then they would have to call it a day, since trying to find anything was a waste of time in the dark.

She surveyed the trail again and followed it down a section of sloping ground and over a jutting section of rock. She continued walking a few yards, carried by the momentum of the hill, but the trail seemed to end in midair. She turned, thinking the runner must have doubled back, and just as she did, she saw something swing toward her out of the corner of her eye. She barely had time to lift her hands to protect her face before the club hit her on the side of the head. The trees spun around her, and a splitting pain spread through her head and neck. Although she could still hear, her vision went black, and her legs would no longer support her. She collapsed heavily to the ground.

Leia felt herself drift through time. She was ten years old again and fishing in the mountains with her favorite uncle. A black bear appeared suddenly and swatted her away from the pile of fish and through the air as though she were no more substantial than a fly. When she opened her eyes, she half-expected to hear the rush of the mountain stream from the bush where she'd landed. But instead, there was only darkness and the smell of wet leaves in her face, and she remembered that she was at Elephant Rock.

Somebody took hold of her hands and bound them together behind her back as she struggled in what seemed like slow motion. How could she have been so stupid?

The assailant finished with her hands and stepped away. What was he going to do? Leia waited, breathing deeply, preparing for her own offense. But his steps receded farther and farther. He was leaving! She gave herself a few moments to recover. Her head pounded as though Elephant Rock were sitting on it.

"Leia?" she heard José's voice—closer, clearer.

"José! Over here!" She tried pulling her hands apart. She wriggled them with the hope of getting loose, but had no success. She rolled onto her back and looked up at the canopy of leaves over her head, through which she could see the dark sky and a few bright stars.

"Leia?" José called, very close now.

"I'm here!" she shouted at the top of her lungs.

José shone his flashlight in her face, forcing her to shut her eyes.

"What are you doing down there?" he sputtered. "Did you fall? Are you all right?"

Leia almost laughed at the confusion and concern in his voice.

"I think I'm okay," she said as José helped her sit up. "Someone came at me and knocked me down. I think he was hiding under that ledge of rock right there. Can you untie my hands, please?"

"My God," José said, "you're bleeding. You're hurt. We have to get you to the hospital."

"I'm okay, really. My head just hurts a little bit," she said, downplaying the pain that was trying to split her head apart.

"He tied your hands with a bandanna," José pointed out as he tried to untie the knot. "Hold on … I need something to help loosen this knot." Leia heard the jingle of keys behind her. "Did you get a look at him?"

"No," she said. "He blindsided me."

Then Leia was free. She rubbed her wrists first and then gingerly touched the left side of her head. A small amount of blood coated her fingertips.

Leia thought of her gun in its holster. "He didn't take my gun," she said, patting it.

"I'm glad," José said, and she could see that he was badly shaken. "Do you have a plastic bag handy?" he asked, holding up the bandanna by a corner. Leia found a bag in her jacket pocket and sealed the bandanna inside.

"So it was most likely the killer, then," José said.

"Most likely. I think he came back to finish something, and we just got in the way."

Leia and José returned to their cars as a team was arriving to cast the footprint Leia had found. They watched the technicians' flashlights bob through the dark woods. Leia leaned heavily on the hood of her car.

"You need medical care," José said. "Please, let me take you to the hospital."

"What about the car?"

"I'll have someone bring it back to the motel."

Leia hesitated, although she knew she shouldn't drive.

"I insist," José said firmly.

He helped Leia into his car, and off they went to the emergency room. Leia did her best to mask her humiliation. Never had she been caught so off guard. She was lucky to be alive.

{CHAPTER THIRTY-TWO}

Friday, Before Midnight

"Look at all these apples!" Naya said euphorically as she twirled among the apple trees. She had never seen so many apple trees and was thrilled to be able to pick some of the fruit that hung low.

Next to Naya stood Janet. She looked different from the last time Naya had seen her. Her body parts were reconnected, and she had string wound up over each joint. Naya thought the bindings would feel uncomfortable; however, Janet appeared to move freely and without much difficulty.

Naya held an apple in her outstretched hand. "You want one?" she asked.

"I don't like apples anymore," Janet said. "They make me sad, because I can't eat my mother's apple pie anymore."

"Oh!" said Naya not sure what to make of this information. She paused, then inquired, "Where's your elephant?"

"He's over there, eating apples." Janet pointed.

Naya could see far away in the distance something that looked like an elephant walking among the apple trees. "Do you have any more string?" she asked Janet, wondering if she could try what Janet had done to herself to see how it felt.

"No, I don't." Janet looked at her hand. "I used it all up. Come on, Naya, let me show you something." Janet took hold of Naya's hand.

Janet's hand was strangely cool, but Naya didn't pull away. She walked along with Janet through the apple trees, feeling the tall blades of grass stroke her knees. They left the orchard and soon were standing in front of a large, red house. It had only one enormous door and no windows. Within the large door was a second door, just big enough for someone Janet's size to go through.

"This is my house," Janet said proudly.

"Can we go in?" Naya asked, excited.

Janet gently tugged the doorknob on the smaller door, and it sprung open. Janet stepped through the door, and Naya followed. To Naya's surprise, inside the red house was a broad field of sunflowers. She couldn't see a roof or any walls. The sun shone brightly there, just as it had outside, and the breeze continued to blow.

"Wow," Naya said, "look at all these flowers! Why are they all facing in that direction?"

"That's because they turn with the sun," Janet explained. "That's why they're sunflowers. Look, here's my bed." She pulled Naya through the flowers.

Naya saw a tall bed on a raised platform in the middle of the field.

"Where are the rooms?" Naya asked curiously.

"I don't know." Janet shrugged. "But we can play here." She climbed up onto the bed and pulled Naya up behind her.

"Why do you live here?" asked Naya.

"Because the big, bad man left me here," Janet said sadly.

"Is the big, bad man here now?" Naya asked, feeling a little scared to be there with Janet by herself.

"No, you don't have to be scared. Jerry is outside, and he is protecting us," Janet said, and Naya felt a little better.

Janet's tone changed. "Did you ask the doctor yet?"

"I think I did," Naya replied evasively. She had showed Dr. Gram the picture, but she hadn't told him what Janet had said.

"And what did he say?"

"I can't remember," Naya said, very uneasy now. She hadn't been sure if Dr. Gram would believe her story about Janet, so she hadn't told him.

"You can't remember, or you're just not telling me?" Janet had a hard grip on Naya's wrist now.

"He won't believe me, Janet—nobody will!" Naya whined.

Janet let go of Naya's wrist. "Ask him a question, and he will believe," Janet said, waving her hand like a magician.

"What question?"

"Come here, let me tell you." Janet pulled Naya closer. "Say this: 'Knock, knock.' And when he says, 'Who's there?' you say …" She whispered a name in Naya's ear.

"Who's that?" Naya asked.

"I don't know," Janet said. "That's for you to figure out." Janet began to cackle uncontrollably.

Naya's fear bloomed under the warm sun. "That isn't funny, Janet."

"Yes, it is," Janet said, continuing to laugh. She fell back on the bed and shrieked toward the sky.

"I want to go home," Naya said, looking around for the door.

"No," Janet said, still laughing. "I won't let you."

Naya jumped off the bed and ran toward the door. When she gripped the doorknob, she found it wouldn't turn. She tugged on the door, but it was tightly closed.

"Let me out! Let me out, please! I don't want to stay here!" Naya screamed.

Janet continued to sit on the bed in the middle of the field of sunflowers and laugh hysterically. Naya pounded on the door relentlessly, screaming and trembling in fear. There was no escape from this strange place of blue skies and sunflowers.

"Mommy," Naya sobbed, and slid down against the door, still clutching the doorknob. Her heart throbbed loudly in her ears. She began to feel light-headed, and finally she lost consciousness.

*   *   *   *

Sheetal Patel and the rest of the night staff stood around the big blue doors of Strauss I, watching Naya Hastings. They had never seen anybody act out so dramatically while asleep. They watched Naya clutch the handles of the big blue doors and shake them with fervor. Her face was dripping with sweat and flushed with fear. Her eyes were wide open, but she didn't seem to comprehend anything around her. They were scared to arouse her for fear of frightening her. But it was unclear whether she was awake or asleep. They waited and watched until she finally collapsed on the floor into a deep slumber.

Sheetal gently lifted Naya in her arms and rocked her gently. The night nurse brought a sponge soaked in cool water. Sheetal wiped Naya's face until she stopped sweating. Once Naya had settled down, they carried her back to her room and tucked her into bed. The MHA doing the sleep observation sat close, watching Naya lie peacefully in her sleep. Sheetal turned off the light and walked quickly to the nurses' station. She wanted to document what had happened in as much detail as possible. She couldn't wait to tell Peter about it. But she would have to wait until Sunday; otherwise, she knew he would cancel his plans. Sheetal and her boyfriend both thought Peter was too serious and needed to have more fun. Besides, he had just finished a rough week.

{CHAPTER THIRTY-THREE}

Friday Midnight

It was almost midnight when the slaaf arrived home. He was exhausted, and it took a great effort to enter his apartment quietly, so as not to draw any attention from his neighbors. Inside, he snatched a half-eaten sandwich from his bare refrigerator and ate it ravenously, washing it down with cold beer. Now, he needed sleep. In his bedroom, he sat on the edge of the bed and stared at the framed black-and-white photograph of his mother.

It was the only photograph of his mother that he possessed. He had been twelve years old, still a boy, when he last saw her. His father had already been gone, wasted away the year before in front of their eyes. A year later, his mother fell gravely ill with the same disease. The boy spent a lot of time tending to his mother's needs, with help from his maternal grandparents, who lived nearby and provided meals. The boy did everything else and tried to bring in some income by working whatever menial jobs he could find at the fish market. He no longer went to school, but still, he remained cheerful and energetic. His mother had taught him that he could always be better. Nothing was going to stop him from making something of his life.

The slaaf couldn't forget the day he had stood next to his mother as she was taking her last breaths. She had drifted into a delirium, barely recognizing her own son. It was agonizing for him to watch her suffer. In a desperate attempt to clear his conscience, he was compelled to reveal the secret that he had closely guarded for so long.

"He was a bad man," the boy told his mother.

But she shook her head weakly. "No," she said. "Nobody's perfect. I still think he was a good man."

The boy felt tremendously guilty and fearful then for having divulged the secret. Had his father heard from beyond the grave? Would he send Anansi to avenge him? His father's words still haunted him: *Believe me, Anansi will kill you …* His mother appeared to fade even faster after he told her the secret. In the end, had his revelation caused his mother's death?

After the funeral, the boy spent his nights lying awake in fear that Anansi was waiting for the right moment devour him. Months passed, and he remained profoundly depressed by the loss of his mother and paralyzed with the fear of Anansi. His grandparents sought help from the local obeah man to rid the boy of his pain and suffering. They believed that the obeah man would use the power of obeah to heal the boy from the inside.

The obeah man stood in front of the boy, towering like a mythical giant. The room was filled with the smoke of incense and camphor. The obeah man chanted in a language the boy didn't know. The obeah man was the magic man who would make his agony go away. He was the best wizard in town. The hundreds of candles around him heated the room to a stifling temperature. The boy sat sweating with anxiety, not knowing what was to come. The obeah man rolled his dice to decide which method the boy should follow.

"You must sacrifice a bird in such a way that Anansi thereby will be tricked into thinking that he has actually cut you into pieces, and thereafter you shall be free," the obeah man instructed the boy.

The next day, the boy set up a wooden platform in the back of his grandparents' shack. He procured a sharp butcher knife from the local meat vendor and purchased a live chicken, making sure it was small enough to control.

By that evening, his anguish was so strong that he knew he could not wait another day, or the fear itself would kill him. Every noise he heard could be Anansi, coming to cut him up. He bathed himself and donned clean clothes. Then, without any more forethought, he slit the chicken's neck and decapitated it swiftly. He held the bird by its feet as blood gushed out of the neck, splashing his clothing and skin. Once the bird had stopped writhing, he put it on the wooden platform and cut off its limbs, one by one. He then completed the task by chopping the bird's feet to pieces.

The boy sat trembling and covered in blood. The shock of having performed his first sacrifice was overwhelming. He felt weak, but free at last from Anansi's fury. His heartbeat slowed, and his breathing became less rapid. He spent the rest of that day in rapturous freedom, working hard at the fish market and then seeking out the friends he'd abandoned when his mother had died.

But that night, when he lay down to sleep, he realized he had not been healed after all. He could feel Anansi's presence on the periphery of his mind ... still there, waiting.

{CHAPTER THIRTY-FOUR}

Saturday

Arcus woke to the sound of the phone ringing. It was his supplier, and he wasn't a happy camper. Arcus owed him almost twenty grand, and it was time to pay up. Most of that was money that Arcus had fronted Everson for his increasingly expensive habit. As soon as he got off the phone, Arcus called Everson's cell phone.

Everson was not pleased to hear from him. "I'm at the hospital," he hissed. "I'll call you back later."

"I need what you owe me. Today," Arcus said and hung up.

Sure, he and Everson were friends, which was why he'd let the money go for so long. He figured the guy was a doctor, so of course he was good for it. Everson must be raking in the cash. But Arcus could no longer support the credit line that he had extended to Everson. If he did, then Everson would become a liability and burden to him. From now on, it was going to be "Pay as you go."

Arcus showered and dressed. He knew where Everson lived. He had been there a few times, usually to pick Everson up to go to a bar or to hang out at the cabin. But that was before Everson had begun seeing Evelyn and disappeared from the social scene—no more late nights, no more double dating. Evelyn had a tight leash on that boy.

Now it was time to pay his customer a visit. Arcus needed that money to keep his own reputation afloat, and he was determined to get it, one way or another. Brute force was sometimes part of this business, and Arcus didn't have a problem with that, friend or not. He was sure that he could persuade Everson to settle this particular debt.

Arcus had been working as a dealer for many years. When he was fourteen, he had come with his grandparents to Newbury, where his grandfather found work with a prominent businessman by the name of Ken Gardner, owner and operator of the butcher shop Fresh Meat. As a teenager, Arcus helped out at the store as well. Mr. Gardner liked him and always said he thought Arcus had a future in meat.

Then, when Arcus was eighteen, both his grandparents were killed when a semi slid across the yellow line on an icy highway and hit them head-on. Arcus took their deaths hard and fell into a deep depression. He had wanted to die too. He could no longer work, and Mr. Gardner had him placed in the university hospital's psychiatric unit.

Arcus was then transferred to a nearby psychiatric institute, where he stayed for six months before the shock of his grandparents' deaths began to fade. When he returned to Newbury, he lived in the house he'd inherited from his grandparents. But he couldn't bring himself to go back to work at Ken's shop.

He had met another young man in the hospital who had access to various illegal drugs, and that young man soon became Arcus's role model. By the time he was twenty, Arcus had connections in New York City who supplied him with cocaine, crack, and meth, for which he found an endless market among the rotating hospital and university crowd in Newbury.

Arcus still felt pain when he thought of his grandparents. They wouldn't like what he'd become. The drugs helped him forget—temporarily, anyway—how he had failed them. They had been so strong, but he was weak.

{CHAPTER THIRTY-FIVE}

Saturday

Peter set out on Saturday morning for the city, glad to have a weekend free at last. His head cold seemed to be abating, but he tucked some antihistamine pills and tissues in his bag just in case. As he drove, his thoughts replayed the previous afternoon's encounter with Agent Bines at Elephant Rock.

After his ordeal, Peter had gone to have a drink at Big Joe's Sports Bar. He'd been there about fifteen minutes, nursing a scotch and watching ESPN, when Detective Rodriguez walked in. Apparently, the detective had also felt a need to unwind before going home to bed.

Peter had been glad to see José and had bought him a drink.

"If it wasn't for you," Peter had said ruefully, "I might have ended up in a jail cell tonight, counting bars. My senator uncle would have been thrilled about bailing me out. At this point in the campaign, the opposition will use anything they can get their hands on."

Peter had realized then that he should call his uncle and tell him what had happened. He looked at his watch. It was late. He'd have to call the senator tomorrow.

Peter and José talked of Peter's shift on the community-policing project. One night, José had summoned Peter to the police station following a report of domestic violence. It was customary for a mental-health professional working with the project to accompany the officers if trauma or abuse was suspected. Sometimes children or other victims needed emergency counseling.

"I hate to admit how nervous I was on that call," Peter said, sipping his scotch.

"Well, it turned out to be a pretty dangerous situation," José said, "so I don't blame you."

As soon as they'd reached the house, they discovered that the father of three children (ages two, four, and six) had locked himself in the house with the children and their mother. The man was threatening to kill his family and take his own life. It took José and the hostage negotiators many hours to persuade the father to surrender without harming his family. Peter had seen the three children over the next few weeks to work through the psychological impact of their ordeal.

José finished his beer and got up to leave. "You know, you don't have to worry about today," he reassured Peter.

Peter raised his eyebrows questioningly.

"Agent Bines is an astute investigator, and she always keeps an open mind. She follows leads, not emotions. Besides, we almost caught someone running through the woods after you left. It was just unfortunate that Leia didn't know who you were beforehand."

Since Peter had grown up for the most part in Newbury and his uncle was such a prominent citizen, Peter had gotten to know officials in every municipal department. He thought again about how it had felt to be in handcuffs. He hadn't liked it a bit.

"Any leads?" Peter asked.

"A few. We might have a partial footprint. The other details I can't talk about. I hope you understand."

"Of course," Peter said. "So what's Agent Bines's story?"

"She's the best at what she does," José said with pride. "Did you know she was the one who tracked down Mary Ann Henderson's kidnapper in Mexico?"

"I remember hearing about that one," Peter said. "Didn't they find her in the nick of time?"

José nodded. "If it hadn't been for Leia, she would have been dead."

"She seems like quite a woman," Peter said.

"She is," José said, nodding emphatically.

Before he knew it, Peter had reached the West Side Highway. He was familiar with the maze of roads in New York City, since he had been there many times before. He found his way to the Upper West Side, where the Iyengars lived, and parked a few blocks away. He jogged three blocks to the co-op complex where the Iyengars resided. The doorman greeted him, then directed him to the elevator, which he was to take to the sixth floor. It was a beautiful old building—even the elevator had carved mahogany ceilings, and the corridor he stepped into featured original dark-stained woodwork. One of the doors in the hallway had been left slightly ajar, and as Peter approached it, a petite Indian woman pulled it open. She appeared to be in her late forties and was dressed in a brightly colored sari.

"Mrs. Iyengar?" Peter said, extending his hand.

"Good morning, Dr. Gram. Please come in," she said, clutching his fingertips briefly. "Could you please take your shoes off and put them there?" Mrs. Iyengar pointed to a corner where various pairs of shoes lay.

Peter sat on a wooden bench and removed his shoes. He smelled the fresh fragrance of incense in the air. The living room had large windows and was aristocratically decorated.

"They're Indian," Mrs. Iyengar said, noticing Peter's interest in the paintings on the wall in the entryway. "From the mogul era."

Peter nodded as if he knew what that meant. "They're beautiful."

"How is Naya doing?" Mrs. Iyengar asked.

"She's actually doing quite well," Peter replied with a smile.

"Please follow me. Mr. Iyengar is expecting you." Mrs. Iyengar led Peter through the living room and stopped beside an open door. "Would you like something to drink?"

"Tea?" Peter said, having liked the tea he'd had at Indian restaurants.

"Go on in—I'll bring you a cup of tea," Mrs. Iyengar directed Peter.

Peter stepped into what appeared to be a home office. Mr. Iyengar was sitting on the opposite end of the room on a raised wooden platform on the floor. In front of him was a low, pearl-white table. As Peter walked toward it, he saw that it was made of marble. Across the table from Mr. Iyengar lay two large white cushions.

"Dr. Gram," Mr. Iyengar said, "I've been expecting you. Please come in and sit with me." Mr. Iyengar gesturing toward the empty cushions. Peter squatted on one of the cushions and crossed his legs. It seemed surprisingly comfortable.

Mr. Iyengar shook Peter's hand firmly across the table. He was a portly gentleman in his late fifties or early sixties—much older than his wife. His almost-bald head was covered with a few strands of graying hair, and a pair of circular glasses sat on the bridge of his nose, making him appear very scholarly. "Tell me, how is our little princess doing, and what do you think is wrong with her?"

"She's safe right now. The problem is that we're not sure about the origins of her behavior."

Peter described the dream that had brought Naya to the hospital in the first place. He explained that they were trying to find out if she had a psychotic disorder versus a sleep-related disorder.

"How may I be of help to you?" Mr. Iyengar asked Peter.

"I was hoping to learn more about her biological parents. That information might help us come to a reasonable working diagnosis," Peter said.

"What would you like to know?"

"Did Naya's biological mother have any significant psychiatric problems?"

"Let me tell you more about our family," Mr. Iyengar began with a deep breath. "You see, Naya's mother was one of three children born to our parents."

"Did she die when Naya was an infant?" Peter interjected, having heard from the Hastings that she was deceased.

"Yes, Naya's mother—my sister Meena—died when Naya was just a few months old. I'm the oldest of the three; Meena was the sister in the middle; and Shalini is the youngest sister. Our parents raised us in a small town near the city of Bangalore.

"My mother was sixteen when she had me, thirty-two when Meena was born, and thirty-four when she had Shalini. As you can see, there is a large age gap between me and my sisters."

"When did you come to America?"

"When I was twenty-five years old. I came to help my family financially."

"How old was Naya's mother when she died?"

"She was thirty years old," Mr. Iyengar replied. "Meena was a gifted woman, but from her teenage years on, she was terribly misunderstood. She left home in her twenties and lived by herself. She cut herself off from our family. I heard she would wander the streets prophesying people's futures. There were periods when she seemed to live in a sort of heightened trance state. I suppose it was during the years when she was away that she met Naya's father."

"Do you know anything about him?"

"Unfortunately, no. Naya's father is a stranger. The only time we ever saw him was at her funeral, and even then, we didn't even know his name. He didn't have any interest in Naya. He told us that he didn't want to be a part of Naya's life and relinquished his parental rights. At the funeral, he gave me a letter that Meena had been writing to me just before her death."

"How did Naya's mother die?"

"She had metastasized brain cancer."

"So young?"

Mr. Iyengar nodded dispassionately.

"Did she ever receive any form of psychiatric help while she was alive?" Peter inquired.

"At the time, there were no mental-health facilities in the town where she lived," Mr. Iyengar said sadly.

"Is there anyone else in your immediate family who may have had a mental illness?"

"No, not that I know of. I have two perfectly healthy daughters who are in their twenties, and my sister Shalini has two teenage boys with no such problems."

"Does Naya know any of this?" Peter asked, as he didn't want to accidentally divulge any private information.

"All Naya knows is that her biological parents passed away when she was a baby and that her mother's wishes were that she be adopted by a good American family. I loved my sister dearly, and I have a special affection for my niece. I wanted to make sure that Naya would be welcomed into a loving family."

"Why an American family?" Peter asked out of curiosity.

"Meena knew that Naya had inherited her special abilities, and she didn't want Naya to face the same obstacles that she had and end up a pariah. She felt Naya would be better understood in an advanced Western society, with a better chance at a normal life."

"How did the Hastings find out about Naya?" Peter inquired.

"Through mutual friends, we learned that the Hastings were interested in adopting an Indian child, as they are extremely fond of Indian culture. We found them to be a genuinely caring couple, and they lived close to us here in America."

"Do you meet Naya often?" Peter asked.

"Yes, we do. She likes to come and spend her holidays with us, especially during the Indian festivals. We also get to see her from time to time when we drive by the Hastings."

"I'm glad that you're in contact with her. Naya talks of you very fondly."

"Can we come and see her while she's in the hospital?" Mr. Iyengar asked with concern.

"Of course," Peter said with a smile. "Just let me know when."

"Maybe tomorrow or the day after," Mr. Iyengar said. He looked at his wife, who was standing behind Peter with a cup of tea.

"How much sugar would you like?" Mrs. Iyengar asked Peter, who was surprised to see her. He hadn't heard her come into the room. *Apparently I'm an easy guy to sneak up on*, he thought, remembering Agent Bines's silent approach.

"Just a teaspoon should do," he said. She handed him the cup, and when he lifted it to his mouth, the scent of cloves and cardamon filled his nostrils. He breathed deeply.

"So what do you do with your time, Mr. Iyengar?" Peter continued his questioning.

"I'm the professor of Sanskrit at the Institute of Foreign Languages. Do you know Sanskrit?"

"No," Peter said, smiling ruefully. "I'm afraid I'm not that great with languages."

"It's one of the earliest languages of the Eastern world," Mr. Iyengar said. "Most Indian languages are derivatives of Sanskrit."

Peter's eyes ran over what must have been hundreds of books in the shelves lining the room.

"I also tell people's fortunes," Mr. Iyengar said.

Peter blanched. Had he heard correctly? "Fortunes?" he said stupidly.

Maybe fortune-telling was an Iyengar family business.

{CHAPTER THIRTY-SIX}

Saturday

Everson paced anxiously around his living room. He walked over to the window and peered through the curtains only to see a familiar car parked right next to his. Ever since Arcus had called him at the hospital, Everson had struggled to tamp down an increasing sense of panic.

"Shit, shit, shit," he said.

He listened for footsteps outside his apartment door. Nothing yet, but he knew there was no point in leaving; Arcus would find him sooner or later. So he just stood at the door in the dimly lit room, startled by the loud knock on the door when it finally came. He rubbed beads of sweat from his forehead with the back of his forearm. He knew he had to let Arcus in.

"What can I do for you?" Everson said with forced cheer as Arcus brushed him aside to enter the apartment. "Can I get you a beer?"

"I need the money now, so why don't you just write me a check or something?"

"Arcus, I can't, man."

"What do you mean, you can't? Quit playing around and just get me the damn money!" Arcus raised his voice and stepped toward Everson in an intimidating way.

Everson backed into the arm of the couch, almost losing his balance.

"Easy … you're in control here," Everson said. He wanted Arcus to know that he had no violent intentions.

"What the hell is wrong with you?" Arcus bellowed. "I need all of it— now!"

"Come on, you should have given me some notice. I don't have that kind of money on hand."

"I called you this morning," Arcus said.

Everson sank down on the couch and held his head in his hands. It was time to quit pretending. He'd been living beyond his means for quite some time. His credit cards were maxed out, he owed several mortgage payments on failed real-estate investments, and his monthly car payment and the rent on his apartment were higher than he could afford.

"Listen," he said. "I don't have it, Arcus. I don't have any of it."

"You think I'm going to buy that shit? You're a damn doctor, and you're broke? That doesn't make any sense!" Arcus slammed his fist down on the kitchen counter, and Everson jumped up from the sofa. Arcus walked swiftly toward him.

"I don't care if you're broke. My suppliers don't care. Just get the money. You have twenty-four hours."

Everson met Arcus's eyes just as Arcus drew his arm back and punched Everson hard in the stomach. The sudden blow caught Everson off guard, and he reeled back onto the couch, wincing in pain.

"That wasn't necessary," Everson tried to say as he choked on his own saliva.

Arcus reached under his long coat and took out a crowbar, which he slapped into his opposite palm a few times.

"This is what I'll have to use next," he said. "It makes pretty faces very ugly." He swung the crowbar at the tall lamp that stood next to the sofa. The glass lampshade and bulb shattered, and Everson covered his face with his arms to protect himself from the flying glass. In a flash, Arcus had the crowbar under Everson's chin. "Remember. Twenty-four hours."

"Where am I supposed to get that kind of money?" Everson said.

"Beg, borrow, or steal. I don't care how you get it."

"I need more time," Everson begged.

"You better start knocking on the doors of all your rich doctor friends." Arcus sneered.

"My only close doctor friend is Peter, and he's so busy with his patients, he doesn't make time for anything else," Emerson whined. But Arcus just turned his back and walked out of the apartment, slamming the door behind him.

Everson sat on the couch for a few moments, waiting for the pain in his stomach to subside. He didn't know what to do. If he ran, where would he go? He had no family. If he stayed, his career was at stake, and his life was in grave danger.

And if he stayed, who would help him?

{CHAPTER THIRTY-SEVEN}

Saturday

"Yes, fortunes," Mr. Iyengar said in a mildly amused tone. "Do you believe in destiny, Dr. Gram?"

"I'm not sure what you mean," Peter answered, puzzled.

"Some Hindus believe that we're born with a life that has been mapped out for us, and that what will happen has already been foretold, preordained. The only problem is that we don't know what that plan might be, and hence we're supposed to live each day doing our very best."

Peter found the idea fascinating, if improbable.

"Many centuries ago," Mr. Iyengar continued, "there was a small group of wise men with the power of foresight known as the Seeked Ones. They wrote the prophecies of a few chosen lineages in the form of scriptures. Over time, this group scattered over India, each taking a handful of scriptures that contained the fortune of a selected group of families. Each Seeked One had the ability to read the scriptures and tell the future. All the Seeked One had to do was to wait for that person—known as the Seeker—to find him."

"It was preordained that at some point in the Seeker's life, he would have an encounter with the Seeked One. Since our lives are short, these wise men took steps to provide their services to the Seekers by handing down these scriptures to chosen pupils, along with the skills to decode them. In that way, if they fell into the wrong hands, the documents would be of no value, and thereby the prophecies would be safeguarded."

"Are you a Seeked One?" Peter asked.

"Yes, I am," replied Mr. Iyengar.

"So, does that mean you can tell me my fate?" Peter queried.

"No," Mr. Iyengar said. "As I mentioned, the Seeked Ones only wrote down that information for a few chosen lineages. And besides, you didn't come here to learn your fortune."

"That's true," Peter said.

"One of the chosen lineages was my own—and, by extension, Naya's. And I think you're a part of Naya's destiny, as foretold by these scriptures."

"Me?"

"Yes. Let me back up a bit," Mr. Iyengar said, standing up. "It was written in the scriptures that I would play an important role early on in Naya's life. Understand, Peter, I was in America, and my sister was in India. How could I play that important part if I was here while my sister and Naya were there? Before she died, my sister requested that I arrange for Naya to be adopted by an American couple. She foresaw Naya's need to be in America, but not within the family. That way, our paths would cross at a different time. And that's the power of destiny. No matter the distance between the Seeked and the Seeker is, their paths will cross as preordained."

"And where exactly do I fit in?" Peter asked, still skeptical.

"Let me tell you what's written about your presence in Naya's fate."

Mr. Iyengar walked up to a handsomely carved antique sandalwood chest and unlocked it with a small key. The hinges creaked as he opened the chest's lid. He gently lifted out an object wrapped in a saffron satin cloth and laid it on the marble table.

Peter watched with a growing sense of excitement as Mr. Iyengar unwrapped a ream of delicate ancient oval leaves.

"In those days," Mr. Iyengar said, "information was written on the dried leaves of a very special plant."

He looked through them one leaf at a time, searching for the right one. When he found it, Mr. Iyengar began to read aloud in a melodic language unlike anything Peter had ever heard. Peter was mesmerized by the sound, even though he had no clue what Mr. Iyengar was saying.

Mr. Iyengar paused and summarized in English what he just read. "It is written that when Naya comes to six years of age, she will begin a period of unrest. This period will grow and is filled with visions and uncertainty. The period will end only after she helps a tall, white healer who tries to intervene."

"Is that it?" Peter asked, let down. He had been hoping to hear the rest of Naya's destiny.

"That's all I can tell you. The rest is for Naya when she comes to seek her destiny," Mr. Iyengar said softly, knowing that Peter was a little disappointed.

"But what did you mean when you said that she would be helping me?" Peter asked.

"I don't know, but that's what is written. It may take some time before you figure it out."

"But I'm the one trying to help her," Peter said.

"Perhaps you must change your perspective," Mr. Iyengar suggested.

"But I don't currently need help from anybody," Peter reaffirmed, "especially not from a patient—one who happens to be seven years old!"

"Everything will make more sense as time passes, and you will see that it's all written in your own destiny," Mr. Iyengar said as he gathered the leaves, carefully wrapped them again in the satin cloth, and returned them to the chest where they belonged.

Peter couldn't make sense of what Mr. Iyengar had told him. He'd had great hopes that Mr. Iyengar could shed light on what was wrong with Naya, but now he felt further than ever from getting his questions answered. He realized that it was time for him to leave.

"Please let me know when you plan to visit Naya in the hospital, so that I can give her the happy news," Peter said, standing and feeling the blood rush through his toes, which had begun to go numb. He wasn't used to sitting Indian style on the floor.

Peter thanked the Iyengars for the aromatic cup of tea and for allowing him to come by on such short notice. As he walked to his car, he tried not to think of what Mr. Iyengar had told him, but he couldn't help himself.

People actually believed such things. The funny thing was, Peter found he wanted to believe them himself.

As he drove toward Broadway, Peter's thoughts drifted to stopping for a bite to eat before the play. It was strangely appropriate that he had tickets to *Bombay Dreams*, a Bollywood musical, considering he had just left the Iyengars' home. The musical had received rave reviews and came highly recommended by Sheetal and her boyfriend. (In her most transparent effort yet, Sheetal had suggested cheerily, "Hey, you could even take a date!" as if the thought had struck her out of the blue.)

Peter hoped the show would help him forget about this mess for a few hours.

{CHAPTER THIRTY-EIGHT}

Saturday

In the precinct office, Leia sat with José and Lieutenant Andrew around a large, round table that was covered with information about Janet's case. She presented Carroll Prize's preliminary report.

"Based on the lab studies so far, she thinks that the approximate time of death was about nine days before the discovery of the body, just as she had initially mentioned."

"What about the mode of death?" José asked as he blew on his hot cup of coffee.

"Jason Kelly, the forensic pathologist, thinks she bled to death," Leia reported. "There were no marks found on her neck to indicate that she was strangled. It was only after she was dead that he cut her into pieces."

"What about the DNA results from the body?" José asked.

Leia looked through the pile of reports and found one from the FBI's DNA lab. The FBI's DNA lab was the largest of its kind in the world. It had two programs; the DNA Analysis Unit I that provided serological and DNA testing services to numerous agencies, and the DNA Analysis Unit II that was subdivided into three major programs. The programs were the Mitochondrial DNA Case Program, the Missing Persons Program, and the Federal Convicted Offender Program. Leia had also sent the bandanna that she had acquired to the DNA Analysis Unit II with the intention of extracting any hair from the assailant and analyzing the mitochondrial

DNA sequence. It was going to take a few more days before they processed any material that they retrieved from the bandanna.

"The DNA analysis of fragments found on the victim revealed no traces of blood other than that of the victim," she summarized.

"Damn it!" José said.

"There were some canine marks inflicted after death, indicating that some wild animals chewed on the body," Leia remarked as she sipped her own coffee.

"So we have a professional killer on our hands," Lieutenant Andrew said, shaking his head in disgust.

"Was there any evidence of genetic material from the killer?" inquired José.

"They did find some hair and skin buried under Janet's nails, but couldn't find any match in CODIS," replied Leia. CODIS was the acronym for the program that blended forensic science and computer technology. The humongous database incorporated data from many participating regional labs. CODIS generated leads using two indexes: the forensic index and the offender index. The forensic index contained the DNA profiles from crime scenes, and the offender index contained DNA profiles of individuals convicted of sexual and violent crimes. The database tried to match crime scenes with known serial offenders.

"So he doesn't have a record," José deduced.

"Except for the case of Debbie Sanders, I couldn't find any other case even with the slightest resemblance," said the lieutenant.

José clutched his hair in frustration. "The million-dollar question is, if this isn't a serial killer, then why do it again after so many years?"

"Maybe she was at the wrong place at the wrong time?" Leia postulated.

The trio finished their coffee as they spent almost two hours pondering the case. They felt they were almost at a dead end; they had no further leads.

"In conclusion, the profile we have so far is a person born well before 1967, who has the skill of a surgeon and who is familiar with this area," summarized Leia. "And that's only if the two cases are connected. What if it was some kind of family ritual handed down through the generations?"

"I think he believes that he got away once, and that he can do it again," José said, obviously wanting to believe the two cases were indeed connected.

"Any suggestions?" asked Lieutenant Andrew.

"We might need to take DNA samples from every professional working in the surgical specialties in the area to begin with, and see if it matches with what we have," José suggested with a slight wince, clearly aware that this would be an enormous undertaking.

Lieutenant Andrew stood up and slammed his hand on the table in frustration. "That is impossible!" he shouted. "Imagine asking people to give a piece of DNA, even if they're not suspects."

"We'll have to get an order from a judge before we do that, then notify the potential people," said José determinedly.

"What judge in his right mind will authorize something like that, especially over the weekend?" asked Lieutenant Andrew impatiently.

"I don't think that'll work, as it's going to take way too long," Leia pointed out. "We have to find another direction to move in."

"What about the doctor?" the lieutenant asked, referring to what had happened the previous day. "He could be the prime suspect because he was found at the scene of a crime. He also has access to his uncle's ranch and has been around for a long time."

"Peter? I doubt it very much," replied Leia. "He's far too young."

"Maybe a cook or a vet," said José, thinking of other people who might have such skills.

"Now you're opening a can of worms. We can't go after everyone who can hold a knife in town," the lieutenant remarked.

"True," said Leia. "What about the ranch—any information from there?"

"I found that a few of the contractors were undocumented workers," José said. "I wonder if we need to report that to the immigration authorities."

"Given the senator's position, let's hold onto that for now," Leia said, rubbing her forehead. She was still frustrated with their poor progress.

{CHAPTER THIRTY-NINE}

Saturday

Naya woke late, but she still didn't feel well rested. The staff had saved a tray of breakfast for her that they allowed her to eat in her room soon after brushing her teeth.

Because it was Saturday, there was no school. Some of the children had a weekend pass and left the unit early in the morning with their families. Naya's parents had told her they would visit her later in the afternoon.

Naya sat in her pajamas at her desk. She had eaten only a portion of her cheese and toast. She didn't like the hospital food. She already missed her mother's cooking, even though she had only been away for two days. She placed her unfinished plate on the tray, which lay on the floor next to where she sat. She remembered her dream from the night before. For the first time she could remember, a dream had actually scared her. It had felt so real that she almost believed it had happened. She felt comforted by the thought that she was safe in the hospital, and that someone was watching over her as she slept.

This was also the first time that the same character had reappeared in her dreams. Naya decided to put her dream onto paper and show it to Dr. Gram. She felt anxious that she wouldn't see him until Monday. She didn't feel comfortable talking about her experience with anybody else.

As Naya was drawing a detailed picture of her dream, Sasha came running into her room without knocking on the door.

"Naya, Naya!" Sasha called, startling the girl. "What are you doing?"

"Nothing," Naya replied, turning her drawing facedown. She didn't want to share her drawings with Sasha.

"Don't lie," Sasha said, bending over Naya's shoulder. "I see you're hiding something from me."

"No, I'm not," Naya blurted out defensively. She didn't want Sasha in her room; she wanted her to go away. But that was mean to say, and Naya didn't want to be mean.

Sasha reached past Naya and tried to grab one of the sheets of paper. "Can I see what you drew?" she said.

"No," Naya said, laying her own arm across Sasha's to prevent her from taking the paper. "It's private." She was beginning to feel very angry with Sasha. She remembered the staff telling Sasha to watch her boundaries, and she wished Sasha would do so now.

Sasha tried to grab the drawings again, and Naya stood up from her chair and pushed Sasha away.

"You bitch!" Sasha shouted. "Then I'm not playing with you again! Ever!"

Naya recoiled, surprised by Sasha's angry tone and the language she was using.

"Then I won't play with you either!" Naya replied angrily.

Sasha reacted by swinging her fist toward Naya's face, but she missed.

Naya stepped back from Sasha in fear and screamed for help. A male staff member ran into the room.

"You're supposed to be in your room, Sasha," the staff scolded Sasha. "You don't have permission to come in here."

"I don't care!" Sasha shouted. She lifted her hand as if to try to hit Naya again, but the staff person grabbed her wrist.

Sasha turned toward him and tried to stomp on his feet. The man jumped back, pulling Sasha with him. Sasha then kicked his knee, and the man winced and accidentally allowed Sasha to pull her wrist free from his grip.

"We need more help here!" the staff person shouted.

Naya stood in the corner of the room, watching Sasha explode as another staff member ran into the room. Maybe, Naya thought, she should have showed Sasha her pictures. Maybe none of this would have happened. The two staff members trapped Sasha in the corner, and she crouched there like a wild animal that was going to pounce on its prey.

"Don't you even dream of it," Naya heard the second staff member warn.

Before Naya knew it, the two staff members were carrying Sasha out of the room, kicking and screaming at the top of her lungs. Naya followed at a distance and watched, trembling, as they carried Sasha toward the Quiet Room.

She heard one of them call to the nurse, "She needs some medication!"

But Sasha's screams drowned out the call for help. Naya ran to the nurses' station. Nurse Jennifer was working in the back. It was obvious she hadn't heard the staff's cry for help.

Naya banged on the Plexiglas, and Nurse Jennifer opened the door.

"They need your help," Naya said, pointing down the hallway.

Nurse Jennifer ran to help the two struggling staff members, but by the time she reached them, Sasha had broken loose and run into her room, where she continued to curse and scream and bang the furniture. Nurse Jennifer stood in the doorway with her arms and legs spread apart, probably to make sure Sasha wouldn't run out of her room again.

Nurse Jennifer said to one of the staff members, "Please page Dr. Patel." Then she turned back to Sasha. "You have to calm down and put your clothes on now," she said.

"Kiss me, you white bitch!" Naya heard Sasha scream furiously.

Naya stepped back from the doorway of her room as Dr. Patel walked swiftly past. "Let's give her twenty-five milligrams of Benadryl IM, stat," Sheetal instructed Jennifer as she walked into the room. Jennifer sprinted back to the nurses' station to draw up the medication that had been ordered.

"Sasha, let's talk about this," Dr. Patel said in a gentle voice as she took a couple of steps into Sasha's room. "What are you upset about?"

"That bitch!" Sasha screamed. "She wouldn't show me her pictures!"

"What pictures are you talking about?"

"Ask Naya," Sasha said.

Naya felt shame rise in her body from her toes to her face.

"I will, once you calm down," Dr. Patel said.

"No, you won't," Sasha snapped.

Then it sounded as though Sasha were spitting. Dr. Patel backed up into the doorway.

"If you can't get control of yourself, we'll have to hold you down and give you some medicine. What's your choice, Sasha?"

"I don't care, I don't care!"

Nurse Jennifer returned with a shot, and she, Dr. Patel, and another staff member went into Sasha's room.

Sasha screamed, "No! I don't want an IM, I don't want an IM!"

In less than a minute, the staff members were back in the hallway, and Sasha was crying as though her heart were broken.

Naya felt sorry for Sasha then. She thought about how no one ever visited her. She would try again to be Sasha's friend, even though she'd said she wouldn't.

"Watch her for a while, and once she settles down, she can have lunch in her room," Dr. Patel said to the staff member.

Naya watched Dr. Patel come toward her. She was afraid that Dr. Patel would be angry at her for not showing Sasha her pictures. But Dr. Patel was smiling, so Naya relaxed.

"Naya, can you tell me what happened?" Dr. Patel asked. She had pretty long hair and sparkly eyes.

"I was drawing pictures, and she wanted to see them," Naya replied softly. "And when I said no, she started to hit me."

"Sasha can become very angry sometimes for no good reason," Dr. Patel said, putting her hand on Naya's head for a moment. "You don't have to talk to her at all if you don't want to."

Naya felt comforted, relieved, and sad all at the same time. She felt sorry for Sasha, but she didn't really want to talk to her anymore. Most of all, she wanted to leave the hospital. This was definitely not the place for her. When her parents arrived, she would ask them to take her home right away.

{CHAPTER FORTY}

Saturday

Senator Thomas Bailey sat in his office, mulling over the information he had received from the lieutenant. He wasn't happy the way the case was progressing—or, should he say, not progressing. He had hoped the offender would be caught by now.

And now, his fool of a nephew had somehow gotten mixed up in the case. The investigators didn't think there was any connection between Peter and the murder; nevertheless, such connections could always be made, and if they were made at the wrong time, it could blow the campaign to smithereens.

"Damn you, Peter," Thomas cursed aloud. He walked out of his office and went looking for his wife, whom he found reading a magazine in the living room.

"Yes, dear," Beth said before he even said anything.

"That nephew of yours has put himself in a delicate situation," Thomas said with some annoyance.

Beth put down her magazine. "What do you mean?" she asked, her eyebrows drawn down. He could tell she was getting ready to defend her favorite nephew against him, just as she'd always done during his growing years.

"I just heard from Lieutenant Andrew that investigators found him snooping around the crime scene yesterday."

"What?" Beth asked, appearing shocked and surprised. "Why would he do such a thing? He wasn't arrested, was he?"

"Gratefully, no," Thomas said. "The evidence they have indicates that the killer is much older than Peter."

"Oh, good," Beth said, apparently completely satisfied.

"How he got involved in a murder case when he should be practicing medicine is beyond me," Thomas said with a scowl.

"Maybe we should talk to him before jumping to any conclusions," Beth suggested. "Why don't you have him stop by tonight, so that we could find out what's going on?"

"Yes, dear. I'll do that," Beth said, standing up and walking to the telephone that sat on a small table in one corner of the living room. She dialed Peter's telephone number. After five rings, his voice mail picked up.

"Hi, Peter. This is your Aunt Beth. Could you please call me or come by the house as soon as you get this message? We have something important to discuss with you. Bye, honey."

Thomas was disappointed that Peter wasn't at home. He wanted to get this matter taken care of. Peter needed to keep a low profile until after the election. What was so difficult about that?

"I'll let you know as soon as I hear from him," Beth said with a soothing smile. "Don't worry about it. Why don't you go back to what you were doing?"

Thomas returned to his office, grumbling under his breath. Beth had always been the responsible one in her family, and the senator had resented the fact that one of its members was always asking her for something. He remembered the night he had opened the door to find Beth's sister Sally standing on the other side with eight-year-old Peter—who, in spite of the cold winter night, was dressed only in his pajamas. The boy had been holding his teddy bear. Sally had a ring of finger marks around her throat, and the senator knew from the look on her face that she had come to the end of her stormy marriage.

At the time, Sally was married to a successful, intelligent investment banker with a fiery temper and a budding drinking problem. They had been married for about two years before Peter was born, but their problems dated back to the day they met. Sally was always calling on Beth with some new sob story, and Beth, bless her tender heart, was always there for her sister.

When Peter was four years old, his father began to have an affair. When Sally protested, Peter's father became physically and emotionally abusive toward her. Still she stayed, although Beth begged her to leave or to at least get Peter out of there. Sally always had hope that things would get better.

Peter began to spend more and more time with Beth and Thomas. Then, finally, on that winter night, Sally left him there with the hope that she would come back for him when she got on her feet. None of them saw her again for ten years. That was what made Thomas so frustrated and angry. He liked Peter, really, but he couldn't tolerate the idea that the boy's mother could just abandon her only child and walk away. Every time he looked at Peter, he thought about what his mother had done to him.

Beth had simply opened her heart and incorporated Peter into the family as if he had always been one of her own. She was a little biased toward him, given the emotional baggage he carried, and Thomas resented that fact too.

He heard the telephone ring and the low murmur of his wife's voice as she answered it. A few minutes later, she appeared in the doorway of his office.

"Peter's on his way back from the city," she said. "He's seen a play! Isn't that nice? Anyway, he'll stop by on his way home. It'll be an hour or so. Do you need anything, dear? Are you hungry?"

{CHAPTER FORTY-ONE}

Saturday

Everson picked up Evelyn at seven o' clock, as promised. He was wearing her favorite outfit: a gray suit and tie with a baby blue shirt. She answered the door in a pretty floral dress that complemented her curvy figure. Her dark, coarse hair was pulled into a full ponytail at the top of her head, and her ruby lips complemented her outfit.

"God, you're handsome," she said, showing him her perfect row of white teeth as she gave him her familiar smile of admiration.

"You're not so bad-looking yourself," Everson joked. She balled up one manicured fist and punched him.

"Oh, all right, all right," Everson said. "You're the prettier one and we both know it."

"Well, don't sell yourself short," Evelyn said. "You're very pretty too."

Everson feigned amusement that he didn't really feel. Every time he looked at Evelyn's beautiful face, guilt threatened to crush him. How had he managed to mess up so badly? He had wanted to be the tough guy, the strong guy, the party guy. And now he felt weaker than ever; his legs trembled at the knees.

Evelyn leaned in close after they climbed into the car. She closed her eyes for a kiss, and Everson gazed at her long eyelashes as they rested against her cheeks. What had he done? He leaned forward and kissed her, softly, with none of his usual bravado or arrogance.

She pulled back and surveyed him in the moonlight that came through the sunroof of his blue BMW.

"Are you all right?" she asked. "You seem … different."

He put a grin on his face and slid his hand up her knee. "Oh, do I?"

She squealed and slapped his hand away. "Not now—I'm starving! Where are you taking me for dinner?"

"The new Italian place, of course," Everson said.

"Oh, I'm so excited. I bet it'll be amazing."

"I'm sure it will," Everson said. *If my card doesn't get declined, of course,* he added mentally.

Evelyn was looking at him again. "Are you sure everything's okay?"

Everson grabbed her hand and kissed it, then put the car into gear.

"Couldn't be better," he answered, swallowing hard. It was going to be a long night.

{CHAPTER FORTY-TWO}

Saturday

Peter flipped his phone closed and adjusted the earpiece in case he received any more calls as he drove home. Absentmindedly, he hummed the vibrant songs from the musical he had just seen.

Boom shakalak … The song played like a broken record in his head.

His aunt's phone call had surprised him. For a fleeting moment, he wondered if something had happened to his mother. Then he remembered that he'd meant to call her and Uncle Thomas about his encounter with the authorities at the crime scene. Now he had to try to convince them that his wild story was true, when no one with an ounce of common sense would believe it. Now he was nervous.

He would have to practice what he was going to tell his aunt. It didn't matter what he told Uncle Thomas—the man would argue with Peter even if Peter said that two plus two equaled four.

Peter's cousins Brad and Richard always went to their father rather than their mother to complain about Peter, because they knew their mother would always take Peter's side, and their father never would. Sometimes his cousins told lies about something Peter had supposedly done, knowing their father would reprimand him because it was their word against his. It hurt Peter that his uncle didn't believe in him, but the unconditional love and support he always got from his Aunt Beth almost made up for it.

Peter had always been grateful to his aunt and uncle for their monetary and emotional support, given the circumstances in which he had grown up. His earliest memories were good ones. He remembered fondly the apartment in New York City where he had lived with his parents those first few years. He was his parents' only child, so he had received their undivided attention. Even when his father was busy at the bank, he would often take Peter to the Central Park Zoo in the summer.

But when Peter was five years old, his father came home less and less often. The kindergartner spent most of his after-school hours with his mother. On the increasingly rare occasions that his father was home before Peter went to bed, he spoke to Peter's mother coldly or angrily, and she scurried around the apartment, trying to make things right for him so that he'd stay. They would sometimes have terrible fights, during which his mother would scream and cry, and his father would yell back at her. Peter began occupying himself in his bedroom, living in his own world of toys and trying not to listen to what was happening on the other side of the door.

Peter remembered one particular night when he was awakened by the sound of his mother screaming.

"No!" she said, and then: "Stop it! Stop it!"

Peter got out of bed quickly and went across the hall to his parents' room. The stench of alcohol and vomit drifted through the bathroom doorway as he passed. Was someone sick?

Peter pushed open the bedroom door. His parents' room was partially lit by the moonlight that seeped through the window. In the moonlight, Peter saw his father hitting his mother with his fist. With each punch, she would fall back on the bed, sobbing, trying to get up or crawl away, and Peter's father would grab her and punch her again, grunting, not saying a word. As Peter watched in horror, his father hit his mother in the stomach, on the back, on the arms and legs—never on the face.

Peter stood frozen in the doorway, paralyzed with fear and uncertainty. If he tried to help his mother, his father would beat him too. His mother had told him, "Just stay out of his way, Petey. Be a good boy."

Peter crept back to his room and closed the door behind him. He sat on the floor next to the radiator, not knowing if he should cry, not knowing if his father might beat his mother until she was dead. He felt cold, numb, not himself anymore.

He spent the entire night in the same spot. At some point, he fell asleep. In the morning, he hesitated to leave his room, unsure of what to expect. He continued to sit there until he heard a knock on the door. It was a cue from his mother that it was time for him to get up for school. He jumped into his bed and huddled under the covers. He pretended to be asleep when his mother came in.

"Peter, it's time to get up," he heard his mother say softly. She pulled the blanket away from his face.

She looked the same as she did every morning … maybe a little more tired. Her eyes were swollen from crying. Her robe covered the new bruises on her arms and body.

Peter got out of bed and followed his mother to the living room. He looked around to see if his father was reading the newspaper, as he always did. To Peter's relief, his mother told him that his father had left early for work. He looked at his mother, who was preparing breakfast for him in the adjoining kitchen. She smiled at him as though nothing had happened. He hurried to the bathroom, pausing at the door as he remembered the smell from the previous night. He pushed the door open only to smell the fresh scent of flowers. It was as though it had all been a bad dream. But he knew that really, his mother had just cleaned up the mess before waking him.

By the time he was eight, Peter could predict the days when his father would arrive home drunk. On luckier days, his father wouldn't arrive home at all. Peter kept himself occupied with his schoolwork and spent a lot of time with his cousins Brad and Richard on the ranch in Newbury.

Then came the night Peter's mother had barged into his room and taken him out of the house in his pajamas. In the car, he looked at her and saw that her neck was ringed with purple welts. After that night, Peter hadn't seen her again for ten years.

From then on, Peter had lived with his aunt at the ranch. As he got older, he had slowly realized that he needed to stop waiting for his mother to reappear. He needed to make a life for himself there at the ranch. He began to work harder in school. He spent his free time exploring Elephant Rock and Willow Lake. After graduation, he left the ranch to attend college and then medical school. When he told his college friends he was going "home," he meant the ranch, which he visited religiously during summer recess and other holidays.

Peter distinctly recalled the next time he had seen his mother. It was at his high-school graduation. He knew she loved him; she had sent him birthday cards every year as he grew up. He had accepted the fact that she needed that time away from him to repair her wounds; after that, his mother could come back into his life. He learned at his graduation that his father had moved away from the city and that his parents were divorced.

Over the next few years, Peter spent time repairing his relationships with each of his parents. He never saw them together and preferred it that way. His aunt and uncle had become parental figures to him, and he deeply respected and admired them. But the memories of what his father had done to his mother always haunted him, often resurfacing during stressful circumstances. He rarely drank, and he avoided dating for fear that hidden deep inside him there was a monster like the one he had seen emerge from his father.

Now, Peter was so lost in memories that he was startled to find himself approaching his aunt's ranch. He drove through the front gate and up the driveway. When he got out of the car, the silence of the countryside reminded him how much he loved the ranch. It had been a few weeks since he had come to visit; the fellowship at the hospital kept him busy.

Before he could ring the bell, the door opened, and Peter's aunt Beth appeared with a warm smile on her face. She was a tall, beautiful, distinguished woman with an oval face, bright blue eyes, and wavy blond hair. The resemblance between his mom and his aunt was striking, and Peter himself had inherited his mother's blue eyes.

Peter knew Aunt Beth was happy to see him, but she seemed a little worried.

"Hi, Aunt Beth," he said. He hugged her and stepped into the foyer.

"Peter, thanks for coming on such short notice," Beth said.

"Anything for you," Peter said, grinning. He walked along with his aunt into the living room and took off his jacket before sitting down on the soft, chocolate-colored leather sofa.

"Where's Uncle Thomas?" he asked.

Beth sat down next to Peter and stroked his hair. "He's in his office—he should be here in any second."

"How are you? What's going on with the campaign?"

"Oh," Aunt Beth sighed, "We've all been very busy. And to make things worse, that poor child was found murdered."

"I know," Peter said. "What a sad story. I actually want to tell you something related to that. You won't believe it when I tell—"

"Won't believe what?" Uncle Thomas said, entering the room.

"It's about Janet Troy, the dead girl they found at Elephant Rock," Peter remarked swiftly.

"I hope you didn't do it," the senator said humorlessly.

At that point, Peter knew that his guardians had already known where he had been the previous evening. After all, he should have thought about them even before he'd considered going to Elephant Rock. It was foolish on his part to think that they wouldn't find out. His uncle was the most well-connected politician in the area.

"Okay, listen, let me explain," Peter stressed before anybody else could say a word.

"Go ahead, we're listening. And this better be good," the senator said cynically.

Peter looked at his aunt, who had sat silently once her husband had stepped in. He knew that he was on his own this time, and rightfully so. He didn't want his aunt to bear the brunt of his actions.

"It's complicated … I'm not sure where to begin." He told the two of them about Naya and the pictures she had drawn of her dreams, omitting Naya's name for the sake of confidentiality.

"So what's that have to do with you and why you were found at Elephant Rock?" the senator interjected.

"Thomas, dear, will you give the boy a chance to tell us what he has to say without interrupting?" Beth spoke out in support for Peter.

"Interestingly," Peter continued as he heard his uncle grumble under his breath, "this girl had a dream on the night before the news of the murder broke out. In that dream, she had an encounter that seemed unexplainable. The next day, she drew a picture of her dream and showed it to me. Amazingly, the drawing depicted Elephant Rock."

"You should have taken the picture to the police first," the senator said.

"All I was doing yesterday was comparing the picture that she had drawn to Elephant Rock."

"Even if it meant going to a crime scene all alone? Without anyone's permission or approval?" the senator inquired with a slight raise in tone.

"I felt I had to go, but I'm sorry I didn't talk to you about it beforehand, Uncle Thomas. It's just that there's no way this girl could have known about Janet Troy. The news had just come out in the papers, which she hadn't seen. She's never been to Elephant Rock. All I needed to do was to check and see if what she had drawn was actually the murder scene." Peter's frustration grew as his uncle's frown deepened. "What's the big deal, anyway? It's not like they arrested me and threw me into the slammer so that the senator's nephew could make headlines all over the country."

Uncle Thomas looked at Peter and said with a sigh, "They found the girl's bag on our property. If they were to connect our family with that crime, even in speculation, it could ruin my campaign—let alone my career and our lives."

Peter was shocked. The last thing he'd ever wanted to do was put the people he loved and respected most in jeopardy. "I am so sorry, Uncle Thomas," he said sincerely. "I didn't know. If I had, I would never have gotten mixed up in all this. I had this wild hunch, and I thought I was doing something important—something that might help the case."

Aunt Beth took his hand and squeezed it.

"I understand," Uncle Thomas said finally, relieving Peter of the pressure to justify his actions and to convey to him that he still cared.

"If you have any more revelations, contact the FBI agent on the case," Uncle Thomas said.

"You mean Agent Bines?" Peter felt his face growing warm.

"I see you've already met her," Aunt Beth commented.

"Yes—she was the one who found me while I was exploring Elephant Rock yesterday," Peter replied, not wanting to discuss the embarrassing details.

"Well, good, then," Aunt Beth said. Peter was grateful to her for believing his explanation without batting an eye.

"Now, Peter, would you like to stay for dinner? I made your favorite dish."

He grinned at his aunt. She always was one step ahead of him. It was almost as though she could read his mind.

"You bet," he said as he stood up. He wouldn't miss one of Aunt Beth's wonderful, hearty meals.

"Would you like a beer?" Uncle Thomas asked with a small smile.

"You know I don't like beer." Peter grinned. "But a scotch on the rocks … that I wouldn't mind."

{CHAPTER FORTY-THREE}

Saturday

"Have a nice evening," the store clerk called out as the slaaf exited the small medical-supply store.

"You too," the slaaf said with a small nod.

In the parking lot, he stowed his new instruments in the trunk, then drove out of town and into the woods, where his next project awaited him. He rolled down his window to let in the refreshing breeze. The sun had almost set. By the time he reached his destination, it would be dark. Darkness was always ideal for his ventures into the wilderness.

The slaaf stepped out of the car into pitch darkness, surrounded by trees and the night sounds of crickets and nocturnal rodents rustling through the underbrush. He collected a flashlight and duffel bag from the trunk and slammed it shut. Then he found the head of a deer trail and followed it into the woods toward the live trap he had set, looking for telltale signs of recent wildlife activity. He spotted some scat and, nearby, some long, narrow footprints: a fox.

The slaaf moved through the bushes and found the trap. He pointed the flashlight toward it, surveying his caged prize. Indeed, it was a handsome red fox with an elongated snout and long, pointed ears. The slaaf stepped closer and admired its full orange coat and hallmark white-tipped tail. The animal turned around, looking for an escape. It grew more restless as he came closer, finally freezing in fear.

But the slaaf had no trouble persuading the fox to eat the meat he laced with hemlock, a poison that would slowly paralyze it. When it shuddered and finally died of asphyxiation caused by paralysis of the respiratory muscles, he took it from the trap by its tail and flung it over his shoulder.

It took the slaaf half an hour to reach the boathouse on the shores of Willow Lake. That night's sacrifice brought only a slight feeling of relief. It was when he laid the body out for Anansi that he felt the anxiety ebb, as though Anansi had backed away, buying the slaaf more time on earth.

He left the tools on the table, covered with blood and fluid. His hands were relatively clean, thanks to skill and practice. The table itself remained soiled, but he was always afraid to disturb it. It seemed sacrilegious, and the last thing he wanted to do was anger Anansi. The evidence lying about made him a little nervous … but then again, decades had passed without any trouble. The boathouse was a safe place, protected from bad luck, curses, and prying eyes.

He left the boathouse and trekked around the lake toward the woods. The sky had cleared, and the heavens shone with stars. He gazed up as he walked, wondering if he could catch a glimpse of Anansi. It was a perfect night for stargazing; neither the moon nor the light pollution blurred the picture of the heavens.

Deep in the woods, he looked around and found an appropriate area to place the remains of his sacrifice. It was only after the slaaf had completely laid out the fox that he felt satisfied with his offering to Anansi. His anxiety levels had dropped; now he was free to go home. He looked at his exhibit to make sure he had arranged everything properly before heading back into the woods. It was almost midnight, and he was exhausted.

He walked slowly through the woods back to his car. Within no time, he was back in his car, cruising toward town. His mind was calmer, and his emotions were at bay.

{CHAPTER FORTY-FOUR}

Saturday

It was five minutes to eleven as Sheetal made her rounds on the unit. All the children were fast asleep, and her footsteps echoed in the stillness as she walked down the hallway. The night nurse was busy reading a magazine in the nurses' station, and the only other staff members present were the mental-health associates monitoring those children on sleep observation. At this point, only two children on the unit were being monitored at night, and Naya was one of them.

Sheetal walked up to Naya's room and stood next to the MHA who sat at the door. She stood there silently for a moment, and the MHA smiled in acknowledgment that Naya was having a good night so far. No one said a word for fear of waking her up.

Just as Sheetal was stepping away from the door, she saw Naya sit up in her bed. The MHA who was watching her instinctively stood up.

Sheetal whispered, "It's all right," and stopped the MHA from entering the room. "Let's see what she does!" she exclaimed softly. This was a perfect opportunity to witness a nocturnal phenomenon firsthand.

Sheetal and the MHA stood motionless and watched Naya as she sat upright in the bed. For about a minute, the little girl just stared straight ahead. Then, suddenly, she turned around, stood up, and squatted, facing the window that was next to her bed. The partially open blinds let in some yellow fluorescent light from the street lamp outside.

From where Sheetal stood, she could see Naya's face glow with a golden radiance as the yellow light shone on her. She looked to Sheetal like a little Indian princess.

Sheetal tiptoed a little closer to Naya, easing silently through the doorway. She could see that Naya was speaking as though she were having a conversation with somebody.

Sheetal advanced until she stood right next to Naya's bed. She could now hear more clearly what Naya was saying. She strained her ears and bent closer to hear what Naya said. She waved her hand in front of Naya's face with no response. It was clear that Naya didn't perceive the motion of her hands.

Sheetal gazed at Naya in disbelief. She had never seen a sleeping child look so awake. Naya's eyes focused on her, but they didn't see her; they saw someone else. Gooseflesh rippled on Sheetal's arms. What, exactly, was she witnessing here tonight?

"Is this your room?" Sheetal heard Naya say in what appeared to be a one-sided conversation.

"I can see your elephant outside."

"I like your bed—it's very soft."

"Sure. Your room smells like flowers."

"Janet, what do you want?"

"How can I help you?"

"Who is the big, bad man?"

"Like what?"

"Why not? That's not fair."

"I won't be scared."

"Yes."

Sheetal watched Naya lie down. She appeared to still be talking, but her speech was inaudible. Naya was much calmer than she had been during the previous night's episode.

The MHA resumed her position next to Naya's door. Sheetal hurried back to the nurses' station, so that she could jot down Naya's words while they were fresh in her mind. She knew Peter would be appreciative of all the information she could gather. This was definitely one of the most interesting children she had come across during her rotation on the unit.

*   *   *   *

Naya found herself in a violet-colored room. She saw Janet standing next to a bed that was draped with colorful sheets. She walked to the bed and squatted on it, feeling the softness of the sheets.

Janet stood silently looking at Naya. This made Naya a little uncomfortable; she decided to start a conversation.

"Is this your room?" Naya asked Janet.

"Yes," Janet replied flatly.

"I can see your elephant outside," Naya said, peering out the window next to the bed.

"I take him everywhere I go," Janet replied.

"I like your bed—it's very soft," Naya offered, feeling the velvety sheets. The fabric reminded her of the sheets on her bed at home. The hospital sheets were not as smooth.

"Can I sit next to you?" Janet asked.

"Sure. Your room smells like flowers," Naya said remembering her previous meeting with Janet.

Janet climbed onto the bed and sat next to Naya. The two of them stared out the window for a moment.

"Janet, what do you want?" Naya asked out of curiosity.

"You're my friend—and I need your help," Janet said solemnly.

"How can I help you?" Naya couldn't imagine how she could be of assistance.

"You need to tell the doctor about the big, bad man."

"Who is the big, bad man?"

"I don't know," Janet said, shaking her head. "But he does lots of bad things."

"Like what?"

"I can't tell you," Janet said reluctantly.

"Why not? That's not fair," Naya whined.

"Because they're scary," Janet said.

"I won't be scared," Naya said, trying to put on a strong façade.

"Would you like to lie down next to me?" Janet asked, changing the subject.

"Yeah," Naya replied.

The two girls lay down next to each other. Naya wondered why Janet only wanted Dr. Gram to help her. She was a little scared to ask.

"Why the doctor?" Naya whispered into Janet's ear.

"Because he knows what the big, bad man has done," Janet whispered back.

{CHAPTER FORTY-FIVE}

Sunday

Peter was up at the crack of dawn. It was still dark in his room. He usually felt entitled to sleep in on Sundays, but he found himself unable to drift back to sleep, thanks to habit. He lay there thinking about the events of the past three days. Until now, he had thought of psychological phenomena in a very straightforward fashion. He wondered how Naya was holding up and if she had had any more episodes. That thought prompted him to get out of bed. He knew Sheetal was on call, and she would probably be awake by now. He turned to the nightstand to pick up his phone, then changed his mind. He decided to first get ready, get some breakfast, and then call Sheetal before going to the hospital. He needed to check in with Naya personally.

He shaved and showered, and since it was Sunday and he was making an off-hour visit to the hospital, he decided to wear a pair of jeans and a casual sweater. He stood at the mirror, adjusting his long-sleeved, cream-colored sweater. He obsessed a little over his thick hair, attempting to control his mop of curls. The piercing blue eyes that gazed back at him from the medicine cabinet looked a little tired.

Peter went over to the kitchen and opened the refrigerator only to find a few leftovers from the previous week. He needed to go to the local market, but only after his stopover at the unit.

He picked up the telephone, tapped in Sheetal's pager number, and waited for her to reply.

"Sheetal, it's Peter."

"I know," Sheetal answered.

"You busy?"

"Very. Good-bye … just kidding," Sheetal joked.

Peter got straight to the point. "Anything interesting happening with Naya?"

"Oh, there's lots to tell," Sheetal answered, and this time, she wasn't being sarcastic.

"I'll be right over—did you have breakfast yet?" Peter inquired.

"No, not yet."

"I'll meet you in the cafeteria in thirty."

"See you soon."

Peter found Sheetal in the cafeteria at a table, already eating.

"What, you couldn't wait for me?" he joked.

"I was starving," she said, smiling.

Peter grabbed a tray and ran over to the buffet line, where he picked up an apple, a bowl of cereal, and a glass of orange juice.

"How was your evening?" Sheetal asked enthusiastically as he sat down. "I hope you liked the musical."

"I loved it—that was something to see," Peter replied with a huge smile. "Thanks for the recommendation."

"Did you take a date?" Sheetal asked slyly.

"What do you think?" Peter countered, and Sheetal slumped in over-dramatic disappointment.

"Peter! You're going to die a lonely old man."

"Yes, but I'm going to die a lonely old man who has saved thousands of poor souls from the depths of mental illness. That's something, right?"

"Hmm," Sheetal mused, crunching on her cereal. She swallowed and finally said, "Well, if you can't cure your own insanity, at least you're willing to help others."

"Ha, ha," Peter said. "Okay, time to change the subject. So what's been happening on the unit?" He wasn't just trying to distract Sheetal; he was really dying to know.

"You have one hell of a patient. She kept me awake most of the night."

"Tell me more," Peter said impatiently.

"Let me begin with Friday night first," Sheetal began, then explained the sequence of events.

"Did Naya say anything the next morning?" Peter asked.

"She drew a couple of pictures that she wants to show you. She wouldn't show anyone else. Then she had another episode last night—though it was a lot milder," Sheetal said as she slurped her coffee.

"Last night, I actually heard a part of the conversation she had," Sheetal said with a big grin, knowing Peter would die for that information.

"And?" Peter prodded, unable to mask his enthusiasm.

Sheetal held out her hand, as if for a bribe. "Just kidding," she said with a laugh and went on to describe what she had observed the night before. She pulled from her trouser pocket a copy of the progress note that she had written. "Here—see for yourself," she said, handing over the paper to Peter.

Peter read the one-sided conversation aloud. "Very interesting," he commented.

Sheetal bent over the table, trying to see the note. "Make any sense to you?"

"It might, but only after I speak to Naya."

"Are you going to see her now?"

"You bet—can I keep this?" Peter said folding the paper.

Sheetal nodded. "It's your copy, and you can do with it what you please."

"You're such a good comrade," Peter said gratefully. He thought again how glad he was to be teamed up with Sheetal. She would be a great asset to whichever hospital in India she chose to work in.

"Peter …" Sheetal paused. "It's not normal, what's happening to her. Is it?" Sheetal toyed with the bottom of her waist-length braid with her hands, and Peter realized with surprise that she was tense.

"No," he said quietly. "I don't really think it is."

"I've never seen anything like that," she continued. "She was … well, it sounds crazy, but I really believed that she was talking to someone. How can a dream be that vivid?"

"When is a dream not a dream?" Peter asked rhetorically, smiling slightly.

"When it's a … vision?" Sheetal tried to change the punch line to suit their situation.

"Good answer," Peter said. "Even if I can't believe it myself yet."

As they walked back toward the unit, Peter recounted his visit to the Iyengars as they walked through the hospital corridors.

"Have you heard of a Seeked One before?" Peter asked Sheetal, fascinated by the concept of preordained destiny.

"I think I have. It's up there with all the other types of fortune-telling, like palmistry and astrology."

"What do you think about that stuff?"

"In India, a lot of people lead their lives and make major decisions based on such information. For example, a friend of mine said that a prominent politician in her town drove his son to become a politician just because a fortune-teller told him that he would be the next prime minister of India. The poor chap had to let go of all his dreams of becoming a pilot."

"I'm not sure what Mr. Iyengar's interpretations mean."

"You'll have to wait and see. Only time will tell. Did he mention anything about you getting a date before you turn forty?"

Peter ignored her friendly ribbing, as usual. "Have you ever been to a fortune-teller?" he asked curiously.

Sheetal burst out laughing. "Only to see if my horoscope was compatible with my boyfriend's."

Peter smiled. "The Iyengars said that they would visit Naya sometime soon. Let me know if they come by this evening. I'd like to talk to them once more."

"No problem," Sheetal said, swiping her card to enter the unit. "Let me know what happens after you speak to Naya, and if I don't see you again, we'll catch up tomorrow."

Peter and Sheetal parted as they approached the nurses' station. Sheetal had to finish documenting notes in the charts. Peter walked down toward

Naya's room, wondering what she would have to say about her most recent experience with Janet.

{CHAPTER FORTY-SIX}

Sunday

Everson woke with a splitting headache. The previous night, he had used the last of his cocaine, trying to forget about the trouble he was in. Now, he felt as if he were caught in an ever-tightening vise. On the one hand, he owed Arcus a large sum of money; on the other, he needed the cocaine that he could no longer afford. He was sure that he wouldn't get any today. He needed to manage his emotional rollercoaster on his own.

He needed to talk to Evelyn, just to hear her voice. She always made him feel better. He dialed her number.

"Hello?" The welcoming tone in Evelyn's deep, throaty voice told him she had looked at her caller ID.

"Hi, baby." Everson forced himself to take a deep breath.

"Is something wrong?" she asked. "You sound weird, and after the other night—"

"No, no, nothing's wrong. I just … I miss you already, that's all."

Her laughter tinkled through the phone speaker. "Well, hey, all right. I miss you too, babe."

Everson couldn't keep himself from releasing a ragged sigh. "I love you so much."

"I love you too," Evelyn said. "But I gotta be honest. You're really starting to freak me out. Are you sure everything's all right? You know I love hearing how you feel about me … but I can tell when something's wrong. You can lie to me if you want, but you can't hide from me."

Everson's heart leapt into his throat, but he forced a laugh. "Oh, all right, you got me. I think I'm catching Peter's damn cold." He sniffled for effect, which was easy enough, considering that he truly felt as if he could cry. "I don't know why I even hang out with that guy."

"Oh, I see," Evelyn teased. "So you're wanting to make sure you've got your chicken-soup chef all buttered up, huh? I knew you wanted something!"

Everson chuckled along with her, even though he'd never felt less like laughing in his entire life. "I can't fool you, honey. I don't even know why I try. So what do you say? Are you going to take care of me? … If I've really caught Peter's deathly germs, I mean?"

"Don't be silly. You know I will," Evelyn promised. "Whatever you need. You don't even need to suck up, though apparently that won't stop you from trying."

Everson rubbed his face with his hands in despair. "Thank you, baby," he whispered.

"What's that?"

"Nothing, I was just clearing my throat. It's starting to get sore, I think. I should probably let you go."

"Well, call me if you need anything. Anything at all," Evelyn stressed.

"I will," Everson lied, feeling like the scum of the earth.

After he hung up, he stared at his phone for several moments. His next call would be far less pleasant—and the person on the other end wasn't likely to be anywhere near as sympathetic as Evelyn had just been.

He dialed Arcus.

"What is it now?" Arcus asked bluntly.

"I need more time," he replied.

"No."

"Please, I'm begging you. I don't know what to do." Everson felt his chest tightening. Ironically, his first automatic thought was that he should find his dealer and buy something to take the edge off. *Old habits die hard,* Everson thought bitterly. *Unfortunately, addicts die a lot more easily. Oh God, help me.*

"I can't help you, man," Arcus was saying.

"Shit, this is fucking insane!" Everson said, his tone creeping higher.

"One more day. That's it."

Everson breathed a sigh of relief. "You got to help me come up with something."

"Don't count on it," Arcus said coldly.

"Thanks," Everson said sarcastically and hung up the phone.

Everson sat holding his head. It only pounded harder. He was too ashamed to ask his girlfriend; besides, he knew that this would end their relationship. He was going to have to ask Peter to help him. If Peter couldn't lend him the money, maybe he could get it from his uncle, the senator. Everson went into the bathroom and popped in a couple of pain-killers, hoping to ease his crippling headache. He had to find Peter. Time was running out.

{CHAPTER FORTY-SEVEN}

Sunday

Naya heard a knock on her bedroom door. She turned around to see Peter standing at the door. Squealing in surprise, she immediately leaped out of her chair and ran to him. "I thought you weren't gonna be here until tomorrow!" she exclaimed joyfully.

Peter stood at the door, glad to see Naya looking so bright and lively. "Well, technically, I'm not supposed to be, but I was in the area and decided to see how you were doing," he replied, altering the truth.

Naya held onto his hand and tugged him into the room. "I want to show you something," she said with a sparkle in her eye.

Peter followed Naya to her desk and watched her take a seat. On the desk was a folder with her name written in large capital letters. The ink glittered in the sunlight.

"I see you have a folder of your own," Peter pointed out.

"Yup—now I can keep all my drawings in one place," Naya said proudly.

"That reminds me—I still have one of your pictures, but I left it at home," Peter said, hoping Naya didn't miss it.

"You can bring it tomorrow," Naya said graciously.

"That's very nice of you, Naya. Thank you for understanding," Peter said, feeling a little guilty. He mentally berated himself for the lapse in memory.

Naya smiled coyly, clearly pleased at his gratitude.

"Did you draw any new pictures?" Peter asked.

"That's what I wanted to show you," Naya said with excitement. She was always proud of her drawings, which certainly worked in Peter's favor.

"Why don't you show me?" Peter asked, settling onto her bed, moving Noodle carefully out of the way.

Naya carried the folder over to Peter, then hopped onto the bed next to him. She carefully opened the folder, revealing a few sheets of paper inside.

Peter stole a peek inside the half-open folder. "Wow, Naya! More than one picture," he commented. "I see you've been working hard."

Naya beamed and ran her petite fingers through the stack. "I wanted to show you this one." She removed a very colorful picture and placed it on her lap.

"Can you tell me what the picture is about?"

"This is Janet's house," Naya explained. "There's tall green grass all around."

"Does Janet live alone?"

"Uh-huh," Naya said, pointing to the large, red house that had only one large door and no windows.

"When did you have this dream?" Peter inquired.

"I think this one was on … Friday night," Naya said, trying to remember the exact day.

Peter thought Janet's house looked more like a red barn.

"I wonder what the house looks like on the inside," Peter commented idly, meeting her eyes.

"I have a picture of that too!" Naya said, glancing through her folder and pulling out another sheet of paper.

Peter saw that Naya had drawn a rather tall bed in the center of what seemed to be a field of flowers. At one end was a red wall with a large, red door.

"Hmm, that's very interesting. She has lots of flowers in her house," Peter pointed out.

"She told me they were sunflowers."

"Who's sitting on the bed?" Peter asked, looking at the two figures.

Naya moved her finger over to the one sitting on the right. "This one is me," she said, then moved her finger over to the other. "This is Janet."

"What did you talk to her about?" Peter gently prodded.

Naya's mood quickly turned sullen. "She told me about the big, bad man that left her there all alone."

"That must have been scary for you," Peter empathized. He wasn't just saying that to placate Naya; such a dream surely must have been terrifying.

"She asked me to ask you a question," Naya said, surprising Peter momentarily.

"What question?"

"Knock, knock."

"Who's there?" asked Peter.

Naya leaned over and whispered in his ear.

"Who is that?" asked Peter.

Naya shrugged. "Janet said once I told you that, you'd believe me." Naya's doubt was evident in her voice.

"Believe you about …"

"Trying to help Janet."

"With what?"

"I don't know," Naya said, shrugging again.

Peter watched Naya as her affect changed. She chewed on a fingernail, appearing a little frightened.

"Did she scare you?" Peter asked softly.

"Yes … she wouldn't let me out of the house," Naya said sadly, "But she was friendlier yesterday."

"You dreamed of her again?"

"Last night. I remember a little."

"What did she say?"

"She asked me to tell you about the big, bad man."

"Does she know who the big, bad man is?"

Naya shook her head vigorously from side to side. "But she said that you knew what the big, bad man had done."

"I do?" Peter asked, astonished.

Naya sat silently. Peter knew that this was emotionally taxing her. But she had discussed this with surprising maturity compared to other children her age.

"Do you want to show me some of your other pictures?" Peter asked, deciding to shift the focus away from Janet.

"Sure. See?" Naya removed other drawings and spent a few minutes describing them to Peter, who patiently listened. Patience had always been one of his virtues; working with children, he needed a lot of it.

"Can I take these two pictures?" Peter asked, pointing to the first drawings. "I promise I'll keep them safe and bring them back with the other one."

Naya handed them over to him without a second thought. She clearly had utmost faith that Peter would be able to help her; he was simultaneously touched at her trust and anxious about what on earth he could do to help.

"It's time for lunch—everybody line up," both of them heard a staff member announce in the hallway. Naya placed her folder back on her desk, and Peter escorted her out to line up with the rest of the children.

Once Naya had joined the lunch line, Peter went to the nurses' station. He sat there by himself, staring at the pictures Naya had drawn. They were well-drawn depictions of her dream, but even their detail couldn't clarify what was going on. Nothing seemed to make any sense. Why would Naya dream of a dead girl? Why would that girl expect Peter in particular to know what the bad man had done? It was pretty obvious that anyone who read the paper knew what that man had done. It seemed as if Janet must have been referring to something else.

"Why would a dead girl want my help?" Peter said aloud. *People will think I'm insane if I disclose this to anybody,* he thought silently.

Peter decided it was time to call Agent Leia Bines before he did something that could get him in trouble. He pulled his phone from his belt, but it rang before he could dial the number. The caller ID displayed Everson's name.

"Yes, this is Peter."

"You have a few minutes to spare today?" Everson asked.

"Maybe a little later," Peter said, looking at his watch.

"Cool … when?"

"I can meet you for a cup of coffee in the afternoon, if that's what you want. Problems with Evelyn?" Peter asked.

"I'll tell you then," Everson said with some urgency in his voice.

Peter hung up with Everson and dialed the number that Leia had left for him. *Maybe she might have some clues about what's going on*, he thought to himself. *It can't hurt.*

"This Dr. Peter Gram calling. I need to speak to you rather immediately. Please call me as soon as you get this message. Thank you," Peter told her voice mail.

Now all he could do was wait.

{CHAPTER FORTY-EIGHT}

Sunday

Leia sat waiting for Peter at the hospital coffee shop. She had been surprised and intrigued by his urgent message, deciding to meet him immediately.

Leia had only been waiting a few moments when Peter walked in. She stood up and shook his hand as he sat down.

"It's nice to see you under better circumstances," Peter said with a smile made overly broad by embarrassment. "You didn't bring your cuffs this time, did you?"

"Always," Leia said. "But this time I think I can trust you. What would you like to talk about?" Peter mused that a federal agent could probably always be trusted to come straight to the point.

Peter felt as if Leia had turned a giant interrogation spotlight on him with the directness of her question. "It's complicated—I don't know where to begin," he told her.

"Start at the point that's least confusing," Leia suggested.

"Remember the little girl that I spoke to you about that day by the rock? Her name is Naya, remember?"

"Yeah—the one who drew the picture."

"She had another dream," Peter said, taking out the two drawings from his pocket. He laid the first one on the table facing Leia and flattened it out, gauging her reaction as he did so. Leia leaned over the drawings, her full lips pursed questioningly.

"And?" she finally asked.

"This is a drawing of where she met Janet in her dream—"

"Wait a second." Leia's eyes narrowed. "Did Naya mention Janet's name specifically?"

Peter nodded. "Yeah. And yes, I know—it's crazy to think that Naya came up with the name on her own, but she did; the newspapers hadn't even been delivered yet when she had the dream."

Leia looked skeptical, but Peter had expected as much. Maybe it wouldn't matter what Leia thought about where Naya got her information; maybe the information itself would be compelling enough. He certainly hoped so.

Peter pressed onward. "She told me this was Janet's house. But it's a little weird for an intelligent girl like Naya to draw a picture of a house without any windows, but rather, just one large door."

Peter eyed Leia uncomfortably. Everything about Naya was turning out to be out of the realm of modern psychiatry. No medical explanation existed for how Naya managed to glean such details about the case, and Peter knew it. He only hoped that Leia wouldn't require one. "The drawing looks more like a barn to me," Leia pointed out.

"That was my first thought too," remarked Peter. "Do you really believe that Naya's dreams could actually mean something?"

"Anything is possible," Leia said. "It seems crazy, of course, but this wouldn't be the first time something crazy happened on one of my cases. It's best not to rule anything out."

"Do you think that ..." Peter hated sounding insane to a beautiful woman, but his need to find the truth won out, as usual. "Do you think that any of this is really relevant—that she's witnessing some hidden reality? Could the person who did this have any association with a red barn?"

"Now that's an interesting interpretation," Leia said as she looked at the features of Naya's red house. She shook her head and chuckled, and Peter didn't need his psychology background to understand that it was a laugh of weary disbelief, not of amusement. "Hey, anything's possible, right? The killer could certainly be using such a place to carry out his killings."

"This is the other picture that Naya drew," Peter said, presenting his second piece of questionable evidence.

"Another barn, with tall grass all around it," Leia said. She leaned back from the table, and for a moment, she and Peter simply surveyed each other. Nervous with the knowledge that what he had just offered Leia was hardly the stuff of criminal prosecution, Peter willed himself not to flinch. He needed to be calm, steady—not for himself, but for a pair of little girls who needed someone to speak for them. Leia regarded him with similar stoicism, and he noticed involuntarily for the hundredth time how pretty she was, with her coppery hair and hazel eyes.

Leia was the first to speak. "In any case," she said slowly, almost regretfully, "this is the only lead we have so far—if we can call a couple of drawings made by a sleepwalker a lead. I can't believe I flew out here to investigate a little kid's drawings, but I have to say that it just might be worthwhile to see if we can actually find such a structure anywhere near Elephant Rock." She shook her head and laughed that dry laugh again. "Hey, you never know, right? Do you recall having seen any such structure anytime? You know this area pretty well."

"Just a single red barn? Not really, but there are a number of private properties surrounding Elephant Rock that are pretty damn big. Having wandered around those parts as a kid, I can certainly attest to that."

Leia steepled her long, delicate fingers in front of her nose for a moment, contemplating everything Peter had divulged.

"This is going to be such a stretch that it's more of a leap," Leia said, "but getting a second aerial view might be beneficial. Would it be possible for me to take the barn drawing with me?"

Peter was hesitant to part with the original drawing, but he knew he had to. "I'll need it back by the morning before I go to the hospital. I have to return it to Naya—I promised her I would, and I don't want to lose her trust as a patient."

Leia took the picture, then said, "I'll meet you first thing in the morning right here—at seven thirty, if that's all right with you." She smiled at Peter's obvious anxiety. "Don't worry, Peter. I'll keep the drawing safe." she promised.

Peter forced himself to relax and offer her a smile. "Sounds good. Let me know if you find anything, would you? I'd love to know for sure whether I'm a quack or not." Leia grinned. "Oh, I don't know ... you could just be a quack who happens to be right this time." Her teasing tone turned serious with startling rapidity, as if she was embarrassed at her sudden lack of professionalism. "Anyway, you have my number if anything else comes up." She folded and tucked the picture into her jacket pocket. "And, Peter ..."

"Yeah?"

"Thanks for the tip." Leia smiled again, then said good-bye. Leia drove back to the precinct to meet José and to get the police helicopter. It was time to go for a second ride; the need to take another look at the landscape nagged at her. As reluctant as she was to act upon the lead from a seven-year-old's artwork, her hunch persisted. *Besides,* she thought ruefully, *there isn't much else to investigate!* She decided that she had nothing to lose—well, except for the cost of a helicopter ride, and that was a fair gamble for the chance to solve a child's murder.

A tentative optimism took hold of Leia, and she pressed the gas pedal closer to the floor.

{CHAPTER FORTY-NINE}

Sunday

José and Leia buckled themselves into the seats of the helicopter, and José tapped the pilot on the shoulder as an "OK" signal. The engines whirred to life, and within a few minutes, Leia was once again hovering far above her crime scene.

Leia held the paper that Peter had given her, then leaned over and stared hard at the landscape around Elephant Rock, trying to spot anything that resembled a solitary red barn. Elephant Rock passed under them, and the pilot veered over to a couple of properties that no one had scrutinized much during their first flight. After making a couple of passes without detecting anything noteworthy, disappointment drove away Leia's optimism, leaving only mounting sheepishness in its wake. She was starting to feel foolish. What was she doing, hovering far above the ground and clutching the drawing of a child currently locked in a psych ward?

Maybe I should have my head examined, Leia thought, smirking a little despite herself.

The helicopter whizzed over the senator's ranch and the large adjoining barns. None of those barns were red, and after circling the adjoining areas for a few minutes, Leia concluded that she had seen every last barn the senator owned.

Leia kept an eye on Willow Lake as it rippled by far below. *Must be nice, owning that kind of lakefront property*, she thought. *I'll bet you can do some great boating here during the summer.* Sure enough, she saw a couple of boathouses in the distance. Leia sat up straighter. She hadn't thought of it before, but a boathouse could resemble a barn if viewed from a certain angle. She quickly directed the pilot to circle Willow Lake. Sure enough, a couple of boathouses along the lake's shoreline could pass for the building in Naya's dreams. After hovering over the lake, Leia and José eliminated a few structures based on architectural or decorative details.

Two structures closely resembled drawing. One was situated on an apple orchard, and the other sat on a smaller ranch. José noted the two locations on a map of the area, then signaled the pilot to return to base.

Stretch of reasoning or no, José and Leia were so desperate for a break in the case that they couldn't contain their excitement. They clambered out of the helicopter and literally hit the ground running, in a hurry to notify Lieutenant Andrew about their findings. The lieutenant didn't seem very happy about the fact that their prime lead had originated from a child's dream, but in any case, he knew that was the only clue they had at the moment.

"What the hell?" he asked over his speakerphone, and Leia could just imagine him throwing up his hands and shrugging. "What else do we have to do all day? I can't spend all my time on speeding tickets."

The lieutenant dispatched two units to pick them up at the heliport. One unit was to escort Leia to the orchard boathouse, and the other took José to the ranch boathouse.

Leia rode with the two officers that she had met on the first day at Elephant Rock, Jeremy and Tony. They briefed her about the owner of the orchard as the police car sped through town.

The cruiser slowed considerably as it drove through a tall set of gates. Leia gazed out the window as the car rolled along a narrow, winding road that eventually turned into the circular driveway in front of a small, white cottage. Leia and the officers stepped out of the cruiser. She instructed the officers to stay by the car while she went and spoke to whoever was at home—preferably Mr. Deed, the owner.

Leia walked to the cottage and up the porch stairs to the front door. She pushed the bell button and waited for a few minutes. Just as she raised her hand to push the doorbell for a second time, she heard the deadbolt slide open. In front of her stood a frail old man who looked as if he was in his late eighties.

"Hello, are you Mr. Deed?" Leia asked him.

"Well, if I weren't, I would certainly want to be now," Mr. Deed joked cheerfully, looking surprised to have company. "What brings such a pretty young lady to my doorstep?"

Leia noticed Mr. Deed squinting through his thick eyeglasses, trying to see the people who stood not too far behind. His expression became less gregarious when he saw the two men behind her. His shoulders hunched forward as he looked up at her with new respect.

"Oh, so this official-type business, then?" he asked. "My apologies."

As infuriating as Leia found the objectification of women, she found it impossible to be annoyed with this elderly man, who really just seemed friendly. Of course, she hadn't become a federal agent because she trusted people. She scrutinized him carefully.

"I'm FBI agent Leia Bines." Leia gestured behind her. "And those are my colleagues." She flashed him both her smile and her badge to set him at ease. Mr. Deed extended his hand with a small smile and glanced at the other two officers. "Would you like to come in?" he invited Leia. "I'd prefer if we spoke inside. Even just standing wears me out. Be good to those knees of yours, doll, or you'll regret it, let me tell you." He peered around Leia. "You can even bring in your boyfriends, if you want."

"Yes, thank you," Leia said, ever the professional. "And I think I'll leave my colleagues behind, but I appreciate the invitation." Mr. Deed beckoned for her to follow, then leaned on his cane as he hobbled slowly down the corridor into the living room.

"Would you like to join me for a cup of tea? I was just pouring myself one," Mr. Deed asked with a crackle in his voice.

"That would be perfect," Leia said, basking in the warmth and coziness of the cottage as she sat on an old, comfortable couch. Across from her was a handsomely carved stone fireplace. A small flame danced there to the rhythm of a cool draft. The walls were covered with ornate, flowery wallpaper that had peeled off in a few corners.

"Do you live by yourself?" Leia sensed a hint of solitude between these walls. "For the past fifteen years," Mr. Deed replied as he poured Leia a cup of freshly brewed tea. "So you understand, you've got to forgive me if I was a little forward. You can't blame a guy for trying, even if he's four times your age, right?" Mr. Deed laughed heartily, and Leia was a little irritated to discover that she wanted to laugh as well. Good grief—she was getting soft these days. "So how can I help you?" he finally asked.

"Have you been following the news lately?"

"I may be old, but I'm not senile," Mr. Deed said with a grin. "In fact, just because I'm old doesn't mean that—"

"Have you heard about the killing at Elephant Rock?"

"Sure did. Read about it in the papers."

"We have a reason to believe that the killer might have been using a red barn or a boathouse. We've looked around the vicinity of Elephant Rock and have found two possible matches."

"So how do I fit in? Am I a suspect now?" Mr. Deed joked.

Leia fought the urge to roll her eyes, instead smiling politely and sipping her tea. The strong aroma tickled her nose. "Your boathouse is one of the buildings that matches our description."

"The old boathouse … I see," Mr. Deed said, nodding. "I haven't used that rotting old thing in more than thirty years."

"Do you know if anybody else uses it?"

"If they do, they're sneaky. It's been locked up for ages."

"Can we take a look inside, if you don't mind?"

"Not at all, if this will help your case."

"Thank you for your hospitality," Leia said, placing her empty cup on a wooden chest that doubled as a table.

"Can you find your way to the boathouse?" Mr. Deed asked. "Much as you'd like an escort, I hate to step out in the middle of my teatime. We old folks love our routines." He winked.

Leia stood up. "I sure can—just tell me which way to go."

"All you have to do is walk around the house and walk through the apple trees 'til you find the lake," Mr. Deed directed.

"Is the boathouse locked?"

"I think it is … but I don't remember what happened to the key. That's not unusual, trust me. Hell, I don't remember what happened ten minutes ago."

"We might have to break open the lock and have it replaced, if that's all right with you."

"It's fine by me. At least then I'll have a key," Mr. Deed said, sipping his second cup of tea.

Leia thanked him once again, then rejoined the two officers outside.

"Do you have a crowbar, by any chance?" Leia asked Tony.

"I think I do," Tony replied a bit too eagerly. Leia's visit with Mr. Deed had clearly left the two officers restless. Tony popped the trunk of the cruiser then rummaged through the equipment that they always carried, just in case.

"Here we go," Tony said, holding a steel crowbar.

The two officers followed Leia through the trees. Once they were closer to the lake, they could see the boathouse. The three of them came to a halt a few meters from it. A faint, but foul odor surrounded the air around. The boathouse looked just as Naya had drawn it, although no tall grass grew around it as it did in her picture.

As Leia had expected, the building was locked. She noticed that the lock had been used recently and didn't appear to be thirty years old.

"Break it open, Tony," she instructed.

Tony stuck one end of the crowbar into the loop of the lock, then busted the lock apart with a grunt and a yank. The broken lock thudded to the ground. He kicked the pieces aside and heaved the door ajar.

Leia unholstered her gun and signaled Tony to open the door further. Tony pushed the door completely open, letting in enough light to dimly illuminate the interior.

Leia instructed for Tony to guard the door, then waved Jeremy in behind her.

Leia crept forward. The stifling air reeked of decomposing flesh. She clapped a hand to her mouth instinctively, trying not to throw up.

It was that smell—the smell that haunted her nightmares. It was the smell of unsolved crimes in San José, of rats and blood and suffering. Sickening memories accompanied the wave of nausea.

It's not like that this time, she reminded herself. *There's nothing you could have done. Forget it and do your job!*

She forced herself to advance slowly, looking all around her. It was clear by the dust and cobwebs that the place had not been cleaned for a very long time.

However, on the dusty wooden floor, Leia noticed footprints and drag marks.

Somebody's been here recently, she thought. *Like I didn't already know that from the stench.* Sunlight seeped through the rotting walls as she scanned the walls for any clues. She walked in slowly past the boat bay to the far end of the boathouse.

"Look at this," Leia murmured to Jeremy. They stood and surveyed a large, wooden platform. Dotting the surface were small, darkened pieces of flesh. Mottled red and brown streaks coated the top and the sides all the way to the floor.

"Good God!" Jeremy exclaimed. "What happened here?"

"You don't look so good," Leia said. "I think you need some fresh air."

"Yeah," Jeremy blurted and ran out. Leia didn't need to follow him to know that his lunch would promptly appear under one of Mr. Deed's apple trees.

Leia reholstered her gun and snapped on a pair of latex gloves. *A sacrificial chamber—that's what this is*, she thought. She noticed the pile of surgical blades on the table. They were covered with dried blood. It was apparent that the killer had recently used them.

"This is insane," Leia heard Tony say as he walked toward her.

"I hate to jump to conclusions," she said dryly, "But I'm gonna hazard a guess that we might have found the killer's hideout." The handkerchief she held over her nose and mouth muffled her sarcastic tone.

"Look at all these blades—we have a professional here," Tony commented.

Leia picked up one of the steel blades and held it to a shaft of sunlight. The honed edge gleamed in the sun. This was a fine instrument, all right, but no personal inscription graced the handle. Leia hadn't really expected one, but if her perpetrator wanted to leave such a calling card, she certainly would have appreciated it. She returned the knife to its original position and looked around for other artifacts. Leia found a small ceremonial wooden stool and a number of intricately carved animals.

"Lions, elephants, and giraffes—oh my," Leia said. "What went on here, Tony?"

Tony didn't answer her rhetorical question, but she knew they both had a pretty good idea of the grisly events that had transpired in this dark boathouse. Located in a corner were a couple of metal hooks that one would find in a hardware store.

Leia couldn't bear the stench anymore. She signaled to Tony to step out of the boathouse. Tony was more than eager to exit himself. He now understood why Jeremy had vomited all over the grass.

Once outside, both officers gulped fresh air. Jeremy stood nearby, a little embarrassed about his emetic episode.

"We won't tell anyone," Tony kidded with his partner. "Especially since I damn near tossed my own cookies."

"I think we should lie low to see if the killer shows up again," Leia said, returning to the matter at hand.

The two officers looked at each other, then nodded in agreement.

After their stomachs had settled a little, Leia and Tony walked back in for another look. This time, Leia noticed small pieces of fur sticking to the platform. "He's been killing animals too," she pointed out. "He has been performing rituals, just like I thought."

"What about the forensic team? Do I call 'em?"

"We'll wait. Tell José that I'll be sending him some samples for DNA testing." Leia dropped several of the smaller artifacts and blades into baggies.

Once Leia was done collecting the evidence, she handed everything to Tony. "You take these for now. I'll speak to Mr. Deed and ask him if he has any idea who might be using his boathouse."

After walking back to the cottage, Leia flipped open her phone. "José, it's me," Leia spoke into her cell phone. "I think we hit the jackpot, my friend."

"I'm glad you did, because we didn't," José replied. "We'll be there right away."

"See you soon," Leia said, and hung up.

Leia paused a moment and caught her breath, overwhelmed by the revelations of the past few moments. How was it possible that one little girl's dreams had led her here? She was grateful that Peter had come forth with the information. She struggled to reconcile the eerie insight of Naya's dreams with her own logical ideas about reality.

How could a little girl have identified a monster's lair in her sleep? Leia's investigative impulses urged her to get to the bottom of it.

{CHAPTER FIFTY}

Sunday

Everson waited for Peter impatiently at the bookstore coffee shop. Finally, Peter arrived, plopping down wearily in the chair across from his friend.

"I've been really busy today," Peter sighed. "And I still haven't gotten groceries."

"What's been going on?" Everson inquired, pretending to be casual. He hoped Peter wouldn't see the rapid pulse fluttering in his neck.

Peter described his patient's nightly episodes.

"That's some weird stuff," Everson said. "Your kid sounds like a loony tune. Is she from some wealthy, screwed-up family?"

"Maybe wealthy, but definitely not screwed up," Peter said—a bit defensively, Everson thought.

"How long is she going to stay in the hospital?"

"Not too long. I think she'll be discharged very soon—even as soon as tomorrow," Peter disclosed. "Anyway, enough shop talk. What was it that you wanted to talk about? Is it Evelyn?"

"No." Everson plunged ahead without hesitation. "It's just that I need some money. I've gotten myself into a bit of a jam, man."

Peter paused, his expression a little guarded. "How much are we talking about?"

"Well, you know how it is, when you fall a little behind, and you think you can catch up in a few paychecks. But then things just sort of snowball on you—"

"How much?" Peter repeated.

"Close to twenty grand," Everson said, wincing and slouching in his chair.

"Twenty *grand*? As in, two zero? Didn't I give you close to five grand six months ago?"

"I'll give it back to you—with interest," Everson pressed on.

Peter paused for a few seconds. "Look, man, I don't have that kind of money just lying around. I've got school loans, you know. And how is it that you have so much more debt than I do? Your student loans would have been paid off years ago!" He couldn't keep his irritation out of his voice.

Everson looked Peter in the eye and said, "You don't have a girlfriend who spends up all your money. And ... well, it's embarrassing to talk about, but ..."

Peter looked at him expectantly.

"... but I've just made a few really bad investments," Everson finished lamely.

"I'm sorry, but I can't this time," Peter said flatly. "I hate telling you that, but come on—you know I don't have it."

Everson's cheeks burned, and he was glad that his dark skin tone hid his shame and fear. "Oh ... well, all right. Thanks for listening," Everson said. His pulse whirred even faster. What the hell was he going to do?

"I need to get groceries," Peter said, rising from his chair.

"I'll see you in the hospital tomorrow," Everson said, trying to conceal his rising hysteria.

"Okay," Peter said, and he was gone.

{CHAPTER FIFTY-ONE}

Sunday

The slaaf followed Peter from the bookstore to the local grocery store. He had seen Peter in the woods with the FBI agent, and he wanted to know what Peter knew. He watched from a distance as Peter made his purchases and walked out of the store. His heart palpitated, and his hands turned sweaty. The slaaf waited for a couple of minutes before pursuing his quarry on foot. Spying was risky, but the slaaf needed to find out whether the FBI was closing in on him.

The slaaf ran around the block, then peeped around the corner to see if Peter was still visible. He was relieved to see the doctor just a block ahead, walking slowly. Now he would be able to follow him at a safe distance.

The slaaf tailed Peter as he window shopped on his way home.

From a distance, the slaaf watched Peter walk into an apartment complex. He couldn't decide whether he was disappointed or relieved that Peter hadn't met with anybody on the way. His body tensed, unable to accept the idea that nothing was afoot. His desperation for answers only grew more intense.

Maybe the police were corresponding with Peter discreetly.

Peter would be leaving for work in the morning. The slaaf decided to invite himself to a little open house while the doctor was busy at the hospital. The answers could be in Peter's apartment.

{CHAPTER FIFTY-TWO}

Sunday

Mr. and Mrs. Hastings sat with Naya in the family visiting room. They were glad she had adjusted to the unit's routine, but they remained concerned about her nightly episodes. When would their daughter's dreams leave her in peace?

"I waaant tooo gooo hooome," Naya whined to her mother, who was consoling her in her lap.

"Soon, my dear," Mrs. Hastings said with a tear in her eye. It was difficult for even the strongest of parents not to respond the way she did to such a cry. The fair woman looked even more pale than usual as she nervously tugged on her delicate pearl necklace.

"Please, I don't want to stay here anymore. Why do I need to stay here? There's nothing wrong with me!"

Mrs. Hastings couldn't tolerate her daughter's psychological pain and frustration. Given the inconclusive results of Naya's tests, Mrs. Hastings wondered whether she was making her daughter suffer for nothing.

Mrs. Hastings leaned over and spoke softly in her husband's ear. "What do we do? We're no closer to answers than when we brought her here. She can't stay here forever—it's killing us both!"

"It's up to you," Mr. Hastings deferred. He too was struggling with the choice of having hospitalized Naya in a psychiatric hospital. What social ramifications would something like this have for her future? He didn't want Naya to endure any more stigma than was absolutely medically necessary.

Mrs. Hastings rose and walked out of the family room while Naya sat eating a snack with her father. She walked over to the nurses' station and asked the unit nurse if she could speak to the doctor on call. The nurse agreed to page the doctor and requested that she wait for a moment.

Mrs. Hastings stood in the hallway near the nurses' station as she waited for the doctor to arrive. Then a young Indian lady walked up to her and introduced herself as the doctor on call.

"Hello, my name is Dr. Patel. How can I help you?"

"Are you familiar with Naya's case?" Mrs. Hastings asked nervously.

"Yes, I am."

"Is it possible for us to take her home today? After all, the test results came back negative."

"Oh, you want her to be discharged today?" Sheetal repeated, surprised. She thought a moment. Peter wouldn't like it if she discharged Naya before he returned, but she couldn't keep the girl here against her parents' wishes.

"Why would you want to take her out today?" Sheetal asked. She had to admit to herself that she was stalling; she already knew the answer. What mother wanted her child in the hospital?

Mrs. Hastings explained how helpless she felt, being unable to comfort her daughter at night. More simply, Mrs. Hastings just missed her daughter terribly.

"It's not uncommon to feel helpless or sad—many parents do." Sheetal could tell that her effort to provide emotional support was falling woefully short.

"Can we take her home?" Mrs. Hastings asked again, wiping her tears.

"If you did, it would be considered against medical advice, since we're still in the process of evaluating her. We don't want her here any more than you do, and we're trying to get her out of the hospital as quickly as we can. I don't recommend taking her home at this point."

Mrs. Hastings didn't seem convinced. "We're also worried about what the other children will do to her," Mrs. Hastings said, clearly referring to Sasha's violent outburst toward Naya.

"That's why we have so many staff members to watch over the children and keep them safe," Sheetal tried.

Mrs. Hastings just stood silently, feeling emotionally overwhelmed.

"I spoke to Dr. Gram today," Sheetal said, after inspiration struck. "He visited the Iyengars over the weekend, and he has some new information about Naya's biological family that might aid with Naya's treatment." Sheetal paused, hoping that the new information might help defuse Mrs. Hastings's current emotional crisis.

"What information?" Mrs. Hastings asked.

"I'm not sure, but I know that the Iyengars are coming here tomorrow to see Naya and talk to Dr. Gram." Sheetal's hopes lifted at Mrs. Hastings's curious expression; perhaps she was gaining some ground.

"Did Dr. Gram tell you this?"

"Yes … and not only that, but Mr. Iyengar also called here earlier himself, and I spoke to him. They were happy to hear that Naya is safe and faring well."

"What time will they be here?"

"Most likely in the morning," Sheetal replied. "You can come here too, if you would like to. But in any case, I think Dr. Gram will speak to you tomorrow to summarize all his findings and make further recommendations based on this new information."

Mrs. Hastings jutted her chin out slightly, and Sheetal noted her determination wearily. "So maybe she could come home tomorrow?" The way she said it, it almost didn't sound like a question.

"Yes, that's a good possibility. But you'll have to discuss that with Dr. Gram."

"What about tonight? Can I stay here with Naya?" Mrs. Hastings inquired.

"You can remain here a little while past visiting hours, but I'm sorry—I can't let you stay here overnight. It's hospital policy, so it's not up to me."

Mrs. Hastings felt a little calmer after talking to Dr. Patel. She was curious to hear the new information Dr. Gram had collected.

"If you need any help telling Naya about having to stay here another night, I'll be more than happy to assist," Sheetal offered.

"Thanks, but I can do that myself. She'll be happy to hear that her uncle and aunt will be visiting her here tomorrow."

"If you have any other questions or concerns, don't hesitate to ask; I'm here all night," Sheetal said with a parting smile.

Mrs. Hastings shook Sheetal's hand and watched her walk away briskly toward a second family who was waiting for her at the end of the corridor. She then returned to the visitor's room, where Naya sat eating her snack.

Naya bounced out of the seat as she saw her mother return. "Can I go home today?" she asked around a mouthful of cookies.

"Maybe tomorrow, after we talk to your doctor," Mrs. Hastings said, running her fingers through her daughter's hair. "Did you know that your aunt and uncle Iyengar are coming to see you here tomorrow?"

"They are!" Naya squealed with delight. "Will they bring me a toy?"

"I think they will, but only if you stay here tonight."

"I'll stay! I'll stay!" Naya hopped up and down, bursting with joy. She liked the pampering and attention that her Indian relatives showered upon her.

{CHAPTER FIFTY-THREE}

Sunday

Mr. Deed's property crawled with police activity as officers investigated their biggest break since the discovery of Janet's body. Officers were scouting the entire neighborhood for clues. Standing slightly away from the flurry of activity, Leia discussed the next plan of action with José and Lieutenant Andrew.

Leia had just filled the officers in on exactly where her hunch about the boathouse had come from. "That's insane," the lieutenant remarked. He couldn't accept that he owed this burst of progress to a little girl in a psychiatric hospital.

"You better believe it," Leia insisted firmly. She herself couldn't really grasp exactly how Naya's visionary dreams were possible, but the bottom line was undeniable: they had made major progress in the case.

Leia looked at her watch; it was almost ten at night. She returned to a previous discussion about possible suspects. "One possibility is that our killer is a surgeon."

"Maybe not," José remarked. "It could be anybody with similar skills."

Leia ignored him without meaning to; she was deep in thought. "Maybe," she mused, "We should check out the physician database for a list of neighborhood surgeons."

"I like that idea," the lieutenant concurred.

"In the meantime, we can search for any identifying evidence," José said, nodding.

"Any fingerprints so far?" Leia asked the lieutenant.

"Yeah, but no matches to anything in our databases."

"Have you looked in the immigration-service databases?" José asked.

"I'll have to check," the lieutenant said. He stepped aside and spoke into a walkie-talkie. "They'll look into it right away," he said, turning back to José and Leia.

"The artifacts at the altar site are Jamaican. This indicates that our killer was performing some sort of Jamaican ritual," Leia said, looking at the newly printed photographs of the boathouse interior. "Maybe our guy is of Caribbean origin."

"Are we looking for a Jamaican surgeon?" asked José.

"Yes, we should," replied the lieutenant.

Leia nodded in agreement. "That's one way to narrow our list of suspects." She was optimistic that they would find more clues once they dusted the entire boathouse. Hopefully, if they were lucky, they would find some incriminating DNA evidence. "Let's identify all the Jamaican surgeons who work in the nearby hospitals."

"We will," replied the lieutenant. "Did Mr. Deed know anything that might help us?"

"No," Leia said. "He was genuinely shocked by it all. He says he hasn't used the boathouse in thirty years, and I believe him. He's got to be pushing a hundred."

Leia's stomach growled audibly. "You haven't eaten since you got here," José observed with concern.

"Yeah, I think my stomach just announced that it's time to go get something to eat," Leia replied. "Would you like to join us, Lieutenant?"

"No, thanks. I'll stay here for now," the lieutenant answered.

"Could you do me a favor and call the department of social services? I think Mr. Deed might need some assistance and protection after all," Leia called from a distance as she headed toward her car, accompanied by José. "I don't want the killer to go after that crazy old guy."

The lieutenant waved in acknowledgment and returned to the boathouse to help his comrades.

*   *   *   *

The slaaf watched from a distance. He had trekked around Elephant Rock after leaving Peter's apartment complex. His growing anxiety had destroyed his previous complacency, and he intended to go back to the boathouse to clean up and collect his tools, even if the desecration of his special altar represented blasphemy. But to his dismay, he could see nothing but a swarm of police activity. He flinched involuntarily when he saw the female agent and the troopers near the boathouse.

The slaaf was frightened and shocked at the same time. He couldn't understand how the police had discovered his well-kept secret. They had never come close to tracking him down after the first human offering, and that investigation had gone on for years. His thoughts flashed back to the day that he had happened upon Peter and Leia near Elephant Rock. Peter must have somehow tipped them off … but how?

"That bastard," the slaaf thought aloud. "He knows. Somehow he knows." It was also possible that something had gone awry during the previous night's sacrifice. Had a new curse been cast upon him?

The slaaf stood behind the tree line, afraid to move any closer. He turned around and ran as fast as he could through the woods. The whole world seemed to be collapsing around him. His eyes rolled madly in his head as he watched for pursuers on all sides. Was he being followed? Confusion and panic engulfed him. His head spun; he began to feel faint and dizzy. He stumbled over a branch falling to the ground. He began to feel as if he owed an impossible debt. He needed to do something quickly. It was only a matter of time before the whole situation would unfold, and he would no longer have any place to hide.

The slaaf passed out.

{CHAPTER FIFTY-FOUR}

Monday Morning

Peter met Agent Bines in the hospital coffee shop again. When he arrived, the waitress was pouring Agent Bines a cup of coffee.

"Good morning, Dr. Gram," she said.

"Agent Bines." Peter set his bottle of orange juice on the table and pulled out the chair opposite her.

"You look better than when I last saw you," she commented.

"Ah ... well ... I had an early night last night," Peter replied sheepishly. Leia's eyebrow twitched upward in amusement. "So were you able to use Naya's picture in any way?" he asked.

Agent Bines leaned across the table toward him. Excitement shone in her eyes. "It was the strangest thing," she said. "We found a perfect match for that red building. Can you believe it?"

"Amazing!" Peter exclaimed, leaning back into the chair. He paused, then shook his head slightly in wonder. "But you know ... somehow, I'm not really that surprised. Though I have to admit, it makes me wonder what's next. Voodoo?"

Leia ignored his joke and concentrated instead on the task at hand, as usual. *My looks give her an unfair advantage,* Peter mused. *If I were as nice to look at as she is, she might wander off topic occasionally too!* "I think we might have some strong new leads, thanks to that picture," Leia said briskly. She went on to describe what they had found at the boathouse.

"So who do you think killed Janet Troy?"

"Well, we know that the individual responsible has surgical or culinary skills," Leia told him, "and we also found a baggie containing trace amounts of cocaine. There was a sort of altar set up in the boathouse that had been used several times before; it seems he killed not only Janet Troy, but many wild animals … and God only knows what else. We found carvings and other tokens there that lead us to believe the killer is obsessed with ritual—specifically Jamaican ritual sacrifice."

"Do you have specific suspects in mind?" Peter asked, startled by her description. An image of Everson flashed before his eyes.

"We're checking with the personnel department here at the hospital to see if there are any surgeons of Jamaican origin or with Jamaican ancestry." She looked at him searchingly. "Do you know anyone who might fit that description? We have to tread so carefully when we ask questions about ethnicity. Any tips you can give me discreetly will keep our inquiries as inoffensive as possible."

Peter didn't want to disclose the name of his friend. But he knew that Agent Bines would eventually find it out anyway, and he wanted her to trust him.

"Do you?" she asked once again.

"I do."

"Who is it?"

"His name is Everson Hunter."

"Do you know him well?"

"Yes."

"Do you think he's in the hospital now?"

"He should be," Peter said, looking at his watch.

"Has he been acting strangely in any way?"

"Not really." Peter hesitated. "Except that he did ask to borrow a large amount of money from me." He recalled how agitated Everson had been. "He said he was way behind on some … investments, or something. He was really vague about it. Frankly, the whole situation was kind of weird."

"I appreciate your forthrightness," Leia said.

"Well, I have to tell you, it's hard for me to listen to you say that my friend is a murder suspect," Peter said with disbelief and angst.

"I didn't say he was. All we're doing is looking for a Jamaican with surgical skills. There could be more than one in the hospital."

Peter sat thinking as Leia sipped her coffee.

"Who's Debbie Sanders?" he blurted.

Agent Bines looked stunned. Peter had never seen her drop her guard that way; it scared him a little. What was so important about that name?

"Where did you hear that name?" she asked sternly. "That's confidential information."

"Naya told it to me," Peter said, and Agent Bines's lips parted in astonishment. "She said that in her dream. Janet told her to ask me who Debbie Sanders was."

"I … I don't know whether to believe you or not," Agent Bines said. "I can't quite get my mind around it." She seemed to have lost her composure, but Peter actually found this comforting; the unstoppable Agent Bines was human after all.

"Join the club," Peter said. "It appears that Naya, through Janet, knows more about this case than all of us put together. Janet's comments suggest that I should know who Debbie Sanders is. Is she connected to Janet in some way?"

Agent Bines took a deep breath. "You won't believe it when I tell you who Debbie Sanders was," she said.

"Was?"

"Debbie Sanders was a murder victim whose dismembered body was found at Elephant Rock almost thirty years ago."

"So, the person you're looking for has killed before?"

"The murders are so similar, it's difficult to think otherwise," Leia said. "The estimated date of Debbie Sanders's death was October 11, 1967."

"Really?" Peter said absently.

"Pardon?" Agent Bines said.

"Oh, nothing," Peter said. "I'm still really struggling with the fact that Naya knows all of this. Is it really possible that she's communicating with a dead girl through her dreams?"

Agent Bines shrugged, then sighed. "It's difficult for me to accept, but if my years as an investigator have taught me anything, it's that mysterious things happen all the time, Dr. Gram, and we spend a lot of time and energy explaining them away. I don't think we can do so under these circumstances, however."

"There's no psychiatric diagnosis for talking with the dead—I know that for sure!"

Agent Bines laughed and Peter, delighted by the sound, joined her. Her cheeks flushed a little with amusement, and Peter had to stare down at his napkin for a minute to keep from blushing himself. He groaned inwardly. *What are you, in grade school? She's an FBI agent, not your recess buddy. Get it together!*

She handed him an envelope. "Here's the drawing I borrowed," she said.

"Thanks for remembering," Peter said.

Leia sat back and sighed.

"What is it?" Peter asked.

"It's just …" Leia paused, then made a sweeping gesture with her slender arms. "All this, you know? I've seen a lot of crazy things in my career, but this …" Her hazel eyes sparkled a little as she leaned forward. "We have to catch this guy, Peter. I have to know if any of this is real."

Simultaneously thrilled by Leia's use of "we" and appalled at his own schoolboy crush, Peter nodded. "We will," he said. "I'll do everything in my power to help you, in any way I can."

His sincerity seemed to set her off-kilter. "Well … thank you," she said a little awkwardly, tucking a wisp of reddish hair behind her ear before clasping her hands in her lap.

Peter sat up straight suddenly, glanced at his watch, and groaned. "Duty calls, as always," he said.

Leia stood up and shot him a knowing glance. "Now there's a phrase I'm already too familiar with—you're a man after my own heart. And anyway, far be it from me to stand in the way of good medicine, especially when I'm starting a full day myself."

They shook hands and promised to keep each other abreast of any new developments.

Then Peter jogged across the hospital lawns toward Strauss I. He was going to miss morning report if he didn't hurry. He was eager to hear about Naya's sleep pattern from the previous night. He was worried about Everson and his possible involvement in this mess. He was absolutely confused about a girl named Debbie Sanders.

Simply put, he needed to talk to Mr. Iyengar again.

{CHAPTER FIFTY-FIVE}

Monday

Everson began his day early, looking for Peter in the hospital. He had decided to simply beg Peter to lend him the money. Time was running out. He had applied for new credit lines with no luck. He didn't have any other options, unless he wanted to consider robbing a bank.

I'll have to tell him the truth about why I need it, he thought to himself.

Through the glass window, he saw Peter sitting in the hospital coffee shop. As he got closer, he saw that Peter was talking to a woman Everson had never seen before. He stood at the entrance of the coffee shop, willing the woman away. Anger and agitation crept over him. He needed to speak to Peter *now*.

Peter was sitting with his back to the door. Everson walked by Peter's table, hoping to be noticed. However, Peter and the woman were so engrossed in their discussion that they didn't even look at him.

Could it be that Peter actually had a girlfriend? If so, Everson had to compliment the man's taste. He eased forward to get a better look. *Well, well. If this is the woman who broke Peter out of monkshood, I can certainly understand why.*

Everson caught a snatch of the conversation, and it momentarily froze him in his tracks.

"The individual responsible has surgical skills," the woman said. "And we also found a baggie containing trace amounts of cocaine ..."

Everson strode away. He should have known that Peter wasn't dating anyone. The woman was obviously a cop. *Is she DEA?* he wondered frantically. Had someone in the hospital discovered his drug problem? Had Arcus been busted?

Everson got out of the coffee shop fast and retreated into the surgery conference room.

He wanted to know what was inside the envelope the woman had handed to Peter. He didn't have much time. He had to devise a plan of action before Arcus confronted him again.

{CHAPTER FIFTY-SIX}

Monday

Peter stood outside the entrance of Strauss I, rummaging in his jacket pocket for the ID card that doubled as the key to the unit. He didn't find it, so he searched in his other pocket. Then he glanced down at his watch, knowing that he would be late for morning report if his ID didn't materialize soon. "Damn," he said to himself as he realized that he had forgotten Naya's pictures at home as well. *So much for hurrying out the door for the sake of punctuality*, Peter thought wryly. *Obviously, that doesn't pay off in the end!*

Peter sighed and pushed the buzzer button intended for visitors. He waited resignedly for a few minutes before he heard a voice through the speaker. "You forgot your key again?" Suzie, the receptionist, sounded like a reprimanding parent.

"Yes, I did," Peter admitted, looking toward the concealed security camera. He ran in before the doors had slid all the way open. "You'll need to buzz me into the unit," he called out to Suzie as he passed her desk.

Peter reached the nurses' station only to find out that morning rounds had finished, and most of the team had already dispersed. He grumbled in irritation, but his mood lightened when he saw Sheetal, who was gathering her belongings and going home after the long weekend call.

"Hi, Peter," Sheetal greeted him as he stepped into the nurses' station.

"Hey, how was the rest of your call period?" Peter queried.

"Nice ... quiet. I managed to get some sleep past midnight."

"How was Naya last night?"

"I think she slept fairly well for the first time," Sheetal said. "The staff member monitoring her observed a little tossing and turning, but nothing more than that."

Peter smiled in relief. "That's good to hear. Things have been a little too eventful around here."

"Mr. Iyengar should be here anytime now," Sheetal informed Peter. Immediately after the words left her mouth, a page from Suzie crackled out of the overhead speaker.

"That must be them," Peter said. "Can you let me out? I forgot my ID badge this morning."

Peter followed Sheetal out of the unit, and she said good-bye over her shoulder before heading home. He walked up to the waiting area and saw Mr. and Mrs. Iyengar waiting for him. They stood up in unison and greeted him with a warm smile.

"Dr. Gram, thank you for taking the time to see us. How is our little princess doing?" Mr. Iyengar asked with pride.

"Naya's doing fine so far, except for one or two nocturnal episodes."

"Do we get to see her now?" Mrs. Iyengar asked.

"Yes. Let's go into the unit. She'll be thrilled to see the two of you."

"Can we give her these toys?" Mrs. Iyengar asked, pointing to a bag on the floor.

"Yes, you may, as long as the nurse confirms that the toys meet the hospital safety code. Regardless, Naya will be able to take them home when she leaves the hospital," Peter explained as he escorted them to the unit door.

Peter's cheeks reddened as he gestured to Suzie once again, feeling a little helpless without his unit key. Suzie remotely unlocked the magnetic blue doors, and Peter led the Iyengars to the unit's family visiting room.

"I'll go and bring Naya. She must be at school this morning."

"They have a school here? I've never heard of anything like that," Mrs. Iyengar remarked.

"Yep—all children get to go to school here, even if some of them don't exactly consider it a perk." Peter smiled, then headed for the school area.

He knew where to find Naya, as every Monday followed the same routine. He stood at the open classroom door and gently knocked on it; all the children in the class turned around and looked at him. "I'm sorry to interrupt," Peter said politely, though he knew the teacher was used to these circumstances. "Could I take Naya, please? She's got a visitor."

Naya was out of her desk and at Peter's side so quickly that for a moment, he wondered if she had added teleportation to her list of unusual abilities. She grabbed Peter's hand. "Is my uncle here?" she asked him enthusiastically. She had clearly been waiting for this moment all morning. She was dolled up in a plaid skirt with tights and a pink sweater.

"Yes, they're here," Peter said. "Are you excited to see them?"

"Yes, yes!" Naya squealed in delight. Peter had to chuckle at the fidgeting little girl. She could barely contain all her excitement. "Even Noodle missed them," she explained. "Can I bring him?"

Peter chuckled. "Well, as long as he promises not to make too much noise."

"He's a stuffed dog," Naya said scornfully.

Peter resisted the urge to laugh, in case he hurt Naya's feelings. "Oh, yes, of course," he said seriously. "You're right. I don't know what I was thinking."

He walked with Naya to the family visiting room. Naya squealed, let go of Peter's hand, and ran ahead of him, straight into her eager uncle's arms. Mr. Iyengar gave her a big hug and showered her with lots of kisses. Naya joyfully repeated the entire process with her aunt.

"Naya, I need to speak to your uncle for a few minutes," Peter said. "In the meantime, you can talk to your aunt. I'm sure she has lots to show you." Peter needed to talk to Mr. Iyengar alone.

Naya was too preoccupied with the bag her aunt was holding to register Peter's words. She tugged at it, trying to see what was inside. "Patience, my dear," Mrs. Iyengar teased in a gentle voice as she handed Naya the bag. Naya plopped onto the floor and rummaged through her gifts with great excitement.

Peter figured she would be occupied for a while, so he gestured for Mr. Iyengar to follow him into the office that Peter shared with several fellows.

"You can sit here," Peter said pointing to a futon at one end of the room. Mr. Iyengar sat down, and Peter wheeled a chair over and sat opposite of him.

"I'm glad you came to see Naya," Peter thanked Mr. Iyengar once again. "However, I was much more eager than Naya to see you today. I need to clarify some of Naya's recent experiences; I wanted to make sure you have the whole story."

Peter went on to narrate the events since Naya's admission and how they had been struggling to figure out what was going on with her psychiatrically. "Did you hear about the girl who was murdered recently in this neighborhood?" Peter asked Mr. Iyengar.

"No, I didn't," Mr. Iyengar replied. "That's terrible."

Peter continued to tell Mr. Iyengar about the murder of Janet and few of the gory details.

"But what has that got to do with Naya?" Mr. Iyengar asked him. He appeared understandably baffled.

Peter took in a deep breath. He wasn't sure how Mr. Iyengar would react to what he was about to say. "This is difficult to say," he began, "but I think the dead girl, Janet, has been trying to communicate with Naya in her dreams."

Peter paused, waiting anxiously to hear Mr. Iyengar's reaction. He watched Mr. Iyengar's face slowly turn pale. His expression wasn't one of disbelief, but of recognition, as if he had heard this sometime before. The silence expanded between the two men as they surveyed one another.

"Are you all right?" Peter asked breaking their silence.

Mr. Iyengar cleared his throat, then managed a yes.

Peter saw a tear glimmering in the corner of Mr. Iyengar's eye. This was even more difficult than Peter thought it would be.

"I have to make a confession," Mr. Iyengar said after recomposing himself. "I need to tell you something about Naya's mother."

Peter was truly surprised by Mr. Iyengar's reaction. Expecting sarcasm or derision, he had steeled himself for criticism and accusations that he was a quack. The strange reaction piqued Peter's curiosity. He keenly listened to what Mr. Iyengar had to say.

"When my sister was about Naya's age, she began to have experiences similar to what you're describing now. People were talking to her in her dreams, she told us. Through extended family and friends, we realized that the people she named were deceased. The family disregarded her pleas for rescue from these nightmares on the pretext that she would grow out of it. After some time, she eventually stopped talking about it. But I think she continued to have such episodes over the years."

"Did they ever go away?" Peter asked, out of concern for Naya's prognosis.

"Nobody really knows," replied Mr. Iyengar sadly.

Peter pulled an envelope from his pocket. He wanted to show Mr. Iyengar the drawing of the boathouse that Leia had returned. He spread it on his lap and tilted it toward Mr. Iyengar. Peter enlightened him on what the picture depicted and its psychological interpretation.

"She's always been such a good artist—just like her mother," Mr. Iyengar said, admiring the drawing.

"There's one more thing that I don't understand," Peter continued. "In one of Naya's dreams, Janet brought up a second girl by the name of Debbie Sanders. It was only today that I found out that Debbie had been killed in the same exact manner as Janet had died, and probably by the same killer—but many, many years ago. What struck me, though, was the date that she was killed."

"And when was that?"

"It was on October 11, 1967—that's the day I was born," Peter said, shivering nervously at his own words.

"I see," Mr. Iyengar said, pursing his lips.

"Do you think there's any connection?"

"Show me your hands," Mr. Iyengar commanded.

Peter had moved beyond questioning anything that happened to him anymore. He extended his arms to Mr. Iyengar without pause.

"Now roll up your sleeves as high as you can."

Again, Peter obliged the odd request.

Mr. Iyengar then grasped Peter's palms and rotated his wrists back and forth. "You see these markings—the lines at your joints?"

"Yeah, sure," Peter said. He had always been self-conscious about the striae at every joint on his body, which were most predominant around his arms and knees and fainter on his fingers and toes. He'd had them since birth, and he usually wore slacks and long sleeves to cover them. He cleared his throat in embarrassment as Mr. Iyengar's eyes moved over them.

"These are soul markings."

"Soul … what?" Peter asked. Just when he thought he had surpassed the last threshold of unbelievability, someone had to test him again.

"Soul markings, which are remnants from your previous life. In other words, there is a good possibility that in your previous life, your *atman*, or soul, inhabited the body of the girl who died on the day you were born."

Peter gaped at him wordlessly, then opened and closed his mouth like a netted fish. Obviously no stranger to shock or disbelief, Mr. Iyengar just looked at Peter mildly until he composed himself.

"Are you saying … that I was Debbie Sanders in a previous life?" Peter managed. "Is that what you're telling me right now?"

"Unbelievable as it may sound to you, yes, I think so. That seems to be the reason destiny has brought you and Naya together. Your special connection may have offered the only way to stop the killer."

Peter couldn't believe his ears … and yet, something about what Mr. Iyengar was saying made perfect sense to him. But he didn't want something that sounded so ridiculous to make sense to him. *What's happened to me?* he thought incredulously. *Haven't I suffered enough? I just can't learn to believe in anything else this week! Hopefully Tinkerbell is on vacation and doesn't plan on stopping by.*

"So let me just make sure I'm getting this right," he said with a defiant note in his voice. "You're telling me that these markings are from having been cut at my joints during my previous life?"

"Yes," Mr. Iyengar said with perfect sincerity. "Your soul was reborn as Peter, but traces of your past life remain. They're probably signs of what happened physically to your previous body during the last moments of your previous life," Mr. Iyengar illuminated.

"This is all really over my head," Peter said, struggling with what to believe.

"Sometimes there are forces beyond our comprehension that we may have to accept without questioning their origins," Mr. Iyengar said softly as he released Peter's palms from his gentle grip.

Peter buried his hands in his thick hair, making it stand up even more wildly than usual. "How am I going to tell the Hastings all of this?"

"You don't have to. Sharing this information won't change the outcome of Naya's future. Maybe Naya will sleep undisturbed once this dead girl's purpose has been met."

"I really hope so, for Naya's sake." A wave of fondness for his patient washed over Peter. "In the meantime, we'll just have to keep Naya safe and monitor her closely."

"There may be a time in her therapy that this phenomenon can be explored, and we can help her understand her role in the greater scheme of life," Mr. Iyengar said.

Peter finally stood up. "I think Naya is waiting for us," he reminded Mr. Iyengar, and the other man agreed. They walked back to the visiting room, each of them thinking deeply about issues they had never thought of before.

*   *   *   *

Everson had been perturbed ever since he had caught a piece of the conversation between Peter and the agent. His thoughts were racing, and his imagination was going wild. What if somehow, Peter had known about his addiction and illicit activities? Word could really get around. Such rumors might explain why Peter didn't want to loan him any money. The thought of being arrested or killed frightened the daylights out of him.

Everson couldn't contain himself. He had to have a face-to-face conversation with Peter. He went to the hospital's children's psychiatric unit and entered it using his ID card. The nurses at the unit told Everson that Peter was busy with a patient's family and wasn't available at the moment.

While Everson stood trying to figure out what to do, he saw Matt and a little Indian girl standing nearby. The girl glanced at him, then looked quickly away.

"What can I do for you, Dr. Hunter?" Matt asked Everson, shaking his hand.

"Could you tell Peter that I was looking for him?" Everson asked as he looked down at Naya.

"Naya, say hello to Dr. Hunter," Matt said.

"So this is Peter's favorite girl," Everson said, remembering that Peter had spoken about an Indian patient when they were at the gym.

Naya replied with a faint hello and smiled at Everson. She then turned away and continued to talk to Matt.

Everson shifted his weight from foot to foot. He didn't have time for this—his life was on the line. He walked out of the nurses' station and out of the building. He got in his car and sped away.

{CHAPTER FIFTY-SEVEN}

Monday

The slaaf was still in shock from the invasion of his boathouse the previous night. Just the recollection of the breach was enough to raise his autonomic activity, shooting up his heart rate. He recalled running away from the scene and into the woods. His sore shins reminded him of the nasty fall he took before losing consciousness, but, he didn't know how long he had been out. He didn't awaken until shortly before sunrise. He had sat up, blinked at the trees above him, brushed himself off, and scrambled to his feet. He then tried agonizingly hard to get back home as quickly as he could, as he needed to be at work as soon as possible.

Later, the slaaf looked at his watch as he drove toward Peter's apartment. It was half past eleven in the morning. "Damn those cops," he said to himself. His body ached from the previous night. The cops were closing in on him; if he didn't act quickly, it wouldn't be long before they trapped him like an animal—and locked him up like one. Now was the time to explore Peter's apartment. If luck was on his side, he might find out what Peter knew and how he knew it.

The slaaf drove along the side streets, looking for a parking spot. Fortunately, he found one on a street just a block away from Peter's apartment.

The slaaf killed the engine, then opened the glove compartment and fumbled through its contents. He was pleased when he found what he was looking for. "Aha," he said, holding up a handsomely carved switchblade that had been passed down through the generations. As he admired the weapon, he recalled how proud he had been on the day his father gave it to him. The handle was made of ivory, giving it a majestic appearance.

He then looked for a small metal spoke that he kept just in case of an emergency. Beautiful knives were capable of amazing work, but sometimes, they needed the help of a crude instrument.

Armed with his favorite knife and metal spoke, the slaaf exited his car. He slipped the switchblade and spoke into his jacket pocket, making sure that they were well concealed. Then he walked slowly toward the apartment entrance, looking around to check if anybody was watching. He sprinted through the lobby to the elevator doors. He jammed his finger into the elevator button about three times and cursed under his breath as he waited restlessly for the twin doors to slide open. As soon as they did, the slaaf darted in. The elevator was empty, decreasing his anxiety that he may look suspicious. He patiently waited until the elevator came to a halt at the eighth floor.

Once the doors opened, the slaaf rushed out into a long corridor, then trod softly along the carpeted floor until he arrived at Dr. Gram's door. He stood next to the door, shifting his eyes to make sure that he was alone. He wanted to make sure Peter wasn't home, so he rang the doorbell. When no one answered, he brandished the metal spoke and inserted it into the keyway of the plug. The plug was the cylinder that rotated when the appropriate key was inserted; it could be manipulated with the proper instrument. He gently pushed and felt the first pin move. With his other hand, he popped open the switchblade and inserted it into the keyway. He maneuvered the spoke until he felt all the pins were in line. At that very second, he turned the switchblade, unlocking the door with ease.

The slaaf stepped into Peter's apartment and gently shut the door behind him. The drawn curtains left the living room dim, and the slaaf peered cautiously around. The air was filled with the aroma of the previous night's cooking. He carefully crept around, making sure not to touch anything. He looked around the living room again blankly, not really sure of what he was looking for. The room was immaculately clean, and he knew that the doctor would be able to tell if he touched anything.

The slaaf stepped into the bedroom, which was brightly lit from the morning sun. He noticed that the bedroom wasn't as clean as the rest of the apartment; the bed wasn't made, and the sheets lay tangled in a large pile, almost falling off the mattress. He walked up to the nightstand. To his surprise, he saw the doctor's ID badge. For a panic-stricken moment, he wondered whether Peter was in fact home—in the laundry room, perhaps.

Relax, he told himself. *He's just forgetful. He's a dedicated doctor—he wouldn't miss his shift.*

Under the badge lay a few sheets of paper. The papers appeared to be the drawings of a child. He pushed aside the badge and picked up the papers. A sharp chill went down his spine as his eyes focused on the first picture. His knees weakened, and he extended one hand out to the mattress next to him, then sat down, holding the papers in the other.

In front of the slaaf was a drawing of a girl who had been cut up using a method that was strikingly familiar. The next picture was more shocking to him; it was of the boathouse that he had guarded so safely for so many years. The third was a picture of two girls in a field of flowers. *This is impossible*, he thought to himself. His dealings with Anansi were his own little secret; he was absolutely sure that nobody had witnessed any of this. His thoughts raced. Maybe this was some sort of a trick that Anansi was playing on him.

The slaaf scanned the artwork, looking for a signature. "Naya," he read aloud in the stillness, and the sound of his own voice startled him in the silence. He repeated it to himself a couple of times, growing bolder. He sat on the bed with the picture still in his hand, staring off into space. He couldn't think; his thoughts appeared to be clouded with fears that his world was swiftly falling apart. He froze in panic, unsure of what to do next.

{CHAPTER FIFTY-EIGHT}

Monday

Peter sat at the telephone in the fellows' office waiting for the receptionist to transfer the call from Naya's insurers. It was Monday, and they had promptly called for a clinical update. He knew that he didn't have much to bargain with, as Naya's symptoms were not really life threatening, and her medical workup had turned out to be normal. Like it or not, the time to discharge Naya was approaching rapidly.

"Yes," Peter concurred, "We'll discharge her later today with an outpatient follow-up appointment." As expected, his attempt to secure more days hadn't been successful. Peter's own personal curiosity remained unsatisfied, but he had to admit that, medically speaking, Naya had completed all the necessary investigations.

Peter opened Naya's chart and looked for the work number that Mrs. Hastings had left just in case the hospital needed to contact her during working hours. He dialed the number and waited for a moment. He instantly recognized Mrs. Hastings's melodious voice as soon as she answered the phone.

"Good morning, Mrs. Hastings. This is Dr. Gram calling from the hospital. I have some good news for you."

"Is Naya coming back home? Mrs. Hastings asked with heightened excitement.

"Yes, she is. You can take her home today."

"Do you have to do any more tests?"

"No."

"I'm so relieved," Mrs. Hastings said. "Have you decided on a diagnosis?"

"We think she has a sleep-related nightmare issue that will abate over time. She does not have any significant psychiatric diagnosis."

"Thank goodness!" Peter smiled at her sigh of relief.

"What time can we come and pick her up," she couldn't contain her excitement.

"You can come anytime after noon," Peter replied, looking at his watch.

"We'll be there by two thirty in the afternoon at the latest," Mrs. Hastings promised.

"Good—I'll see you then.

"Dr. Gram?"

"Yes?"

"Thank you so much for all of your help." Mrs. Hastings sounded a little teary.

"You're truly welcome," Peter answered.

After hanging up, Peter called Matt to give him a heads-up about the upcoming discharge.

"I'm going home ... going home!" Naya shrieked in delight as she saw Peter walking onto the unit. She was standing with Matt at her bedroom door. Matt had informed her of the happy news and had helped her pack her belongings. She ran up to Peter and flung herself at him.

"You need to ask for a hug first," Peter reminded Naya while he made an understandable exception and reciprocated with a gentle hug. He was delighted to see her reaction to the news and was thankful to Matt for having helped prepare Naya for her discharge.

"Have you finished packing your bags?" Peter asked Naya.

"Yep! There they are." Naya pointed to two duffel bags on the floor of her room.

"Did you take all your drawings?" Peter asked.

"Except the ones you have," Naya said politely.

"Yes, that's right—I have to go home and bring them back to you."

"Are my parents here?" Naya asked anxiously, and he had to smile. She just couldn't wait to go home.

Peter looked at his watch, then reassured her, "They should be here any minute now."

"I want to go *home*," Naya said, clearly restless.

"That must be them," Peter said, responding to a page from the reception at the front desk. "I'll need to talk to them for a few minutes before you can leave."

"Can I come too?" Naya pleaded.

"I think the grown-ups need to talk first, and then I'll come and get you," Peter promised. "Matt, could you watch Naya for a few minutes while I speak to her parents?"

"Sure," Matt replied, indicating to Naya that she could sit with him in the nurses' station while she waited.

Peter scurried off to the reception area. He was greeted by Mrs. Hastings, who looked just as eager as her daughter. He looked around for Mr. Hastings, but didn't spot him.

"Her father is at work; he hates that he couldn't be here. But he's very busy with a major project at the office. He'll meet her as soon as he gets home. He's planning to bring a special gift for her on his way back from work," Mrs. Hastings said with a smile.

"There's one more thing we'll have to do before Naya is discharged."

"Okay … will it take long?" Mrs. Hastings asked, obviously feeling pressed to leave soon.

"No, not at all," Peter said, and then asked her to sit down. "We need to discuss the aftercare plan." He knew she wasn't familiar with what would happen upon discharge.

"What would that be?" Mrs. Hastings queried.

Peter sat down as well, then explained the need for the continued monitoring of Naya's symptoms, but on an outpatient basis. "I'll be able to see her for individual therapy at the clinic. For starters, it will be once a week; in that way, I can monitor her symptoms and make sure that she's getting the best care possible."

Mrs. Hastings paused, then nodded. "I don't mind monitoring, as long as Naya gets to live at home with us," she said. "I'd like for that to happen."

"I'll make an appointment for an intake at the clinic for her next week, after which I'll be able to follow up on Naya until we decide that she no longer needs those services," Peter further explained. "It's good to communicate to Naya that she'll still be visiting. Let's explain it to her together when we get to the unit."

"Of course," Mrs. Hastings replied.

"There's one more thing," Peter said with some hesitation. He wasn't sure how to explain Naya's symptoms in the context of a paranormal phenomenon.

Mrs. Hastings seemed to read Peter's mind. "Your meeting with Mr. Iyengar."

"Yes," Peter said, grateful for an opening into the discussion of Naya's experiences. "Mr. Iyengar mentioned to me that Naya's biological mother had similar experiences when she was about Naya's age."

"She did?" Mrs. Hastings said with some surprise.

"Do you know what a paranormal experience is?" Peter knew he was moving away from mainstream psychiatry.

"I've heard about people who have had out-of-world experiences. Does Naya have something like that?"

"The good news is that she doesn't have any psychiatric or medical illness that could account for her symptoms. The only other nonmedical explanation is such a phenomenon," Peter said. "Mr. Iyengar indicated to us that Naya's biological mother had an unusual ability to communicate through her dreams with—"

"The dead." Mrs. Hastings completed his sentence even before Peter could say it himself.

Startled, Peter remarked, "You knew what I was going to say."

"Well, there was one thing we didn't tell you, Dr. Gram, because it sounded too crazy and far-fetched," Mrs. Hastings confessed. "We were sure that if we told you, our report would be considered unreliable, which might affect Naya's care. But … remember the day Naya came in because she was trying to jump off the balcony?"

"Yes," Peter said and paused expectantly.

"A day later, we found out that our neighbors' pigeons had died of a viral illness. After we saw the picture she had drawn while she was in the ER, we began to wonder whether Naya was trying to fly away with the pigeons—whether those dead birds were somehow talking to her in her dreams. We were never going to bring this up until you just mentioned it," Mrs. Hastings said with a sense of relief.

Peter sat dumbfounded. He didn't know what to say. He hadn't expected Mrs. Hastings to so willingly concur. This discussion had turned out to be much easier than he thought it would be.

"In any case, we think Naya might have other such dreams," Peter said. "We'll have to keep an eye on her and make sure that she doesn't hurt herself during those episodes."

"Most definitely. I've been praying that it doesn't happen again," Mrs. Hastings said with undue faith. She stood up, anxious to take her daughter home.

Peter escorted Mrs. Hastings through the blue doors of the unit. He wondered if he needed to tell Mrs. Hastings about Naya's involvement in the FBI investigation of Janet's murder. He decided to hold off until he had more information. He wanted to make sure Naya's drawings proved to be accurate and helped to catch the killer.

Naya ran to her mother from the nurses' station as soon as she saw her. She jumped in joy and wrapped her arms around her mother's waist. "Where's Daddy?" she squealed.

"He's at work, dear. You'll see him when he gets home," Mrs. Hastings said with a big smile.

Mrs. Hastings gave her daughter a hug. Once Naya settled down, she explained to Naya that she would come to see Peter in a week's time for a quick checkup. Naya was much too preoccupied with going back home to understand what her mother was trying to tell her.

"I'll tell her again when we get home," Mrs. Hastings told Peter with a nod.

Peter called the nurses' station and notified Matt to page him if he needed anything, since Peter was going to be out of the building for some time. He told them he was running home to get his ID badge and would be back in time to say good-bye to Naya. He instructed Matt to guide Mrs. Hastings to the administrative office to complete the discharge process. He grabbed his jacket and left the fellows' office, dashing out to the parking lot.

Once in his Jeep, he sped toward his apartment. Thinking about Naya's discharge made him a little sad. He was going to miss her lively personality. But on the other hand, he was glad that tests had revealed her to be a healthy little girl. He could still follow her in the outpatient clinic as one of his therapeutic cases. That consolation put a small smile on his face.

Peter reached his apartment a few minutes earlier than usual, since midday traffic was light. He scrambled from his vehicle and ran straight to the main entrance. Once in the elevator, he waited impatiently to reach his floor. He exited the elevator, removing a bunch of keys from his pocket as he hurried across the hallway. He stood in front of his apartment door, fumbling with his keys as he tried to find the right one.

Peter opened the door to his apartment and walked straight into his bedroom. He was pretty sure he had left his ID badge next to the nightstand. He spotted the ID, picked it up, and clipped it to his jacket. He also looked for Naya's drawings, which he distinctly remembered placing under his badge. But nothing was there.

Peter stood staring at the blank spot on his nightstand in silent bafflement. Suddenly, a strange chill rippled down his back. The feeling was eerie and intense. He shuddered and felt his body hair rise and fall as the chill traversed his spine. He looked around instinctively, checking to see if somebody was watching him. He shook off the feeling, dismissing the silly thought and attributing the chill to the cool temperature of the room. He scanned the bed and spotted Naya's drawings lying in the center of the bed. *Oh, well,* he thought to himself as he knelt on the bed and extended his arm to pick up the papers.

Peter tucked Naya's pictures safely into his pocket and headed out of his apartment. He had to get back to the hospital as soon as possible if he was going to get to say good-bye to Naya.

{CHAPTER FIFTY-NINE}

Monday

The slaaf had been startled by the sound of keys jingling at the front door. He snapped out of his trance and cocked his head. In haste, he dropped the pictures that he held onto the mattress and ran into the living room to confirm his perceptions. He heard the resonance of the chamber moving and the door unlocking. He bolted back into the bedroom in horror, looking for a place to hide. He scanned the room quickly and spotted a walk-in closet in the corner. He ran into it and closed the bifold doors partially behind him.

The slaaf now stood in the dark silently, waiting for the uninvited intrusion to leave. His nose twitched in the dust, and he felt large beads of sweat trickling down his forehead. His heart throbbed all the way to his temples. Wasn't Peter supposed to be at work? But if this unidentified visitor wasn't Peter, who on earth was it?

The slaaf heard footsteps enter the bedroom. From where he stood, he could see a silhouette pass through the room and pause in front of the nightstand. He bent his torso so that he could get a glimpse. To his surprise, he saw Peter. He watched Peter pick up the ID badge and clip it on his jacket. Then the doctor stood motionlessly for a moment before leaning over the bed and picking up the papers that the slaaf had just dropped.

Within a few seconds, the doctor was gone. The slaaf stepped out of the closet after he heard the front door slam shut. His hands still trembled, but he began to feel a little better. The claustrophobic closet had nearly forced him to reveal himself. He stepped toward the living-room window and peeked through the curtains. Within moments, he saw Peter run to a red Jeep parked in the parking lot. He waited for Peter to drive away.

Once Peter was no longer visible, the slaaf rushed out of the apartment and down the corridor to the elevator. He saw that the elevator was still at the ground floor. He couldn't wait for another moment; he ran to the emergency stairwell. He clambered down the stairs two at a time. When he burst out of the apartment complex, he could still see the red Jeep driving away in the distance.

The slaaf took a deep breath. That had been a close call. He had to get to Naya.

He dashed to the parking lot and jumped in his car.

*   *   *   *

Peter drove through town on his way to the hospital. He thought about how much he would miss Naya. He had become quite fond of her. She had brought a new meaning to life and death, as well as to his identity. Without her drawings, the police could have not progressed in their investigation of Janet's murder. Thanks to Naya's special abilities, the case might be solved before Peter's uncle's election. Peter was still smarting over the way his stunt at Elephant Rock had greatly upset his uncle. Now he could breathe easy because his name was cleared.

Despite his rushed schedule, Peter spontaneously decided to stop at a greeting-card store to buy Naya a gift. It took him a few minutes to find a parking spot that wasn't too far from the store. Once he stepped out of the car, he realized that he was going to be late.

Peter pulled out his phone and dialed. "Matt, this is Peter," he said.

"Are you coming soon?"

"Yes, but I'll be delayed by at least twenty minutes. Can you tell Naya and her family that I'm running behind?"

"Sure! See you soon."

Peter ended his conversation and walked into the store. He browsed for an appropriate gift for Naya. Out of a seemingly endless offering of cards and trinkets, nothing captured his eye. He walked to the end of an aisle and found a small section of stuffed animals. *A teddy bear would be an ideal gift*, he thought to himself. *Someone to keep Noodle company.*

Peter picked up a golden brown teddy bear with soft, curly fur. Naya would like it, he decided. When it was his turn at the cash register, he added a pack of gum to his purchase. He collected his change and headed back to his vehicle. He was looking forward to giving Naya her teddy bear.

{CHAPTER SIXTY}

Monday

"What do we do now?" Lieutenant Andrew asked the senator. He floated the idea of randomly collecting DNA samples from the surgical community, as they didn't have any positive leads that would guarantee the killer's capture any sooner.

"I'm sorry. You'll have to find another way to screen the potential suspects," Senator Bailey replied over the telephone.

Lieutenant Andrew briefed the senator on the latest findings. "Two teams are heading out as we speak to check out this suspect," he told the senator. The senator wished him luck. "Thank you," he replied before ending their conversation.

The lieutenant was genuinely grateful for the senator's well wishes; he needed all the luck he could muster. He looked at his watch with increasing tension. Leia and José would reach their destination any moment now.

*　　*　　*　　*

"He isn't home," Leia said, walking inside Everson's apartment. She had found out that Everson was the only Jamaican male surgeon in the hospital. Given the personal information she had gathered from the hospital, he fit the description of the suspect.

"Well, look here," José said, picking up a crumpled piece of aluminum foil. "I think our surgeon is doing drugs." Remnants of the white powder stuck to the foil. "Looks like high-grade coke."

"No wonder he couldn't pay his debts," Leia commented.

"I wonder what other crimes he's got under his belt," José mused, implying that Everson could very well be the killer they were looking for so desperately. "He clearly doesn't concern himself with the ethics you'd expect from a surgeon."

Leia looked around for more clues. The apartment was disorganized and poorly maintained. She walked up to a small magnetic photo frame that stuck to the refrigerator. "This must be him."

José joined her, and they both gazed at an old photograph of Everson. A small imprint showed the date.

"This is fairly recent," Leia commented. "Good."

Without any warning, someone knocked on the apartment door.

Leia put her finger to her lips, and José nodded. She walked up to the door and peered through the peephole. "A woman," she whispered. She opened the door and stood in front of a housekeeper who was holding a bucket.

"And who are you?" the woman asked.

Leia flashed her FBI badge, leaving the woman both surprised and confused.

"Has he done anything wrong?" the housekeeper asked Leia nervously.

"We're just here to ask him a few questions. That's all I can tell you" Leia said sternly.

"H-he's at work in the hospital," the housekeeper stuttered.

"Why don't you come back later to clean the apartment?" Leia asked, though it wasn't really a request.

"All right," the housekeeper said tersely and hurried away down the corridor.

"Send someone to the hospital," Leia told José. She hadn't been able to track Everson down after her morning meeting with Peter. "I need to know everything about this man, including the car he drives," Leia continued.

"I'll get on it right away," José replied.

Leia ordered José to have a criminal-investigation team come and sweep Everson's apartment for fingerprints and DNA samples.

{CHAPTER SIXTY-ONE}

Monday Afternoon

Everson drove frantically, not knowing what to do next. His thoughts were quickly interrupted by his cell phone ringing. "Yes?" he answered. The phone call heightened his anxiety; he was already jumpy enough without any more complications. He recognized the voice instantly.

"Doc, I need you to do something very important for me," the caller said. "You're the only one who can do it, and you have no choice." Everson sat silently as the caller made his request. He paled as the speaker revealed the details of the task.

"I can't do that. I refuse to do that!"

"If you don't, then you know what I can do to you ... or rather, your girlfriend," the speaker threatened. "Do you want off the hook or not? Think about it—you have two seconds to make a decision. Remember, you owe me money ... and her life is at stake."

"Two seconds?"

"One second. Zero seconds. Okay, I guess I'll just—"

"Wait! Okay. I'll do it."

After he hung up, a million things flashed through Everson's mind, but the lasting thing he saw in his mind's eye was a beautiful, curvy woman in a floral dress. Evelyn ... how could he let anything happen to Evelyn? He had always thought he would do whatever it took to keep her safe, and now that sentiment was being put to the test.

"This is crazy," he said to himself. He rotated the steering wheel forcefully, causing the car to swerve and turn about with a screech. Everson had to return to the children's psychiatric unit.

It took Everson about fifteen minutes to reach the parking lot. He jumped out of the car and ran into the unit, straight to the nurses' station. "Has anyone seen Peter?" he asked a busy staff member.

"He left the unit a little while ago, and he's not back yet," the staff member replied.

Everson walked down the hallway by himself, peeping into every room as he walked by. He stopped at the room he was looking for, then looked around to make sure that there was nobody behind him.

"Hi," Everson said to Naya, who was standing by the bed with her back to him.

Naya turned around and smiled. She had seen him before. "You're Dr. Gram's friend," she said.

"Yes, I am."

"Do you know where Dr. Gram is?" Naya asked him.

"I sure do. He asked me to take you to him. Will you come with me?"

"Sure," Naya answered. "What about my mom? I'm supposed to wait for her here."

"It'll be only for a little while. Dr. Gram wanted to show you something special. He couldn't bring it here, so he asked me to get you," Everson lied.

"Can I bring these pictures?" Naya asked, picking up a folder from the table.

"Yes, you can."

"Okay … let's go," The trust in Naya's voice made Everson want to vomit.

Naya walked up to Everson and slipped her small hand into his. Everson swallowed hard, then said, "Well … all right then. Off we go." Everson led her quickly down the hallway while the staff member at the nurses' station was distracted with measuring medications. Naya waved at the oblivious employee, while Everson stared straight ahead, praying that no one saw him. He had sent the receptionist on a wild goose chase for a nonexistent memo, so that helped. Everson led his quarry out of the building as quickly as possible.

Naya quietly followed him through the parking lot.

"Where is he?" Naya asked.

"He's near my car."

"I don't see him."

"You have to be patient."

Everson stopped at his blue BMW. "Get in. I'll take you to him."

"No, thank you … I'll wait here." Naya's manners didn't hide her anxiety. As much as she wanted to see Peter, she didn't want to leave the hospital.

"Get in now, you little squirt!" Everson shouted at her. He flung open the door and shoved her into the backseat.

Naya fell face-first into the car. Her folder slipped out of her hand, and the drawings inside spilled out onto the asphalt. Everson grabbed her legs, shoved her the rest of the way inside the car, and shut the door. She heard the door slam. Her abductor had gotten into the driver's seat and started the engine. She sat up and tried to open the door, but it was childproof and couldn't be unlocked from the inside. She was so stunned that she could barely react.

Everson shifted the gear and drove away. Any second thoughts evaporated as he adjusted to the new plan. He looked in the rearview mirror to see if anybody had seen what he had done. The parking lot was as quiet as when he had first arrived.

He focused on the task at hand. It was simple enough; all he needed to do was take Naya to the cabin. After that, he could go on with the rest of his day, a free bird. The thought of a carefree life brought a smile to his face.

{CHAPTER SIXTY-TWO}

Monday

Peter heard the commotion and the screams from the nurses' station just as he entered the area. He ran to the nurses' station and saw Mrs. Hastings frantically sobbing and flailing her arms. Her usually porcelain skin was blotchy and red, and her sleek blond hair was badly disheveled. He dropped the bag that held Naya's teddy bear onto the floor.

"Mrs. Hastings … what happened?" Peter asked her in bewilderment as she trembled with fear.

"I can't find Naya … I can't find my baby! I looked all over the unit. The staff members don't know where she is. I think something has happened to her—something terrible! All I did was go to the admission office, and when I got back, she was gone."

"What?" Peter was astonished at what he had just heard. He had no clue where Naya could be. He walked around the unit, asking various staff members if they had seen her. No one had.

"Well, she couldn't have just disappeared," Peter said. "How would she have gotten through the metal doors without a key? And Naya doesn't seem like someone who would wander off anyway."

Everyone stood around a hiccupping, choking Mrs. Hastings, completely stumped.

"I know how she got out," a small voice said.

Everyone turned, and standing in the hall behind them was Sasha.

She smiled, pleased to be able to help. "Your friend took her away," she said to Peter. "He thought I didn't see, but I did! He was real tall and bald!"

"Everson …" Peter was surprised. *What would he want with her?* he thought to himself. *Unless he really is the killer* … "Oh, my God, I think he's kidnapped her," he said out loud. He ran back to the nurses' station to see how Mrs. Hastings was holding up.

"Somebody please help me," Mrs. Hastings wailed, breaking down in tears again and collapsing to the ground.

"I think he took her out of the building," Peter said, looking at the blue doors of the unit through the Plexiglas of the nurses' station.

Mrs. Hastings could barely lift her head to look at him.

"Ask the EMTs at the adult ER to come here, stat—Mrs. Hastings is passing out," Peter shouted to Matt, who bolted down the corridor, along with a few other staff members. He placed Mrs. Hastings's head into Matt's hands as soon as Matt reached his side. "I'll go look for Naya," he told Matt.

Peter was now convinced that Everson was the killer, just as Leia suspected. Why else would he take Naya off the unit? It made sense that the killer would be enraged at Naya's participation in the case, and who else even knew about it besides Everson? He ran out into the parking lot, trying not to panic. He looked all around and in between the cars, but just as the fluttering feeling in his stomach had predicted, Naya was nowhere in sight. Then he spotted a familiar folder lying on the ground, next to an empty parking space. Papers lay scattered across the asphalt. He quickly ran over and gathered the loose sheets of paper with shaking hands.

Peter stared down at all of Naya's drawings. He put them back one by one into the folder, looking at them as he did. He spotted a drawing that he had not seen before.

Stunned and increasingly terrified, Peter gaped at the shocking artwork. The picture was of Naya lying strapped to a bed as a large person stabbed her with a knife. Blood spurted out of her body as if from a water fountain. The entire paper was covered by bright red crayon. There were no inscriptions, nor had she signed her name.

Peter knew with terrible certainty that Naya was in grave danger. He couldn't understand why she had not shared this particular picture with him. The most likely explanation was that she feared she wouldn't go home if she showed it to him. He put the drawings back in the folder and ran back into the unit.

"Naya has been kidnapped," Peter told Matt in a shaky voice. "God, this is all my fault!"

"What? Kidnapped?" Matt was still confused about what was going on. "Does Everson have something to do with this?"

"I'll explain it to you later," Peter replied and whirled around.

"Where are you going?" Matt shouted after him.

"To find my patient!" Peter screamed over his shoulder as he ran toward his vehicle.

Once inside his Jeep, Peter flipped open his cell phone and looked under his outgoing calls, hoping that Leia's number was still registered. He pressed the send button as soon as he found it and listened for Leia to answer.

"This is Peter. I think Everson has kidnapped Naya!" he said once again, emphasizing Everson's name.

"When did this happen?" Leia could always be counted upon to catch up quickly, without asking irrelevant questions.

"A few minutes ago, here at the hospital."

There was a brief silence before Leia spoke again. "Are you sure it was your friend Everson who did it?"

"I haven't seen him all day, and I think he's the one. Sasha was the last one to see Naya—and she was leaving with Everson."

"We also think he might be involved."

"Well, I'm sure he is," Peter said firmly. "My best bet is that Everson has taken Naya to Elephant Rock. If he wants to kill again, he'll do it there. I'm going after them."

"Oh, no you aren't," Leia said with alarm. "That's the worst possible thing you can do at this moment. He may be armed and dangerous. We'll handle the situation. Just wait for us near Elephant Rock. I don't want you to—well, I mean, I don't want anyone to get hurt."

"Okay," Peter replied, pleased at her concern for him—which was absurd, considering the unpleasant circumstances. In any case, nothing could stop him from looking for Naya on his own—not even a beautiful woman with a gun.

Peter sped out of the hospital campus in pursuit of Naya's kidnapper. He blamed himself for the incident. If only he had remembered his ID card and discharged Naya sooner, this wouldn't have happened. Peter pushed the thought out of his mind and focused on getting to Elephant Rock as quickly as possible.

*　　*　　*　　*

Leia ran to her car, which was still parked in front of Everson's apartment. She noticed that a police officer was citing her for parking in a no-parking zone. She whipped out her FBI badge as she approached the officer. "FBI—this is my car!" she yelled. The police officer stepped away from the car, and even before she could say anything, Leia was strapping herself into her driver's seat. "This is an emergency," she shouted out to the officer, who still stood frozen, dazed by her actions. She drove away, leaving the police officer with a ticket in his hand. She had instructed José to keep an eye on Everson's apartment and to notify Lieutenant Andrew of the new events. She needed one squad to go to the hospital to confirm that Everson wasn't there. She dispatched another squad to Elephant Rock, hoping that Peter's hunch was right. If not, Naya's life was in even greater danger.

{CHAPTER SIXTY-THREE}

Monday

Matt and the other staff members continued to tend to Mrs. Hastings.

"What happened?" Matt heard Mrs. Hastings cry out softly. "Where's Naya?" She had slowly realized that her daughter was nowhere in sight.

"I don't know how to tell you this, but … Dr. Gram thinks someone has kidnapped her," Matt said softly to her.

"Oh … no," Mrs. Hastings said, her eyes widening to full alert as she looked at Matt. "No! Why would somebody do that? She was just here … please bring her back." She moaned a few more incomprehensible words just before losing consciousness.

"Did someone call the police?" Matt asked a nearby staff member.

"Yes—I did," the staff member responded.

It took less than five minutes for an ambulance to arrive at Strauss I. Luckily, it had been parked at the medical ER when the distress call had gone through, so the vehicle could immediately be dispatched to the scene. Matt watched the EMT personnel lift Mrs. Hastings onto a stretcher and strap an oxygen mask across her face. He climbed into the ambulance and rode with them to the medical ER.

*　　　*　　　*　　　*

En route to the hospital, the lieutenant got a call from José informing him that someone had kidnapped the girl. Upon his arrival at the hospital campus, Lieutenant Andrew drove straight to the medical emergency room. At the front desk, he inquired about Mrs. Hastings. He was led to the fast-track examination rooms, where he found Mrs. Hastings recovering from her panic attack, if not her broken heart. She had regained consciousness, though she remained a little disoriented.

He introduced himself to Mr. Hastings, who stood next to his ailing wife.

"Do you know where Naya is?" Mr. Hastings asked frantically. He had rushed to the medical emergency room from work as soon as he had received the information about his daughter's disappearance and wife's hysterical episode.

"We're looking for her kidnapper," the lieutenant replied, trying to reassure them that everything that could be done was being done. "Can I speak to your wife?" he asked.

Mr. Hastings turned to Jane. "Are you up to it?" he asked.

"Yes, dear … anything for Naya," Mrs. Hastings said weakly.

Lieutenant Andrew tried to get as much information as possible about what had happened, but all Mrs. Hastings knew was that her daughter was gone.

"Will they find her?" Mrs. Hastings asked, hiccupping into sobs once again.

"We will, we will," Lieutenant Andrew said. *My God, when will it end? Why can't we just go back to the way things used to be?* The lieutenant was determined not to have another murder happen on his watch. He thanked the Hastings and walked out with his comrade back to the police cruiser.

The lieutenant headed to the main hospital building, looking for Everson. He needed to confirm the doctor's absence. It didn't take him long to find out that Everson was definitely gone; the murder suspect made no response to several pages, and no one had seen him. There was no doubt in the lieutenant's mind that Everson was guilty.

{CHAPTER SIXTY-FOUR}

Monday

Naya was bound at the hands and legs. She tried to sit up, but she was unable to move. She wriggled, trying to set herself free. She tried to scream, but her lips were sealed shut. Blackness surrounded her. Fear overwhelmed her, and she lay sweating, even though she didn't feel hot. The air felt cool around her as though she was standing in front of a refrigerator.

Naya lay still, exhausted from struggling. She was sure that the big, bad man had brought her to this place. She was angry that Janet had not kept her promise to protect her. Naya fought tears as despair set in. She wanted her mommy.

Naya heard a door open, followed by the striking of a match. She flexed her neck and tried to look in the direction of her toes. She could see the faint flicker of a candle approaching her. The candle appeared to float in midair; only when it got closer could she see the monster who carried it.

Naya tracked the candle with her eyes. The person who held it came close and stood next to her. She knew it was the big, bad man, just from the size of the shadow that his body cast onto the wall behind him. She couldn't see his face, as the candlelight blinded her.

The man placed the candle behind her head. Naya could feel the flame's heat on her scalp. Her head began to feel much warmer than the rest of her body. She couldn't tell what the man was doing behind her. She could hear the tapping and scraping of metal. She tried to tilt her head backward; she arched her body as much as she could, but to no avail.

The man breathed heavily as he came and stood next to her. She could only see the whites of his eyes glimmering in the candlelight. She felt him untie her arms; he held her right arm and lifted it into the air, mumbling what sounded like a prayer under his breath. She then saw him lift one of his hands straight into the air above her face. In his hand, she spotted a sharp and pointed knife. The blade reflected the golden glow of the candle flame behind her. She watched the knife swing down and make contact with her arm. She wanted to scream, but she couldn't. She felt the knife pierce her delicate skin with shearing force.

Her cry went unheard, and her screams just echoed in her head.

✳   ✳   ✳   ✳

"Stop screaming," Naya heard Everson say to her. His sharp tone startled her momentarily. Naya blinked hard and turned her head toward the person who had just spoken. She hadn't realized that she was yelling in her seat. She was a little confused by the fact that she was no longer bound at her hands and legs. It took her a couple of seconds to realize that she had been reliving the dream she had the previous night—the dream that nobody knew about, including Dr. Gram.

"Are you the big, bad man?" Naya asked Everson after a few minutes of shell-shocked silence.

"For you, I'm the big, bad man," Everson said impatiently, just wanting to keep his victim quiet. "Don't say another word!" he yelled for good measure. She was distracting him as he tried to come up with a proper plan.

Naya sat silently, feeling very scared but at the same time telling herself that she needed to be brave.

Naya mustered the courage to speak once more. "Where are you taking me?"

"You'll see," Everson said sarcastically.

Naya started to cry.

"Stop that!" Everson yelled at her. Her sobs seemed to drive him closer to the edge.

Naya wiped her tears with her sleeves. She was truly petrified. Why weren't Janet and the elephant keeping her safe from the big, bad man? She felt betrayed.

The man had driven out of town and into the woods. They finally came to a stop where the road ended, and they could drive no further.

Everson got out of the car and came around to where Naya sat. He opened the door and held her shoulder with a rough grasp. "Get out," he ordered rudely.

Naya stepped out, not wanting to make the man any angrier. She looked around her and saw many tall trees stretching toward the sky. The man held her by the arm, pulling her hard as he walked toward the woods.

Everson took her deeper and deeper into the woods. This was a place he had been before. Naya began to resist, but Everson was strong, and he didn't hesitate to drag her through the underbrush when necessary, digging into the tender skin on her arm. She began to wail more loudly in horror and excruciating discomfort. Unfortunately, there was no one in sight to hear her cries. This wasn't a dream. It was reality, and it was the scariest moment of her life.

{CHAPTER SIXTY-FIVE}

Monday

Peter parked in his usual spot behind Elephant Rock. He jumped out of the Jeep so quickly that he nearly fell down. He sprinted toward Elephant Rock, then climbed its familiar terrain. It took him a few minutes to reach the top. Once on top, he looked around, scanning the woods in front of him. Yellow police tape still wrapped the area, undisturbed since the last time he had been there. He strained his ears for any kind of unusual noise. The only sound was that of his heart beating rapidly behind his eardrums.

Peter walked up to the very edge of the rock and scanned the area once again. There was no one in sight. He squatted on top of the rock, wondering if he had missed something. *Everson must have brought Naya by now*, he thought.

Peter waited restlessly on top of the rock. Strange, how the significance of the landmark had changed for him. Once, he had come here for peace and serenity as he fled his turbulent home life. Now, he came here for confrontation. He came looking for a fight. He wasn't running away anymore.

He got up and paced back and forth, clenching his fist and grinding his teeth. He looked at his watch to see how much time had passed. It had been only three minutes, but it felt like eternity. Still he saw no sign of them. He stood up and climbed down the rock in the direction of his Jeep. He tried calling Leia on his cell phone, but he received no wireless signal. He quickly clipped the phone onto his belt and hurried to his Jeep with a feeling of intense anxiety and helplessness. He unlocked the door and sat in the driver's seat. He opened the folder that lay in the passenger seat next to him. He looked at all of Naya's pictures once again, stopping at the gruesome picture she hadn't shared with him. He carefully scrutinized the drawing for details that he might have missed.

Peter stared hard at the rendered features of the large man. Peter had the feeling that he had seen such a face somewhere before, but he couldn't tell if this was Everson. Peter felt a chill go down his spine, and his palms broke out in a cold sweat. It was the same eerie feeling that he had felt earlier in the day. He couldn't explain the feeling, but he suspected it had to do with Naya's picture. He thought really hard, trying to recollect one other time he had felt such a dreadful feeling. One such memory suddenly surfaced in his mind.

Six months earlier, Peter had been trekking by Willow Lake. He distinctly remembered feeling thirsty after his long hike. He had taken a couple of swigs from his water bottle. He deviated from the trail for a moment and walked toward the lake. He bent down to splash some water on his face.

Peter remembered looking at his reflection. Just as his fingers touched the water, the strangest feeling seeped into his entire body. He had scrambled to his feet, feeling scared. At the time, he couldn't explain why he felt that way, because there was no reason. He had hurried back to the trail, no longer wanting to be in the vicinity of the lake.

Now, Peter was once again experiencing that awful feeling. The thought of Willow Lake made him realize that Everson would have taken Naya to the cabin. That was a safe place that the police wouldn't have known about. He started his Jeep and started backing out from under the tree. He stopped in his path momentarily as he changed the gear from reverse to drive. At that moment, he remembered that Leia would arrive soon. He reached for his phone only to discover that it wasn't on his belt.

"Damn—I must have dropped it!" Peter said in frustration, there was no time to go look for it.

With no phone, there was no way to reach Leia. Peter's sense of urgency was immense. He needed to reach the cabin quickly. It was the only hunch that he could work with at the moment. He knew that if he didn't act right away, Naya might join her friend Janet permanently. He decided not to wait for Leia; time was running out.

Peter took his foot off the brake pedal and drove along the unpaved road as fast as he could. The shores of Willow Lake were two miles away.

*   *   *   *

Leia reached Elephant Rock within eight minutes of receiving Peter's urgent call. She had to depend on the GPS that was in her car. She realized that she had taken longer than she had intended. Once she reached the woods, she pulled her car to the side of the unpaved road and parked. She stepped out of her car and toward Elephant Rock, weaving through the crisscrossed police tape all the way there. She looked toward the top of the giant rock, hoping to spot Peter somewhere.

To Leia's surprise, the area was quiet, with no signs of any recent activity. She remembered the direction in which Peter had climbed up Elephant Rock. She rushed in that direction and began to climb the rock herself. Once on top she stood looking around. She walked to the back of the rock, trying to spot Peter's red Jeep; she remembered that he had parked it on the other side of the rock last time. But his vehicle was nowhere in sight. She climbed down to the area where Peter had once parked. She noticed a shiny object on the ground—a cell phone. She flipped it open and saw Peter's name on the screen. Now there was no way of reaching him.

Leia climbed back up and spent the next four minutes pacing restlessly on the rock. Her hands were cold and clammy, and she pressed them to her face.

This couldn't be happening again. Against her will, she flashed back yet again to the rat-eaten face of that little boy in San José. She hadn't been able to save him, and now she was failing again, and she didn't know what to do. And now, Peter was out there somewhere as well, possibly in danger.

To her disbelieving horror, her eyes began to sting.

You have got *to be kidding me. Come on, snap out of it!* she told herself harshly. *This isn't the time to give up. You're a federal agent chasing a murderer, not a little kid getting bullied on the school bus. If you choke when Peter—when everyone—needs you the most, you'll really have something to cry about, won't you?* She took a deep breath and squared her shoulders, forcing herself to calm down. *Okay. Think about your next move. What's your next move?*

All of a sudden, she heard footsteps emerging from the trees in front of her. She quickly stood up and pulled out her gun from its holster, not wanting to take any chances. She held her breath and waited to see who would come into her sight. Her hands trembled as she held her arms stretched out.

"Don't shoot—it's me," Leia heard a familiar voice shout out to her. To her relief and disappointment, she saw José walk toward her.

"Did you think I was Everson?" José called out to Leia as she put away her gun. She climbed down the rock and walked to where José stood. Her anxiety receded; she was glad to see him.

"The apartment was covered by other officers. I heard on the radio that you were coming here."

"They're not here," Leia said with an uncharacteristic despair. She was exhausted.

"If Peter isn't here, then where is he?" José asked.

"I don't know. He said he would be here," Leia said anxiously. "I found his cell phone on the ground. I think Peter had a hunch that the killer would bring his victim back here … and I think he was wrong."

"Maybe he realized that too and decided to go somewhere else," José theorized.

"But where?" Leia thought aloud.

The two of them stood looking at each other, stumped. They had to act fast, but neither of them knew what to do.

Leia suddenly had an idea. "Ask the aerial team to look for a red Jeep in this area!" She knew Peter drove a brightly colored vehicle that could be spotted easily.

"Everson drives a blue BMW," José added. "I just got that information today."

Leia and José walked back to José's car, which was parked next to hers. José climbed in and used the police wireless set to radio in. "Lieutenant, they're not here."

"What do you mean?" the lieutenant bellowed angrily out of the dashboard speaker with a distorted crackle. "This is goddamned frustrating!"

"I know it is," José acknowledged. "But listen: I need the aerial team to scout the area around Elephant Rock and the lake for a red Jeep or a blue BMW."

"Got it," they heard the lieutenant say before he ended his transmission.

"We'll just have to wait here for further information, I guess," José said with an irritated shrug. They had no other leads to follow. Everson wasn't at work, not at home, and not at Elephant Rock. They had no clue where he could be. Their best bet was to track Peter. He was their only hope now.

{CHAPTER SIXTY-SIX}

Monday

The lieutenant raced in his cruiser toward Elephant Rock. Behind him, cruisers fanned out on side roads to engulf the entire area. He was really frustrated and worried at the same time. He had the entire police department roaming aimlessly around Elephant Rock; that was definitely not a good sign. Now José had to tell him that neither Everson nor Peter were at Elephant Rock.

"Dispatch the chopper right away," Lieutenant Andrew ordered at the top of his lungs through his walkie-talkie. He drove with his sirens screaming and blazing toward Elephant Rock. He spotted two cars parked on to one side and pulled in right behind them.

Lieutenant Andrew asked his fellow officer to stay in the car and listen for any incoming information. He walked over to Leia and José, who stood against one of the cars. "Goddamn it!" he cursed loud enough so that they could hear him.

"Any news?" Leia asked the lieutenant.

"None so far," the lieutenant replied.

Leia knew she had the support of José and the lieutenant, but she still felt tense and worried.

"We have to find Everson's car from the air," the lieutenant said.

"I think we have a better chance of finding Peter's; his red Jeep can easily be spotted," Leia said. "I think he knows where Everson is taking Naya."

The officer who had accompanied the lieutenant came jogging up. "Sir," he said, "we just received a call from the aerial team stating that they've spotted a red Jeep driving down toward the lake about four and a half miles south of here. There's also a blue BMW parked half a mile from a log cabin."

Lieutenant Andrew went back to his car and grabbed a topographical map of the area. "This should be the location," he said, tapping on the map. The cabin wasn't within the current police search area.

"I know how to get there," José said with some enthusiasm. He knew where the cabin was located. "I'll take Leia while you keep a lookout over here."

Leia and José didn't waste another second. They sped away, kicking up a large cloud of dust behind them. The lieutenant watched and hoped that they were right. It wasn't much, but hoping was all he could do at that moment.

{CHAPTER SIXTY-SEVEN}

Monday

Everson pulled Naya along the muddy path to the cabin where he and Peter had spent time together when they needed to relax. There were times when Everson had met Arcus here without Peter's knowledge to conduct his prohibited dealings.

Naya struggled to escape Everson's tight hold. She tried to keep up with his pace. She fell a few times and found herself being dragged. Her arm hurt tremendously as he yanked her along the way.

Everson came to a halt in front of the log cabin. The cabin had a large window in the front and two smaller windows on the sides. A number of shrubs surrounded the cabin; a few creeping vines reached the roofline. He could see a light shining inside the cabin.

Everson knocked on the door. "Come in," he heard a voice boom. Everson didn't hesitate to obey. He had hardened himself to the idea of handing over Naya in order to save his girlfriend's life.

Everson pushed the door open and stepped inside. He pulled Naya from behind him and pushed her forward.

"This is who you wanted," Everson said angrily to the man who stood with his back facing him.

"Now leave her here, and get out," the man ordered.

Everson knew that his own actions would surely make him sick with regret later, when something awful happened to Evelyn, but he just couldn't take any more chances. He was already knee deep in problems that he had to resolve. He shoved Naya into the cabin and stepped out. As he turned to exit, he noticed a bunch of knives on a small table. He closed the door behind him and walked away from the cabin. When he walked a few yards, he heard a bloodcurdling scream. "No!"

Everson was shaken by the scream. Deep down, he had suspected what the man wanted with Naya, but the entire situation had suddenly become very real to him when he saw those knives.

Everson feared for his life and for his girlfriend's life. He was scared of losing everything he cared about: his job, his love, his freedom. But what was about to happen behind that cabin door was terrible, and he had to stop it. It was wrong to save his own skin at the expense of a little girl. He turned around and headed back into the cabin. He pushed open the door, which was still unlocked. He saw the man tying Naya's hands with tape as she sat on a small cot in the corner of the cabin. The man turned around with a gun in his hand.

Before Everson knew it, a bullet went through his right shoulder. He winced in pain and fell back out of the cabin, thrown by the shot's impact. He rolled on the ground, holding his shoulder. He was bleeding profusely and in agonizing pain. He writhed on the grass, helpless to save anyone, including himself.

*   *   *   *

The slaaf's plan had worked. He had blackmailed Everson into bringing Naya to him. Somehow, he had convinced a man of medicine to hand deliver a small child to him! It was amazing, what people would do to protect their own happiness, whether they deserved it or not; this was his lucky day! Now he could end the matter of the little girl who had signed her name to incriminating drawings. The slaaf had once limited himself to small sacrifices made through his work. However, as time went on, the masqueraded offerings had failed to keep his fears at bay. Having spent four years in the area, he had become well acquainted with Elephant Rock and its geographical vicinity. He began to hunt for other small animals and work on their carcasses in Mr. Deed's unused boathouse. Within no time, the boathouse had become a secret altar where he deceived Anansi and performed the tools of his trade.

In spite of the change in tactic, the slaaf had felt utterly dissatisfied. He began to spend more time looking for larger animals, such as dogs and cats. He gradually began to believe that maybe the ultimate sacrifice of a human being would quell his fears. Finally, he could resist temptation no longer. One day in 1967, he had abducted a girl he saw trekking near Willow Lake. She became the ultimate sacrifice to end this divine torture.

The slaaf had never known who she was and didn't want to know. After keeping her for a few hours in the boathouse, he took her to Elephant Rock, along with his armamentarium of steel blades. It took him only an hour to sacrifice and display her for Anansi.

That night, he had slept peacefully for the first time in so long. The rituals were no longer necessary, he reasoned. Life returned to what he considered normal. He was happy working at Ken's shop and the local farms.

It was only after the media splattered the headlines with the killing did the slaaf learn who his victim really was. Over the next few years, the memory of his human sacrifice had faded. The killing had gone unsolved by the police and forgotten by the community. He continued to live in a low profile.

Then, one day, the slaaf met Tayshia, who worked at one of the neighboring ranches. They fell in love, got married, and had a good life. At that point, the last vestiges of his need to use the boathouse ceased entirely, and he became a content man with minimal fears and discomfort.

But misfortune had finally struck the slaaf again only a year ago, when Tayshia was diagnosed with a highly invasive cancer. She died within two months of her diagnosis. This put him back in a spiraling bout of depression. Memories of lost ones engulfed his thoughts day in and out. Old habits and practices slowly reemerge. He returned to the old, dilapidated boathouse in secrecy. He began to hunt for cats and dogs to sacrifice. It was during one such ritual when the white girl stumbled into his path. She was just an unfortunate soul who showed up in the wrong place at the wrong time. He had tried to refrain from doing what he had done many years ago, but the urge to do so had overpowered him. He had thought of the tranquility that had followed his first human sacrifice. He felt justified to carry it out again, as the opportunity had dropped right into his hands.

On that fateful day, he had acted swiftly, taking the white girl by surprise. Once she had passed out, he took her to his altar and sacrificed her. He then returned to Elephant Rock and placed her in the exact arrangement he had used in 1967 in hopes that the curse would pass away, just as it had the previous time.

"How did you know what I did to Janet?" the slaaf asked Naya in a calm tone as she lay on the cot.

"She told me," Naya murmured softly.

"You're lying!" the slaaf screamed at her, scaring her further.

"No, I'm not!" Naya replied and began to cry.

"Do you know how I know you're lying?" the man asked Naya.

"No," Naya said, quivering with fear.

"Because she's dead, you fool," the slaaf said with a snarl.

Naya began to tremble. She couldn't understand what the man was talking about. "I want to go home," she cried out. She couldn't help but beg, though even her young mind knew it was of no use. "Please let me go …"

Now everything had become a lot more complicated. The slaaf's plan to make additional sacrifices on his boathouse altar had been thwarted by the doctor and the FBI agent. When he realized that Everson had access to Naya, he decided to make use of him. This was a chance to find out how much the girl knew before making the ultimate sacrifice.

The slaaf taped Naya's mouth to dampen her screams. This was the moment that he had been waiting for. Now he could please Anansi once and for all.

{CHAPTER SIXTY-EIGHT}

Monday

Peter ran faster when he heard a gunshot. Had his worst fears come true? He sprinted toward the cabin. As he got closer, he spotted Everson rolling on the ground.

"Where is Naya, you bastard? What have you done to her?" Peter shouted in fury, ignoring the fact that Everson was possibly bleeding to death. "Did you kill Janet too?"

"What?" Everson sounded confused.

"Did you kill Janet?" Peter repeated as he stepped closer to the man who had once been his friend.

"I didn't kill anybody," Everson said defensively. "But ... I think I know who did. Naya's inside the cabin—hurry!" Everson tried to point.

Slowly, the logic sank in: if Everson didn't have Naya, someone else must. "Who has her?" Peter asked.

"Arcus."

"You mean, from the health club?"

"Yes."

"Why did you do this?" Peter didn't know whether he was enraged or heartbroken—maybe both. But he quickly realized that now was not the time for this conversation—not when Naya's life was at stake.

"If I didn't, he was going to kill Evelyn. You better hurry," Everson called weakly.

Peter dashed into the cabin and kicked the door. The deadbolt on the inside ripped apart, and the door swung open. He saw the man standing by the cot turn around in surprise. The man held a long, serrated knife in his right hand.

"Arcus! No! I won't let you do this!" Peter lunged forward, trying to grab the other man's hand.

Taken by surprise, Arcus dodged Peter's attack. Peter couldn't stop himself from hitting a small table in front of him. A ceramic vase and its contents fell. Peter winced in pain as it shattered on contact with his left shoulder.

"Doc," Arcus said mockingly, "I'm glad you're here. You'll make my job easy. Somehow, you and Naya know my secrets. In one stroke, I can get rid of both of you once and for all. Then Everson and I'll be in the clear. No one else knows about me." Arcus smirked, enjoying his control of the situation.

"You killed me once, and I won't let you kill me again!" Peter screamed back. "This time, I'm not a defenseless young girl. I'll stop you for good!"

"What do you mean?" Arcus huffed as he stepped away from the cot. Naya watched them from the corner of her eye. She couldn't say a word. Peter tried to sit up. He could see that Naya was helpless and terrified.

"Remember Debbie Sanders?" Peter asked tauntingly, watching Arcus for any reaction. Arcus stood frozen, stunned.

"How do you know that name?"

"It was October 11, 1967—wasn't it?"

"How do you know that?" Arcus said once again. He muttered to himself, clearly on the edge of sanity: "That's impossible ... nobody knew."

"You let her go, and I'll tell you," Peter said firmly.

"I won't! She's mine!"

Peter felt he had no other choice but to lie. "I'm Debbie Sanders, and I know everything you've been doing for the past thirty-six years."

"You're lying!" Arcus rebutted.

"No, I'm not. Look at my arms," Peter said, pushing up the sleeve of his jacket. You see these marks? This is what you did to me." He pointed to the faint bands of discoloration around his elbow. "You killed me by the lake!"

Arcus stepped forward, trying to get a closer look.

"You can't possibly know this," he breathed. "You can't!"

"But I do," Peter bluffed. "You cut me up, just like you did to the other girl."

"No! You're not Debbie!" Arcus howled.

"Yes, I am. I was born on the same day that you killed Debbie Sanders."

"Noooooo!" Arcus screamed out in agony. His body trembled with fury. "Yes, I did it—yes, I killed her there!" he confessed at the top of his lungs. "But how did you know that?"

"I didn't," Peter said. "You just told me."

Arcus was now burning with rage. He couldn't stand listening to Peter anymore. He tightened his grip on the serrated knife and came toward Peter.

Peter realized that he had successfully distracted Arcus. He instinctively lunged forward, tackling the heavyset man and knocking him to the ground. He struggled to avoid Arcus's blade as they wrestled. Arcus lost his grip and dropped the knife to the floor. The two of them grappled, each trying to get ahold of the knife. Arcus forcefully shoved his elbow into Peter's face. Peter lost his balance and fell to the floor. Arcus stood up and snatched the knife back off the floor. Peter sprang forward, taking Arcus through the side cabin window and onto the ground outside. The window shattered, spewing glass all over the cot and Naya.

Peter and Arcus continued their fight outside the cabin. The man who got the knife was the one who would survive.

*   *   *   *

Naya whimpered as glass rained down onto her body. She squirmed and struggled to get loose. She managed to pick up one of the larger pieces of glass with her fingers. With bleeding hands, she worked to slice the tape that bound her hands. She felt the glass sink deeper into her fingers as she tightly gripped the piece. Once her wrists were loose enough, she wiggled her hands and freed them. She scrambled to remove the tape from her legs. She pulled the tape off her mouth and gasped for air, then ran out the cabin as fast as she could.

{CHAPTER SIXTY-NINE}

Monday

Arcus was much stronger and larger. He managed to pin Peter flat on the ground, choking him with his robust left hand. With his right hand, he forced the knife closer to Peter's neck.

Peter tried to loosen Arcus's grip around his neck with one hand while trying to stop the advancing blade with the other. He felt faint from a lack of air. His vision blurred as he fought for his life.

Just at that moment, Peter saw a distorted figure strike Arcus from behind with a dark object. Arcus reflexively removed his hand from Peter's throat and winced in pain. Peter seized the opportunity, pushing Arcus's knife hand away from himself and toward his attacker.

Arcus couldn't stop his own hand from swinging toward himself. He felt the razor-sharp knife slice through the side of his neck. He cried out, dropped the knife, and knelt on the ground, holding his bleeding neck. Blood gushed and spurted like a fountain. Within seconds, Arcus collapsed flat on his face.

Peter sat up, coughing from the stress on his windpipe, and looked at the person standing close to him. It was Naya. She was trembling in horror as she watched Arcus's life slowly ebb away. On the ground was the big, black rock that she had used to hit Arcus on the head. She stood catatonic with fear, her eyes wide open.

Peter knelt and extended his arms, pulling Naya to his chest. She closed her eyes and began to sob. "You're safe now," Peter whispered, "and there is no big, bad man anymore. It's over ... so let's go home." He felt tears well up in his eyes. He held her tight and wept along with her. He was indebted to Naya; without her courage, he would be dead.

Peter and Naya walked away from Arcus and the pool of blood. Peter recalled what Mr. Iyengar had said in terms of Naya needing to save Peter's life first before he could help her heal. Somehow, their fates had been intertwined in this convoluted way.

*   *   *   *

Leia reached the blue BMW and red Jeep that were parked at the end of the road. She saw Everson trying to get into his car. She noticed that he was bleeding from his shoulder.

"Stop!" Leia shouted with her gun aimed at his chest. "What have you done to Naya? Where is she?"

Everson could barely speak. He pointed toward the cabin. She saw Peter and Naya slowly walking away from the cabin. She felt a rush of relief knowing that Naya was safe.

"Oh, thank God!" Leia crouched down and touched both of Naya's shoulders, gazing into her face. A much more grisly face dissipated from her mind at the sight of Naya's smooth, untouched skin. Leia glanced up at Peter and realized that he was staring at her in astonishment.

Leia cleared her throat and stood back up, smoothing her clothes and regaining her professionalism.

"What happened?" she asked, a little more evenly.

"The killer is dead," Peter said, trying not to look at his injured comrade. Clearly, they were both tremendously shaken.

"What do you mean?" Leia asked, looking at Everson. "He's right here!"

Peter went on to explain to Leia what had happened.

Leia was astounded by what she heard. She couldn't believe that the investigation had incriminated the wrong man. Of course, Everson's innocence in one area didn't let him off the hook for what he had done that day.

"Are you sure this man you call Arcus is the killer?" Leia asked once more. She had never even heard the name.

"Yes," Peter said, and Naya nodded in agreement.

"I'm very sorry," Peter heard Everson say. "I didn't mean for this to happen."

Peter turned away from his friend. Holding Naya's hand, he walked to his car. He lifted her and placed her on the hood of his Jeep. "Are you all right?" he asked Naya softly, examining her lacerated fingers.

"Yes, I am," Naya said, then buried her face into his shoulders. She felt safe in his arms.

Now they just had to wait for the rest of the circus to arrive.

{CHAPTER SEVENTY}

Three Days Later

Leia and Peter entered the psychiatric institute where Arcus had been hospitalized several years ago. Arcus's sudden death had left so many questions unanswered, especially regarding the large gap between the murders. Leia had invited Peter not only because he was a psychiatrist, but also because he was part of the events that had occurred.

They sat in the record room, scanning Arcus's old psychiatric chart.

"Here, look—it says he was delusional."

She paged farther along and found a transcript of a session between Arcus and his therapist:

Arcus: He forced me to do it. He tricked me into it.

Therapist: Into what?

Arcus: I can't tell you.

Therapist: Who asked you to do it?

Arcus: I don't know.

Therapist: You keep saying you've done bad things and that someone is making you do bad things, but I'm not going to be able to help you if you can't tell me what you've done or who has forced you to do it.

Arcus: I had to—I had to.

Therapist: Go on, I'm listening.

Arcus: You'll never understand.

Therapist: I could try, and you might feel better if you talk about it, get it out in the open.

Arcus: I'll be punished.
Therapist: By whom?
Arcus: By Anansi.
Therapist: Who is Anansi?

The therapist had documented that there was only silence after that point. He had also written that such incomprehensible conversations occurred regularly.

"What do you think?" Leia asked Peter.

Peter sighed deeply. "I think he was very ill," he replied. "Who's Anansi?" he asked. "An accomplice?"

"I think he's a character from African folklore," Leia said. "I'm pretty sure he's like Coyote in Native American stories—he plays tricks on people. Maybe Anansi lives in the sky. That would explain why the victims were laid out in that way—so Anansi could see them."

Peter continued to page through the two-volume record.

"It looks like he had a tough childhood," Peter said. "In a way, I pity him."

"Well," Leia said, "Not everyone who has a rough or violent childhood feels the need to go around killing people."

Peter smiled sadly. "No. Some of them become so protective of children that they become workaholic doctors who see a personal life as an unforgivable waste of time, so urgent is their need to keep busy and save the world. Oh, and also, they're scared to date, because they irrationally fear that they will end up beating a woman to a pulp because they're their father's son. So, you know, it can go either way. You never know how trauma will affect someone's mind."

Leia's expression was careful. "Do you want to talk about it?"

Peter sighed. "It's not that interesting, really. We all have our stories, you know?"

Leia nodded. "Yes. I do."

Peter smiled. "Somehow I figured you would. But no, I don't feel the need to rehash all of it again. Maybe I'm finally getting over it, or maybe I just bore myself with my rambling. But someday, when we're in the mood, we can grab a beer and swap gritty stories."

He was only half-kidding about going out with Leia, but he couldn't stop himself from nervously adding, "Or, you know, just sell the movie rights for big bucks," just to keep Leia from having to answer.

"What makes you so sure that I have any gritty stories?" Leia asked. "Maybe I grew up in the suburbs with two loving parents and a dog named Lady. I could have gone to a respectable Catholic school and taken horseback-riding lessons on Tuesday and Thursday afternoons."

"Oh, come on," Peter said. "I work in psychiatry. That's how I can tell you that the traumatized kids who don't become murderers or doctors end up as tough-talking cops who can spit nails and kick ass."

Leia ducked her head and laughed, and Peter found the sound as charming as ever.

"Maybe you're right," she said. "But I have to agree with you: I don't want to hear those stories come out of my mouth again. I think that maybe I'm ready to move on."

"So you won't be a tough-talking, nail-spitting federal agent anymore?"

"Well," Leia said, "Too much change at once can be a bad thing. I might stick with that part."

"Good," Peter said, propping his elbow up on the metal table. "Justice just wouldn't be the same without you. Speaking of which ..." His expression turned serious. "What's going to happen to Everson?"

"Right now, he's being held on charges of kidnapping and accessory to attempted murder," Leia replied. "He won't be practicing medicine again."

"What a shame," Peter replied, shaking his head. Despite his old friend's horrible choices, Peter couldn't help feeling very sad for him. Peter had been shocked to discover Everson's secret life with cocaine. "We had become good friends," Peter said wistfully. "He should have asked for help." He shook off his concerns and changed the subject. "I'll need some time to read the whole record."

"Take your time," Leia said. "Meanwhile, I'll try to find his last therapist."

Peter sat in the record room and read Arcus's chart from beginning to end. He wanted to understand what had driven Arcus to kill those two girls.

{CHAPTER SEVENTY-ONE}

Five Days Later

Peter sat flipping channels on the television set. He had been restless and down all day. Even though Naya was safe and the killer dead, his mind couldn't relax. He struggled with the act of having killed a man. Even though the act had been one of self-defense, he felt that his duty was to save lives, not take them. The recent events played over in his mind like a broken record.

Then Peter realized that there was one person who could help: Mr. Iyengar.

"Mr. Iyengar, this is Peter."

"Peter! I've heard you've had a lot to deal with over the past few days. How are you, my dear lad?"

"Not good," Peter replied sadly. "I helped save Naya and made the world safer for children. Why don't I have peace of mind?"

"Peter, you have to know that it was incumbent upon Debbie as the murderer's first kill to put an end to Arcus's gruesome acts for good. During the final moments of her life, she must have made it her mission to return and end this violent streak. That is why her atman came back to this world as you."

Peter couldn't answer around the lump in his throat.

"This was your destiny, Peter," Mr. Iyengar said. "You couldn't have changed it."

"But I took a life."

"I understand your oath to preserve life," Mr. Iyengar said gently, "but in essence, you've saved many more lives and have done a great service to this world."

"That's true," Peter acknowledged. He felt his mood lighten a bit. "Thank you. I feel a little better now."

"I'm glad you called. We're indebted to you after what you did for Naya."

"Not at all," Peter said. "Anyone would do the same."

"Please call us anytime you wish—for anything at all. I mean that, Peter."

"Thank you," Peter said. He felt his spirits begin to rise. He felt relieved knowing that this had been his destiny.

*   *   *   *

Naya found herself in a familiar field of flowers. This time, there were no doors behind her. She skipped through the tall grass toward the singing she heard in the distance.

Janet was picking apples from the short apple trees, a pretty tune on her lips.

"Hi, Janet," Naya said.

"Naya!" Janet squealed with joy. "I'm so glad to see you!"

"Where's Jerry?" Naya asked, looking around without spotting the mammoth beast.

"He's gone to visit his friends," Janet said with a smile.

"What about the big, bad man?"

"He's gone. Thanks to you," Janet said and patted Naya on the head. "We don't have to worry anymore."

"The string—it's gone," Naya observed. "You look whole again!"

"I told you Peter could help."

Naya smiled. "Can we play now?"

"For a little while."

"Will I see you again?" Naya asked, already sensing the answer.

"Actually, it's time for me to leave," Janet said softly.

"But I don't want you to go," Naya said with a frown.

"You don't need to feel sad. I'll always be your friend."

"I'll miss you."

The two girls stood silently for a moment. "Let's play," Naya said. She reached out to Janet and tagged her. "You're it!" she said and ran around an apple tree.

The two friends played happily until the sun began to set. Then Janet bid Naya farewell and walked away into the bright sunset.

Naya stood waving with a smile on her face as Janet faded away in the distance.

{CHAPTER SEVENTY-TWO}

Two Weeks Later

Peter rolled toward his uncle's ranch, his fingers thumping the steering wheel to the beat of the radio. The week had been full of buzz about Everson's arrest and Arcus's death. The event had become a sensation for the local media and gossipmongers. Now that the case was solved, Peter was going to meet with Leia for one last time, so she could update him on what the forensic evaluators had revealed.

Peter stopped at a traffic light under a bridge a few miles away from the ranch. He saw a man known around town simply as the flower man selling roses to those who stopped there. Though Peter was familiar with the man's offerings, he had never had the opportunity to purchase any. He rolled down his window and bought a large bouquet of roses. Once the light turned green, he proceeded down the road toward his uncle's ranch.

Peter spotted Leia's rental car parked outside the house. She had always been prompt in keeping her engagements. He grabbed the bunch of roses and ran into the house. He spotted Leia sitting in the family room by herself, waiting for the senator to arrive.

"These are for you," Peter said, handing them to Leia.

"You shouldn't have," Leia said with a slight blush. She thanked Peter for his gesture.

"It's only a small token of gratitude for having helped Naya," Peter replied with a soft smile. Try as he might, he could never stop himself from noticing her beauty.

"Congratulations, Agent Bines," they heard the senator say as he walked into the room.

"Peter was a big help in solving the case," Leia pointed out, willing to share the credit.

"I'm glad it's over; now we don't have to sample an entire town for DNA," the senator chuckled.

"We have all the DNA evidence we need that links Arcus to the case. He was the one who assaulted me in the woods," Leia said confidently. "Everson is off the hook for Janet's murder."

"What possessed Arcus to do such a gruesome act is beyond my understanding," the senator thought out loud.

"After combing through the records and putting all the pieces of the puzzle together, I discovered some interesting facts," Peter said. "Arcus was born and raised in Jamaica for the first few years of his life. His parents were East Indian and of Jamaican origin. He witnessed the rape and killing of a woman by his father. This was compounded by the trauma of losing his mother a little later. He immigrated to the United States with his grandparents after his mother died. He lived and worked on Mr. Deed's property and found a job at the local market."

"But … why kill?" asked Leia. "Not everyone with a violent childhood ends up a murderer."

"I believe that he was delusional, and those delusions revolved around his integrity. He believed he was indebted to the Jamaican deity Anansi. He felt he needed to carry out sacrifices to ward off misfortune—heck, even to survive."

"What about the two girls?" the senator asked.

"I think he ended up killing the two girls after two separate critical and traumatic events in his life," Peter explained. The first murder was just after the death of his grandparents when he was around eighteen years old. That was the day Debbie Sanders was killed. And the second event was when his wife died, months before Janet was killed. I think it was their misfortune to be at the wrong place at the wrong time."

Leia and his uncle stood fascinated by the narrative. Leia was impressed that Peter had been able to put together the rationale behind the gruesome killings.

"How does your shoulder feel?" Leia asked Peter, changing the topic and eyeing the bulky, bandaged area under his clothing.

"It still hurts," Peter said. "That was a heavy vase. They had to put in eight stitches."

"In any case, I'm going to let the two of you catch up," Leia said, standing up. Leia thanked the senator and Peter for their support. She had a flight to catch back to the West Coast.

She picked up the roses that Peter had given her and smelled them. "I love the smell of roses," she said, smiling at Peter. She turned around and started to walk toward her car.

Peter watched her walk away, the picture of casual grace, that auburn hair tumbling down her back.

"Agent Bines!" Peter called suddenly. "… Leia!"

She turned around and waited for him as he crossed the lawn rapidly. When he got to her, a little out of breath, he didn't seem to know what to say.

"I know that you have to go," he finally managed.

The hazel eyes surveying him had become familiar to him, but now he didn't see even a hint of the cold, careful professionalism they had always held.

"Yes, I do," Leia said. She paused a moment, then reached slowly out to grasp both of his hands. Their faces were inches apart. Seeing Peter's obvious nervousness, Leia broke into a full grin.

"My God, you have a beautiful smile," Peter said. "You should do that more often."

Leia recomposed her delicate features into her typical serious expression, but the smile still tugged at the corners. "I'll think about it," she said sternly. "Maybe."

"Do that," Peter said.

"There's something you should think about too, Peter," she said, more gently.

"There is?"

She squeezed his hands tighter, then leaned forward and pressed her full lips to his. The kiss was brief, and more tender than sexual, but it left Peter speechless nonetheless. She pulled back, studied his face, and smiled again.

"Go on a date, for heaven's sake," she said finally. "Enough of this workaholic stuff. Make some woman really happy, okay?"

Peter laughed, and they could both hear the note of sadness in it. "Look who's talking," he forced himself to tease. He didn't want this moment to be a sad one.

Leia sighed and shrugged. "What can I say? You've got me there. How about this: I'll try the dating game if you will, all right?"

"All right," Peter said softly, and gave her one more smile. "Take care, Agent Bines."

"You too, Dr. Gram," she answered, and turned away.

She waved one last good-bye before she closed her car door behind her, and moments later, she was gone. Finally, the case had come to an end.

{CHAPTER SEVENTY-THREE}

Three Months Later

"Are you sure you want to go?" Peter asked Naya with a smile.

"Yep!" Naya responded confidently.

Hand in hand, they walked to the parking lot. Naya was excited to go for a ride in Peter's SUV.

Peter had been seeing Naya in individual therapy ever since the incident, working through the trauma secondary to the kidnapping and Arcus's grisly death. He also helped Naya understand who Janet Troy was and what had happened to her. Even at her young age, Naya understood that in some unknown way, she had communicated with Janet in her dreams and helped catch the person who had caused Janet harm. Now Peter had arranged a field trip to bring some closure to this chapter in Naya's young life.

They drove through town to the Troy's residence.

"This is where Janet lived," Peter said as he pulled into a narrow driveway.

Mrs. Troy's face was calm but serious when she answered the door. "Please come in," she said.

When Naya and Peter had taken off their coats and settled on the couch in the living room, Mrs. Troy asked Naya, "Would you like a slice of apple pie?"

"Did Janet like apple pie?" Naya asked.

"Yes, she did," Mrs. Troy said with a small smile. "Very much."

A man came down the stairs to greet them. His clothes seemed to billow on him, as though he had lost a lot of weight suddenly.

"This is Janet's father, Herbert," Mrs. Troy said.

Mr. Troy held a family photo album.

"I thought maybe you'd like to see these," he said to Peter and Naya. He sat between them on the sofa. "Here's our Janet," he said fondly, flipping through the pages. "She was a very happy girl."

"She told me she would always be my friend," Naya said proudly.

The Troys looked at each other and smiled, but their eyes were clouded with tears. "Look!" Naya said to Peter, pointing out a picture in which Janet was holding a little white mouse.

"That's Jerry, Janet's pet mouse," Mr. Troy said.

"I thought Jerry was an elephant," Naya said innocently.

"Yes, in your dreams he was," Peter said gently.

As they browsed through the album, laughing at pictures of Janet dressed as a ballerina at two, with birthday cake smeared across her mouth or at seven, and dressed as a pumpkin for Halloween at nine, the Troys shared memories of the happy moments they'd had with their daughter. Peter felt it was important for Naya to have a positive image of Janet after the scary dreams she'd had.

"Would you like to see her room?" Mrs. Troy asked Naya.

"Yes," Naya replied with excitement.

Mrs. Troy escorted Naya and Peter upstairs to Janet's bedroom, which hadn't changed since the last day Janet had inhabited it.

"It's just like it was in my dream," Naya commented as she went in and sat on Janet's bed. "The sheets even smell the same." She looked out the window next to Janet's bed, then looked at Peter with an impish smile. "There's no elephant outside, though."

Peter nodded in agreement. Mrs. Troy stood in the doorway, as though it were difficult for her to enter, and watched Naya as she sat on Janet's bed.

Naya returned to where Mrs. Troy stood and looked up at her. "Thank you for showing me her room," she said. "I'm sorry you're sad."

Mrs. Troy looked down at Naya and nodded repeatedly, her hand at her throat. Then Naya slipped her hand into Mrs. Troy's and walked with her back downstairs. Peter followed.

"Are you happy you met Janet's parents?" Peter asked Naya as they walked back to his Jeep.

"Yes," Naya said with a big smile. "Now Janet can always be my friend."

{CHAPTER SEVENTY-FOUR}

Six Months Later

Peter checked his directions. He was pretty sure he had the right street. He hunted for the address numbers as he drove slowly through the quiet neighborhood. He had traveled three hours into the state of Pennsylvania on a bright Sunday morning, happy that winter had passed and that spring was in full bloom.

"Ah, there it is: number twenty four," Peter said aloud when he spotted a white mailbox with the numbers painted in bright red. He parked in front of the ranch-style house and walked past colorful flower beds and a manicured lawn to the front door. He rang the doorbell and soon heard the clanking of a set of locks from the inside.

"Yes?" said the elderly lady who opened the door. Their eyes met and held, and Peter felt an electrical pulse run down his spine.

"I'm Peter Gram, the doctor who spoke to you a few weeks ago," Peter replied.

"I recognize your face from the papers, Dr. Gram. Please come in," the lady invited. "I was surprised to hear that you wanted to talk to me about Debbie. Would you like to join me for some tea?"

"Certainly," Peter said, following her into the kitchen.

Mrs. Sanders filled a teakettle with water and put it on the stove to boil. Peter looked curiously around the bright kitchen.

"Do you live alone?" he asked politely.

"Yes, I do—ever since my husband passed away five years ago," Mrs. Sanders replied. "Please, sit down." She pointed to a round table.

She served the tea, then sat down opposite Peter at the table.

"So, what is it you'd like to know about Debbie?" Mrs. Sanders asked Peter.

"This might sound strange, but I was wondering if you could share a few thoughts about who she was," Peter requested.

Mrs. Sanders hesitated a moment. Peter held her brown eyes steadily as déjà vu washed over him. Then Mrs. Sanders began to talk about her daughter Debbie with immense fondness. Peter could tell that the memories were still very painful for her, even after all these years.

"She disappeared much like the little girl we read about in the paper—Janet Troy. She was coming home from a friend's house one afternoon. There's nothing like that—losing your child." Mrs. Sanders rose from the table to dab at her eyes with a tissue. "We couldn't stay in Newbury after that. I just couldn't bear to see Debbie's friends … their parents … these families we had once been close to. It just hurt too much. So we moved out here."

"I was born on the very day Debbie died," Peter said.

Mrs. Sanders looked at Peter with a warm smile. She tipped her head a bit to the side. "You remind me of her," she said, putting her cup down on the table. She leaned closer to him and peered directly into his eyes, and Peter was taken aback by an intense desire to be pulled into a hug. "You have very similar eyes."

And maybe the same soul, Peter thought to himself as a strange sensation of warmth enveloped his body. Could she once have been his mother?

Mrs. Sanders leaned back in her chair. "I'm glad you came to see me," she said, smiling with genuine happiness.

"So am I," Peter said with a deep sense of contentment.

Made in the USA